Hungry For You

Michelle Kay

To: Sebastian
Dalways
Michelle Kay

ISBN: 1518671233
ISBN-13: 9781518671234

ACKNOWLEDGMENTS

To Raegan Quinn, my best friend and biggest cheerleader, who has always supported me and loved me. To Amanda Cooke, who deserves gold medals in the arts of Hot Model Hunting and Leading the Blind (I mean me...). To Kizzy, who provided me with a beautiful cover. And to my North West Florida NaNoWriMo group that has proven to be the best sounding-board around.

MICHELLE KAY

1

No matter how many times it happened, breathing was always hard when Milo was on top of him—*inside* of him. Cole's body shuddered and his back bowed, pressing him into the steady thrusting that fed him.

"You okay?" Milo's breath was soft as ever against the shell of his ear, but Cole could still hear the quivering arousal in his voice, the restrain as he fought the basal desires Cole knew he brought out in the other boy.

"Yeah." Cole shifted on the mattress beneath his friend, spreading his knees apart and rolling his hips back. "More."

Milo shuddered and pressed his face into his friend's neck, inhaling the scent they both knew was laced with a drug that flamed his arousal. Cole knew that his body was booby-trapped, and even though Milo tried to make light of it, the guilt of what he did unconsciously still twisted at Cole's stomach.

Shifting onto his knees behind the other boy's sprawled figure, raising up where Cole's tantalizing scent couldn't reach him, Milo moved his hands to the slender hips that shivered and rolled back against him.

"Please... Milo, hurry."

With more power than he'd intended, Milo did exactly as he was asked. A perfect cry rose from Cole's throat as his back arched, his face dropping to the pillows again as Milo let the dam of his restrain break.

Through the sound of their bodies meeting and their ragged breath, Cole heard himself begging for more, even as his own hand snaked between himself and the comforter. Milo must have felt him tighten as he gripped himself, because the young scientist shuddered and dug his fingers hard into his hips.

"Fuck, Cole. I'm coming."

"Please!" Cole felt his own euphoria teetering, needing a push that his own feeble, lust-numbed hand couldn't give him. "Please, hurry!"

In a well-practiced dance, Milo wrapped an arm around the smaller man's waist, holding him steady, driving as deep into him as he could. His other hand came up in the same moment to close around the fist that Cole was already using to coax out his own climax.

Milo shook and grunted against Cole's ear, then the lithe, dark-haired boy felt the heat of his friend's lust erupt inside him, and for that long moment as he released into his own hand, he felt his constant hunger disappear.

Cole had no memory of his childhood. In fact, he was fairly certain he had no childhood *to* remember. What he *did* recall was waking up in a dark, wet place, only to emerge in New York's subway system. He remembered the hunger that woke up with him, and the disgust and shame he'd felt the first time he'd fed.

Marla, the woman who had saved him and had given him a home, had never called him a monster, despite how he felt about himself. Cole didn't know what he was, and if Marla did, then she never told him. All Cole knew was that he was a creature with no past who needed sex to live, but who hated it every time.

"Are you alright?" Milo's voice had the hint of guilt it always had after a feeding.

"Yeah." Cole knew he could sound more convincing, but hiding things from Milo was hard, so he'd stopped faking a long time ago.

"How are you feeling?" Milo had already found his pants and was moving toward the computer rig he had set up in the corner of his room. It was a beast, with three monitors and dozens of cords that ran to equipment Cole had no hope of ever identifying.

"Can I have a second to recover first?" Cole was already sitting on the edge of his friend's low bed, his pants on as he tried to find the front of his shirt. He liked to dress as quickly as possible after his feedings with Milo.

"No. we need to log this now. The more data I have, the sooner I can perfect the medicine."

Cole sighed as he pulled his shirt over his head, the neck hole catching for only a few seconds on his horns. Milo had been working for months on the medication that helped to ease the hunger that Cole felt. They both had hopes of turning the concoction into a full replacement, but for now it helped lengthen the time Cole could go before he had to feed again.

"Come on, Cole. Help me do this."

The horned boy felt heat rising to his face. "I feel the same way I did last time."

"We went a bit longer this time. Do you feel *more* full because of that?"

"I dunno... Maybe a little. I don't usually feel full or not. The hunger just goes away?"

Milo scrubbed his chin as he struck a few keys with his other hand. "Maybe I shouldn't have finished inside you." He had no hint of embarrassment in his voice or face as he finally located his glasses and shoved them onto his face. "I still wonder if you get more from the sexual energy or from the sem—"

"Could you *not* think that part out loud?" He felt flushed all over as he snapped at his too-nosey friend.

Milo went quiet, looking at him over the rim of his glasses for a while. Cole looked away. He felt like Milo's eyes could strip flesh from his bones when he looked at him like that.

"I understand that you're embarrassed about all this, Cole. But this can help. You know that's all I want, right?"

Guilt, in several flavors, speared Cole through the gut. He hated having to rely on his friend for meals while he knew it hurt the other boy every time. He was bad with his own emotions, but he would have had to be blind to not see how Milo felt.

"Alright." In the end, compliance was the least he could offer him.

Haven was a large underground compound created and run by Marla Clairemonte. None of the boys who lived in the compound knew exactly what she did—Scientist, politician, vigilante—any one of these things could be used to describe her. The details didn't matter much to Cole, though. To him, she was his mother and his savior. Like many of the boys that passed through haven, Marla had found them unwanted, hated and often in danger. Psychics, witches, even creatures that haunt bedtime stories, passed through Marla's enormous half-way house. Some were taught to blend in and were let loose; others, like Cole and Milo, chose to stay.

At the moment, Sabin was the only other resident inside Haven—a nineteen-year-old who had outgrown the foster system because of the "devil-work" his foster families had caught him doing. He'd been there for a year, but still kept to himself most of the time. He only sat at the breakfast table now because Marla had made it obligatory.

"Morning, kiddies." Marla often felt more like a cool aunt than a mother, and everyone seemed to like that more. She was tall for a woman and usually wore pumps to accentuate it. Cole thought she might have been older than she looked too, but he'd never been good at gauging ages.

Despite knowing they were there for a briefing, no one questioned her as she sat down and scooped eggs onto her plate. Milo gestured toward Cole with the plate of pancakes that were being passed around, but Cole only smiled and declined.

Milo knew he didn't need to eat—not regular food, anyway—but he always offered, and it always made Cole feel a little more accepted. More than anything, Cole wanted to be normal, and he was sure Milo knew that.

"So is it monsters?" Sabin asked as he poured syrup over his pancakes and eggs.

Cole and Milo both perked up, waiting for the answer they all knew they'd been woken up for. Haven was more than some boarding school for freaks. They had every perk and every amenity, all paid in full by the government. All they had to do was discreetly handle a few "infestations" now and then.

"No. Well, sort of no." Marla smiled at them, her red lipstick as perfect after her mouthful of food as it had been when she walked in. "Visitors."

There was a general groan that passed over the table. It had been a while since any new blood had come through Haven and they had all gotten used to their private routine.

"What rude children I have." Marla was grinning even as she scolded them.

"Who is it?" Milo asked. He didn't mind as much as the others since he usually got to do some research on newcomers. At least he got to *help.*

"Who are *they*," Marla corrected. "A colleague of mine is bringing some of her boys over. Our boss bought them out, so they're coming to join our crew.

"There are other places like Haven?" Cole hadn't meant to sound so hopeful, but he noticed Milo looking at him from the corner of his eye. He always wondered if there were others like him. Others who might have answers to some questions even Marla and her research team couldn't answer.

"There are more Havens than you could ever imagine, Cole. It just so happens that Haven:UK has grown enough that they can service some of the other European nations. My colleague was stationed in Germany, but now it's cheaper for them to pay Haven:UK than it is to support their own. We've picked them up."

"What are their assets?" Sabin asked, knowing he probably wouldn't get an answer.

"Classified." Marla bat her lashes at him. "Same as always, Sabin, my pet."

They all knew that Marla never discussed the abilities of Haven members. They usually disclosed the information themselves once they were comfortable, but it was always left up to them. Cole hated it, but was glad that his own secrets were guarded with the same fervor.

"But what you're telling us is that these aren't guests, but permanent residents." Sabin, like the rest of them, had become immune to her innocent eyes.

"More than likely."

"Are they nice?"

"Well…they're German." She shrugged.

2

No lies had been told about the perks of Haven:USA. Bastian and the two others who had been picked up by the United States facility had spent four hours touring the compound and he still felt like he'd not seen everything. Training rooms, classrooms, gaming rooms, TV rooms, a kitchen, a swimming pool, research labs, armories...it was like a bunker and a preschool had collided.

"They're probably soft from all this pampering," Berlin said as he nudged Bastian with one shoulder.

"I thought we agreed on English only." Venja scolded them as she heard her boys whispering in German.

"Aren't we the ones who were just kicked out of our home and forced to come here?" Alistair, the delicate gem of Haven:Germany popped his hip as he continued in his native tongue. "They should learn German. We *are* the ones who are guests here."

"You're assuming that Americans *know how* to be kind to foreigners," Berlin chimed in, and they both had a laugh.

Venja didn't find it funny, though, and immediately stopped her tour. "I know you are all upset." She caved at least enough to stop speaking English herself. "Coming into a new country is hard. But this really is a grand opportunity for us. Our new funding will give us a chance to help so many more people."

"*American* people," Alistair said, then clicked his tongue when Venja shot him another scolding glance. He shifted his weight to his other leg and propped his hands on his hips, but said nothing else.

"You don't have to speak English all the time, but no pretending you *can't* speak it. Getting along is important for our friendships and for our safety on missions." She paused. "At least I know that Bastian will keep you two in order."

Bastian didn't like being singled out as a tattle, and even though he was the tallest in the group he could feel the other two looking down on him. "I'm sorry," he said after their stares persisted. "But if they ask me, you know I have to tell them."

Berlin and Alistair huffed and threw up their hands before following Venja down another hallway. She smiled proudly at him and continued the tour.

Bastian had never understood the pride she felt. She seemed to think that being incapable of lying was a good thing. Bastian would be the first to tell anyone who would listen that it was a curse.

They saw no one until the tour took them toward the dormitory hallway. In a small sitting room lined with couches and a massive TV, another woman rose to meet them.

"Marla." Venja moved to the other woman and they kissed cheeks in a way that suggested closeness.

"Venja, it's good to see you. Oh, and what handsome boys you have."

Alistair smirked, always pleased for more compliments, but the others did nothing.

"I'm sorry to hear about your facilities."

"Well, you know how politics are." Venja's English was perfect. "We're just glad to be amongst friends."

"Friends is sort of a strong word, don't you think?" Berlin had leaned close to Alistair, whispering to him in German and smiling as the other boy chuckled.

"But it *is* the correct one," Marla said, smiling as the three boys jumped in their shoes. "No need to be secretive. After all, German really isn't *that* hard to learn." She smiled, but all of the boys seemed to have gotten her message. "Your shipped belongings are due to arrive tomorrow, so for now, why don't you all take your carry-ons and I'll get you settled in some rooms."

Grabbing the small over-night bags they'd dropped set aside when they'd arrived, they followed the tall American woman into the hall that smelled an awful lot like home.

The hallway itself was unremarkable—a long corridor with doors on either side. Many were closed and unmarked, but clustered around the half-way point were a handful of rooms bearing nametags. The doors stood open and they got their first glance at their new American teammates.

Bastian nodded politely, though unsmilingly, to a black-haired boy who would have the room just beside his. The nameplate read "Sabin."

Well, he seems sulky. Bastian could feel a dark aura on him, though not a powerful one. He could tell instantly that his soul was mostly good, if not tainted by what smelled an awful lot like dark magic.

Across the hall from him, though, was something much darker than a little witchcraft. Two boys stood in a single doorway marked "Milo," though he didn't know which boy the room belonged to. The tall boy who looked passive enough gave off no aura of any consequence. He was brunette and attractive but average in his dress and gesture. Behind him, though, was a much shorter boy with dark eyes and horns that coiled behind his ears like spindles of glass. Bastian could smell sin on him.

A shiver snaked its way up Bastian's spine as his gaze met the black pools that were this other boy's eyes. Even his pupils had been lost in the void that seemed too deep for any person.

"Man, get a load of that kid's horns," Berlin muttered in German as he turned his back to the room marked for Milo.

Bastian grunted in a vague acknowledgment, but he had to look at the horned boy again—had to be sure he was real.

The tall brunette said nothing, but moved his body further in front of the smaller boy, his face and body both telling Bastian to leave his friend be. He nodded the same way he had to Sabin and then entered his own room, the dark aura trailing after him.

The rooms they had been given weren't fancy, but they were nice. Each had a small half-bath that supplied a toilet and sink, but the only showers available were in the locker room attached to the gym and training area. Otherwise, it was a normal room—bed, desk, computer, dresser. It wasn't that much nicer than the one Bastian had left back home, but it certainly wasn't worse.

When he returned to the hallway, the horned boy was gone, possibly hiding in the room behind his tall friend.

3

Cole had felt something like electricity crackle in his stomach when the tall blond had laid eyes on him in the dorm hallway. Much in the same way that he felt naked under Milo's calculating stare, the blue eyes of this new boy had left him feeling stripped. And while he'd noticed the other two boys gawking at his horns, those miserable parts of himself that he could never hide, he got the impression the boy called Bastian had not been looking at his horns at all. He'd been looking at something much deeper and more intimate inside him.

Cole hid in Milo's room, listening while his friend guessed wildly at what abilities the others might be hiding, until they were all called down to dinner. Meals weren't usually "family" events like this, but Marla and Venja seemed intent on making them get along.

"So, have things been quiet for you here?" Venja asked, trying to keep conversation going.

Both women paused as if to give one of the boys a chance to answer. When no one did, Marla spoke up.

"We've had a quiet month. A few disturbances have gotten close to our borders, but Canada was able to contain the worst of them before we had to step in."

Cole thought that maybe Marla had fixed him a plate of food to keep him from standing out, but now as he sat staring at his plate of roast beef and spätzle he thought it made him even more conspicuous. He pushed some of the spätzle around with his fork when he noticed the broad-set Berlin watching him. If he kept his eyes down and his fork on the plate, maybe no one would notice.

Eventually, the table grew quiet, and that silence stretched on long enough that even Marla and Venja gave up. After what seemed like hours, Marla stood.

"Why don't I show you our research lab, Venja? Milo, come along with us. I think you and Venja will have a lot to talk about."

Cole looked over at Milo more quickly than he'd meant to and was sure the others could read his panic. Milo's lips pressed into a thin line, but he got up, squeezing Cole's shoulder once before following the two women out of the room.

Forks continued to clink as the others ate. Cole tried to gauge how long he would have to sit there before it was considered polite to leave, but just as he was thinking it was getting close, Berlin broke the silence.

"Scheiss-ami," he said in a voice that was naturally deep and gravely. The dark-skinned boy's tone was clear, though—he was addressing Cole. Berlin nodded when Cole looked at him. "Yes, yes. You. You on a diet? Or you just don't like German food?"

Cole's face flushed, knowing the red always stood out against his pale skin. When he looked at his plate he saw that he'd done nothing but stirred it into a globby mess.

"No...I-I mean," Cole's face burned hotter as he heard Alistair snicker under his breath.

"Just ignore them, Cole," Sabin interjected, his attention still on his own meal.

"And what's *your* problem? My Chemical Romance cancel their gig?"

Sabin's lip ring flicked as his tongue ran across the inside of his mouth—a sure sign that he was pissed. "My problem is that you seem to think we don't know what 'scheiss' means. If you want answers, maybe you shouldn't call people 'shit,' ya asshole."

Cole's heart leapt into his throat as he sat quietly between the two forces.

"Well, I think if your friend is so insulted, he should tell us himself."

Every pair of eyes fell on Cole then, and that was the exact opposite of what he'd wanted. He knew that they were waiting for him to make a choice. He found it hard to meet Sabin's eyes as he fiddled his fingers against the side of the table.

"I'm…not insulted or anything."

Alistair actually laughed out loud and Berlin slapped the table once, then gestured sweepingly toward him like he was presenting his answer to Sabin.

"There, you see? You're the only one upset here, Mr. Manson."

Sabin huffed and pushed himself away from the table. "Whatever. I'm out."

"Hope your coffin's cozy," Berlin called after him.

"Was ein Verlierer," Alistair muttered before Berlin turned his attention back to Cole, who was suddenly feeling very alone.

"You're skinny. Why don't you eat?"

"I'm…just not hungry. I'm sorry, I didn't mean to offend you or anything." He ran his fingers along the tip of his horn where with curled behind his ear—a nervous habit he wasn't sure where he'd picked up.

"Er ist so schüchtern." Berlin chuckled as he looked at Bastian, who seemed less entertained. "Those real?"

Cole's fingers paused on his horn, then he moved his hands to his lap, holding them there before they got him into any more trouble.

"Um…yes."

"What are you?"

The pounding of Cole's heart turned into a slow tremble that he hoped he was controlling. What could he say?

"Um…honestly, we're not entirely sure yet."

Bastian's chair scraped the ground. "Er lügt." The others watched him as he walked to the door. "Er ist böse. Sprich nicht mit ihm."

Berlin and Alistair watched the doorway for a while after their friend left, then exchanged glances with one another. After another moment, their eyes fell on Cole again, but they looked less amused this time. Whatever Bastian had said, they seemed to be taking it very seriously.

"I guess I should learn some German." Cole smiled the best he could and tried to laugh, but Berlin and his willowy friend only got up and left the room.

4

Bastian lay awake in bed for a long time after their dinner. He could feel a film of darkness crawling over his skin. He didn't feel sick, but he felt...tingly. It made him restless. Being in a new room probably didn't help.

Needing the comfort of familiarity, Bastian got out of his bed and moved into the hallway. Everything was still, and in a way he'd done many times before, he cracked Berlin's door open and slid inside.

"You awake?" He whispered as he walked through the darkness to his friend's bed.

"Mm. Am now." Berlin's voice was thick from sleep and as Bastian crawled into the warmth of his blankets, it almost felt like they were back home.

Berlin turned onto his side so he was facing the blond man who made his bed suddenly seem much smaller. Their knees bumped and they shifted closer together until their noses almost touched.

"It's been a while since you've done the sneaking." Berlin was smiling, even if Bastian couldn't see it through the darkness. "And here I was being a gentleman and letting you rest since we did all that traveling."

"I don't like it here," Bastian said, ignoring the flirtatious joke.

Berlin frowned and moved a hand into the mess of blond curls on his friend's head. "Is it that kid? He seemed to freak out you at dinner."

"I don't like him," Bastian admitted. "There's something evil about him."

"Well he *does* have horns." Berlin laughed and wrapped an arm around the other man's waist, pulling him close so he could bite his neck. "Maybe he's the devil."

Bastian rolled his eyes and snaked a hand between their bodies, grabbing the other boy's growing erection through the thin fabric of his boxers. He smiled when he heard Berlin's laugh turn into a sudden exhale as the muscles in his chest and stomach tensed. It was Bastian's turn to chuckle as he outlined his friend's shape under his fingers.

"I didn't come in here to talk about devils, Berlin."

With a sigh, Berlin leaned back on an elbow, stretching himself out like a giant cat. Bastian's eyes had adjusted enough that he could see the dark lines of the tattoos that coiled up his friends arms and swirled onto his chest in great netted circles. Sometimes people were shocked by the tattoos that cover nearly all of Berlin's body, but Bastian had always found them pretty. He could see them stretch and undulate as Berlin rolled his body against the palm that was still pressing down on him.

"You got hard awfully fast for someone claiming to be a gentleman."

"Don't get cocky." Berlin was smiling, even as he tangled his hand into his friend's hair and pulled him down into an open kiss.

Bastian spent more of his free time than he would ever admit questioning whether kissing Berlin was a good idea. He definitely liked it, and even now he was shifting his body closer along his friend's side, tracing the insides of his lips with his tongue as his hand pushed his boxers out of the way. He *liked* kissing Berlin, especially when he had the darker boy underneath him. But they weren't a couple—not really. Admittedly, they were as close as two people could *get* to being a couple, and a hand job was the tamest of the dirty things they'd done while sneaking back and forth into each other's rooms, but they weren't in love. They had talked about it, and at times Bastian had even *wanted* it—but Berlin had been very insistent that it would never happen. Bastian wasn't sure if he wanted it to happen anymore.

Berlin's hand came up and gripped him through his shorts and Bastian realized that he'd been slacking, lost in his own thoughts.

"I'm gonna do it myself I you don't get started." Berlin loved arrogant talk when they fooled around, but Bastian could hear the smile on his face.

"Well maybe you need to do a bit more to get me motivated."

Berlin moaned against Bastian's mouth as he moved up so he rested on his side, leaving them facing each other. A smile played on his lips as Bastian shifted out of the boxers that his friend's hand was now shoving off his hips—he knew exactly how to bring out the competitive streak in the other boy. Then a calloused hand squeezed the bare flesh of his dick, and he gripped Berlin hard in response and revenge, all while he tried to bury the moan that rumbled deep in his throat.

"You better live up to your sass-talk, Bastian." The tattooed boy smiled at him and leaned forward to suck a bruise into the skin at the base of Bastian's throat.

"Shit, Berlin." With one hard shove, Bastian pushed the other boy onto his back so he could lean over him. Even though he knew it was no real punishment, he reached down and squeezed him again, harder this time. "What have I said about leaving marks?"

Berlin caught his breath around a smile as Bastian's hand started working him, and he knew that he'd just been intentionally provoked by the darker boy. Normally he would be irritated, but it didn't matter as Berlin's hand matched his pace. Then they both forgot about their challenging words, and Bastian forgot about the nebulous nature of their relationship. This was what he'd gone to Berlin for—distraction—so he closed his eyes and surrendered himself to the rough hand that squeezed him, twisting up his shaft; he surrendered himself to the thumb that pressed down against the slit of his dick where he'd slowly started seeping. He could feel an answering moisture on his own hand as Berlin's body reacted to him.

Vaguely, maybe even subconsciously, they were still competing with each other, trying to bring the other to the peak of their ecstasy before they lost themselves in their own pleasure. Bastian didn't want to lose, not to Berlin, not again, so when he felt the other boy start to tense he descended on him, locking his mouth over the other boys. He pressed into the hard body beneath him, stealing the space Berlin's hand needed to move properly. The tattooed boy's muffled voice vibrated against Bastian's lips, but he refused to let him up—instead, he pulled at him harder, using the ring made by his forefinger and thumb to squeeze him just the way he knew Berlin liked.

A bruising hand gripped Bastian's shoulder just before Berlin's body stiffened, his head pressing back into the pillow as he shot himself onto his own chest. Bastian couldn't help but laugh as he wrung the last few drops from the other boy's now shivering dick. The moment he let up on the weight he'd used to push Berlin into the mattress, though, Berlin shoved him away.

"Christ, Bastian!"

Bastian knew immediately that Berlin was pissed—he rarely "used the Lord's name in vain." Of course, since Bastian wasn't Catholic, he didn't quite understand his aversion to it, but he knew his friend well enough to know that he was probably going to have to finish himself off in his own room now.

"Why the fuck did you do that?" Berlin snatched a tissue from the table beside his bed and wiped the mess he'd made off his stomach.

"I don't know. Why are you such a sore loser?"

"This isn't about winning or losing, asshole. You know I don't like it when you do that."

"When I do what? Take the lead instead of lying around like a rag doll while you fuck me?" Bastian didn't feel much like jerking himself off any more.

"You spend all this time telling me that I'm too competitive with you when we do this, but that's exactly what you're doing. We could have just done this normally without you getting weird and forceful."

Bastian rolled his eyes and turned onto his back, his arms splayed out to either side, his erection deflating where it still laid exposed. He and Berlin argued on an off about who should be allowed to take the lead, and the more they talked about it, the more it frustrated him. But when Berlin called him things like "forceful," it did make him feel bad. He didn't want to do anything that would make Berlin feel uncomfortable or like he had to give up something he wasn't ready to give. But he also felt like he was being forced to do exactly that, just because he was afraid of forcing the other boy. He supposed he couldn't complain too much. If he didn't want to relinquish control or bottom for the other boy, then he could just say no and stop sneaking into his room.

He didn't realize how quiet he'd been until Berlin leaned over him. He still looked annoyed, but not angry any more.

"You always take this stuff so seriously."

Bastian clicked his tongue. It was annoying to hear Berlin say that when he was the one who'd just thrown a temper tantrum because Bastian had made him come first.

"I don't see why you have to worry about it so much," Berlin continued. "The way we do things now feels good, right? We both get off on it, so why mix it up?"

As his friend leaned over him to kiss him again, Bastian wanted to tell him that mixing it up was exactly what he wanted, because the way they did things already *wasn't* enough for him. He knew that would cause a fight, though. Instead, he sighed, closed his eyes and focused on the hand that moved up his thigh to his neglected dick. He would just not think about it for the night—he would come, and then he would go back to his room. At the very least it was better than masturbating on his own.

5

Just like a vegetarian might have problems keeping grotesque hunks of cooked flesh out of their takeout meals, Cole was faced with his own dietary problems. Unfortunately for him, a vegetarian could pick the bits they didn't want out, but when presented with his own special kind of "flesh meal" he could only lose control and gorge himself whether he wanted it or not. That is to say, he might not want sex, but if presented with it, his body would never let him pass it up.

It was because of this that he'd developed an awkwardly detailed understanding of his friends' "intimate" schedules. Milo tended to masturbate most often in the mornings, Sabin in the evenings. Cole worked his schedule around these two factors. If he left his room in the morning and Milo's door, which was to his right, was closed, he would turn left and spend his morning hours in the training room. If it was open, he would go right and meet him, and sometimes Sabin, in the TV room. At night, Cole made sure to be in the library between the hours of eleven and twelve. Being in a room next to a sex-piqued Milo wasn't too hard, but Sabin was noisy. Maybe not noisy enough for anyone else to hear, but Cole's ears would hone in on the panting and the muffled groans, and he would start to feel the buzzing in his head that made it hard to think straight.

Showering was another struggle all together. He'd thought before about asking Marla for a private shower, but could never bring himself to do it. She'd already done so much for him. It seemed silly to ask for more just because he had to adjust his showering schedule. Again, Milo was a morning-shower kind of guy, and Sabin was the opposite. That meant he had the majority of the day to snag his in private. All he had to do was make sure neither of them would be using the gym while he was there.

He had everything down to a finely tuned routine. Until the others from Germany had shown up, anyway.

It had been two days since the new recruits had arrived and already things were more-or-less back to normal. The two groups kept to themselves and everyone seemed okay with that. Rolling out of bed, Cole checked the date on his clock. He had a few more days before he would have to feed again, but he still fetched a small vial of medicine from his dresser. It would take the edge off and make the next three days much more bearable.

As he left the room, he saw that Milo's door was closed, so he hung a left. Noon was still the best time for him to get a shower, but he figured if he was quick he could be in and out before anyone else showed up. He'd woken up a bit earlier than normal and the hallway was quiet, even as he entered the locker room. Everything was normal. There was no noise, no steam—the perfect, *private*, early morning.

Then Cole took the corner to the open space that housed their lockers and he realized things weren't as perfect as he thought. Well, he supposed the body he was looking at could at least be called "perfect." He would never have taken Berlin, with his too-relaxed attitude and gruff sense of humor, to be a morning person. Yet there he was, wide awake and naked as the day he was born.

He'd not thought much about the dark-skinned boy's choice in clothing, but now his consistent use of long sleeves struck him. Because Cole could see what he'd been hiding—*aside from those pecs,* Cole felt the darker part of himself noting—dark, inky-black lines spiraled down Berlin's arms and legs, the coil opening up in places for intricate designs, and between those dark lines were rows and rows of fine writing, though it was impossible to say what language it was in.

The lines looped and snaked up his body, converging over his heart where a starburst pattern seemed to swell with his heart beat.

Cole would have been shocked by the extensive reaches of those tattoos, if the smell of the other man's hormones hadn't also hit him like a freight train of lust. It was a slow burn kind of affect—the remnants of some sexual afterglow.

Berlin didn't even look at him, and Cole realized that there shouldn't have been anything unusual about this encounter. In a facility of only boys, nudity should never be an issue, but the smell clouded Cole's mind despite the medicine he'd just taken, and his eyes were drawn down past the starburst and the rows of muscle to the V that lead to what he was really interested in. He turned on his heels and fled the locker room before his mind could finish imprinting the other boy's shape to memory.

Cole returned to his room, but didn't stay. His heart rate was up and now he could smell Milo in the room beside him. Grabbing a small notebook from his desk he left again, going to the nearest TV room instead. He turned up the volume, his mind convinced he could still hear soft gasps from the other boys who he was sure were all doing something indecent just to fuck with him.

This was okay, though. It wasn't a huge deal. Cole opened his notebook on his lap and found a column listed "Morning: 6am-7am" then wrote "B: M & S." The last thing he needed was someone getting hold of his notebook and finding something like "Dear Diary, today I learned that Berlin likes to masturbate and shower between the hours of 6am and 7am," so he always kept his notes short.

The next day, Cole tried to steal the showers at noon, which had always been a safe time for him. He would have to change that. Alistair seemed to be the sleep-late-shower-late type. Cole also learned that he was the leave-the-curtain-open type. He was still trying to shake the image of long, pale limbs from his mind when he walked in on Sabin later that evening in the gym. Training wasn't usually too hard to deal with, but the compound felt heavy with the sexual hormones of the extra boys and he ended up running back to his room, his body too stimulated by the sweat-slicked skin of his friend as he'd worked the pull-up bar.

Figuring his safest bet would be to shower in the wee hours of the morning, Cole forced himself out of bed at 4am the next morning, certain that Marla would just hose him down if he didn't bathe soon. There wasn't a teenaged boy on the planet who liked waking up early, so his head was still groggy as he slipped out into the hallway. The last thing he'd expected was to not be alone. His heart stopped a second as another figure loomed in the corner of his eye.

Bastian.

The blond had been avoiding him a little more obviously than the others, and for a second, he looked even more shocked than Cole was. Then again, that was probably because he wasn't sneaking out of his own room, but out of Berlin's. For a second, Cole thought he was about to get yelled at, or even threatened, but then their eyes met for the first time since the boys from Germany had arrived, and the tension seemed to be sucked out of the hall like air from a vacuum.

Despite their poor interactions, Cole found it hard to pull his gaze away from Bastian's, and in another first, the blond didn't scowl at him. In fact, he didn't even look embarrassed anymore, which was surprising given the smell of sex that hung on him. Now he just stared, his mouth softening and his lips parting in a strange mirror of the expression Cole could feel on his own face.

He wondered if Bastian felt the same thing he did looking into the tiny, infinite seas the other boy somehow passed as eyes—a beckoning, a soft familiarity.

Everything held still for a few long moments.

"You..."Bastian's voice was a whisper, the first English he'd spoken since his arrival, and for a second, Cole thought he was going to tell him some secret that he never knew he'd forgotten.

Then, as unexpectedly as the moment had taken them, it shattered with the siren that filled the compound. The lights flashed red and, after a few seconds, the doors that lined the hall opened and the other boys hurried out in varying stages of undress. Marla's voice came on over the intercom a moment later.

"Rise and shine, kiddoes. You know the drill. I want everyone suited and in the hanger in five minutes."

It was unusual to be called for a mission on such short notice, but not unheard of. Cole and Bastian looked back at each other for one more second, as though to see if they'd been imagining whatever had just happened, then Berlin caught his friend by the arm, barking something in German before the blond finally turned and ran down the hall. Milo's hand was in Cole's a moment later and the haze he'd felt dissipated.

6

They had received no briefing as they had pulled themselves into the black jumpsuits, and even now as they sat facing each other on the sleek jet that could get them from one side of the country to the other in an hour, they had no idea where they were going. As they had boarded, they'd been given a small pack and a parachute. It wasn't the first time they'd jumped out of a plane, but as Marla appeared from the front and had them all prepare for the jump, a general sense of uncertainty washed over Bastian.

"All of the information about the mission is included in the pack we gave you." She shouted over the wind as the side hatch was opened. "You will be dropping in pairs and will be working different angles of the mission. You have been matched for a reason, so there will be no rendezvous to swap partners."

Milo and Alistair were the first pair to be called and Bastian tried to figure out what benefit they would have working together. There was little hesitation from them as they positioned themselves and then leapt into the still-black sky of early morning. He waited, expecting his name and Berlin's to be called next. They had learned to work as a flawless pair in Germany, so it made sense, but it didn't work out that way.

"Berlin and Sabin, you're up." Marla shouted, holding onto the railing above her head to keep the wind from toppling her.

Bastian looked toward his best friend and caught his eye immediately, then he got an inkling of what was happening. Before he could say anything, the other two boys had been shuffled off the plane, which left him and the dark-eyed boy, Cole, alone. Neither of them looked at each other as they waited the few moments it took the plane to move to their designated drop point. Despite his size and apparent timidness, Cole paused only a moment at the door to look at Marla who nodded to him, then jumped.

Bastian took a breath. He didn't like airdrops. Particularly, he disliked the falling part, but he couldn't wait more than a second, or he and Cole would land too far apart. So he braced himself on the door and when he felt Marla cuff his shoulder, he launched himself from the plane.

The sun was just beginning to rise when Bastian and Cole finally managed to reign in their parachutes and hide them away. Covering their tracks was important no matter what the mission. Crouching in a small space created by thick foliage, they located the small tube inside their packs beside a conservative collection of tools.

Bastian felt strange crouched over the other boy's shoulder, especially after the unusual encounter they'd had in the hallway earlier that morning, but no matter how he felt, he had to focus, even with the fluffy strands of black hair threatening to tickle his nose.

"What does it say?" He asked quietly and felt the smaller body beside him flinch ever so slightly at the sound of his voice.

Cole had not bothered to put on his flashlight to read the paper, but as his black eyes passed over the page, Bastian got the impression that he had no trouble reading it.

"It says that we've been had." Cole handed him the page, then stood up, all pretenses of secrecy gone.

Bastian removed the tiny LED flashlight from the breast of his jumpsuit and moved the light across the typed page.

We're sick of you guys not getting along. You're a team now, so start acting like it.

Beneath those words were numbers that they would all recognize as longitude and latitude, and at the very end there was one more blurb of writing.

P.S. We may or may not have released mutant wolves into the area. Be safe.

Kisses,

Marla and Venja

Bastian read the note several times, then flipped it over to see if there was information about their real mission on the back.

"This is a joke?" he asked.

Cole sat down in a nearby clearing where the light was a bit better and began digging through his pack. "No, it's definitely not a joke."

"They're just leaving us here, then?" He huffed and glanced at the paper one more time. All this to just make them get along better? "Do you know how much money it costs to airdrop us like that? Is she really just throwing your funding around for shits and giggles?"

"You get used to it." Cole sighed and looked up at the grey-blue sky that shone through the tree branches. He seemed disappointed, like his pack had been missing something. "Let's just figure out where we're going and get there as soon as we can."

He seemed different now that they were outside the compound. Cole, with his dark eyes usually downcast, had come across as being overly timid—the type who would bend over backwards to please everyone else. Now he seemed stronger, or at the very least experienced. He also seemed to know the area little better than Bastian would have expected.

"Marla dropped us in these woods last year to test some homing beacons she'd engineered from local woodpeckers. A few of them went rogue, though, and we spent two weeks combing this place collecting them so they wouldn't mate with the local population."

"What an irresponsible woman..."

"I didn't see your boss-lady stopping this." Even as he was speaking, Cole removed a map from his bag and laid it out on top of the dead leaves that littered the ground. With a small charcoal pencil, he marked their destination. Marla had at least been generous enough to put a vague red circle around where they should have landed. He sat back on his knees. "Assuming her comment about the hounds is either false, or we're lucky enough to not run into them, we should be able to get there before nightfall."

The part of Bastian that always bristled in the presence of this dark child wanted to argue. He wanted to ask, "who made you the boss?" He knew that would be counterproductive, though, given the other boy's prior experience with the area. So instead of arguing, Bastian kept quiet and followed the smaller boy deeper into the woods.

7

It was well past noon and Cole was reminded that it was, in fact, the middle of summer—it was easy to forget when they lived underground. He and Bastian had initially planned to make a speed-run of their trip and just jog straight for their destination. After all, if they were only going to be out there for a day, basic survival rules didn't seem that important. But by the time the sun hit its highest point they both decided they needed water more desperately than they'd expected, considering Marla hadn't been kind enough to include any in their packs. Following the land downhill, they began checking nearby gullies until they found a small running stream. It was shaded and the water was cold, but they were both still sweating.

In the hours they'd spent running through the forest together, neither of them had spoken. It didn't help much though. Even keeping in front of Bastian, Cole could still smell the sweat coming off him, could still hear his labored breath, and it made his whole body ache. He should have taken the few minutes to go back into his room to get some medicine. He was hungry, but he realized, more specifically, that he was hungry for Bastian. He'd never felt preferential hunger before, so he chalked it up to being trapped with him.

"This is ridiculous. How much further is it?" Bastian wiped the cold water from his mouth as he spoke.

"We've got a long way still. I told you, nightfall if we're lucky." Cole had sat himself on a rock by the stream and was rolling the sleeves of his jump suit up, needing to feel wind on his actual skin. The suits were made to breathe, but the heat was brutal.

A zipping sound caught Cole off guard, and when he looked over to his companion he could do nothing but watch as the blond peeled the fabric away from coppery-tanned skin.

"What are you doing?" The question sounded a little more scandalized than he'd intended.

"What? There's no way I'm keeping this thing on if we're going to be running around this forest all day playing some *team builder* game." He used the sleeves of the jumpsuit as ties around his waist and Cole realized that his eyes had followed the fabric all the way down. "I'll file a formal complaint if I have to; this is unacceptable." Now he was pulling his shaggy hair away from his face. It was slick with sweat and just long enough to be twisted into a small bun atop his head that he held in place with a piece of cord that had been included in their survival pack.

Cole ducked down to refill his collapsible canteen again. He wanted to turn his back to the show he'd not bought a ticket for, but he appreciated it too much to look away completely. Anyway, turning around completely might have been too obvious a reaction. He didn't want to draw attention to himself. The last thing he needed was for his teammates to start feeling uncomfortable around him.

"Well you can worry about all that *after* we get back home." He placed the full canteen in his pack and pulled it onto his shoulders. "We should get moving again. Besides, if Marla did drop something out here with us, it'll be best if we keep moving."

"She was kidding about that part, though. Right?" Bastian crouched to get water, seeming to forget his dislike now that he hated the heat more than he hated Cole.

"You have a few rude awakenings coming if you think she's joking." Cole watched the other man's back flex subtly as he stood and secured his canteen. "But I say we keep going before we find out."

8

It was late in the afternoon when Bastian finally decided he had to stop. He'd been surprised by the smaller boy's endurance. They'd kept at a steady jog for the majority of the day, and Cole had stopped to rest only a handful of times, always going only for his canteen.

"Stop," Bastian finally slowed his pace, putting his hands on his knees.

"What? We're really close." Cole was winded as well and wiped the sweat from his chin as he spoke.

"I need to eat something." It hurt a little to say those words out loud. He didn't *need* to eat, he supposed, but he was exceptionally hungry, and this *was* only a drill, as far as he could tell.

"It's just another couple of hours. Can't you wait? I mean, we've already come this far." He propped his hands on his hips, taking deep breaths to restock himself with oxygen.

"Look, I can run all day if I have to, but this stupid drill that your mama-bird is putting us through is not worth it for me." Bastian pushed a few stray hairs back up onto his head and turned off the path they'd found.

"What are you doing?"

"Finding myself something to eat."

Bastian could hear Cole huff from the trail—heard him pace back and forth a few times—then the other boy followed behind him.

"Can we at least make this quick?"

"You can't exactly decide how long it takes to forage." Bastian knew enough about plants that he wouldn't poison either of them, but luck was definitely a factor in finding something substantial. "Relax; I don't want to be stuck out here together any longer than you do."

"It's not like I—" Cole swatted a branch away from his face, seeming a little less graceful now that they were in a thicker part of the woods. "—dislike you, you know."

"Then why are you in such a hurry."

There was a long pause, then Cole said, "I'm just ready to be back home."

Bastian knew immediately that he was lying, but sensing that lie meant that his previous declaration that he didn't *dislike* him had been true. Bastian didn't bother calling him on his fib, since it seemed unimportant. Instead, he kept his eyes on the plants around his feet. He was relieved when he stumbled upon something familiar after only twenty minutes of silent searching.

"Here we go." He knelt beside a green, clover-leafed plant that was peppered with tiny white flowers. Pulling his knife from the holder at his ankle he dug the root out of the soft dirt.

"What is that?" Cole wasn't breathless anymore, but he was hanging back at least two yards, and even as he craned his neck in curiosity, he kept away.

"Wood Sorrel." Bastian lifted a string of roots that was dotted with little lumps ranging from acorn sized to walnut sized. "They'll actually taste pretty good once we cook them."

"Cook them? We don't have time to sit around here and *cook* them. Just rinse them off and chew them up and let's go. We're wasting daylight."

Bastian took his time digging up several more strings of the roots, wondering why he was getting enough for two when the other boy was being so blatantly ungrateful.

"Does it really matter if we don't get back this second?"

"It doesn't if you're okay with running into a bunch of dog-shaped killing machines."

"We've not seen one trace of those things. She was bluffing." Next,

Bastian turned his attention to finding kindling.

"This is ridiculous." Cole was muttering to himself, pushing his hands through his hair and then holding onto his horns like they were the edges of a hat he was pulling down hard over his head. Bastian could tell that he was stressed, and he was getting the impression that it wasn't just the dogs. His temper was uneven, like someone grouchy due to heat or hunger. It could have been either one of those things really. They were both still sweating pretty badly, and Cole hadn't had any more to eat than Bastian had.

"This will take less than an hour, alright? I promise."

By the time Bastian had made his small fire, Cole had settled himself on a large stone that sat along the stream they'd relocated. It had widened into a faster moving river that now whooshed loud in Bastian's ears. Cole had reminded him a few times that the noise of the rapids would make it nearly impossible to hear anything that might sneak up on them, but Bastian was still convinced Marla had been bluffing. They had been in the forest all day and the closest thing they'd seen to a mutant dog was a pissed off tree squirrel.

Cole seemed high strung, but he had done nothing that justified the dark aura around him—if anything he seemed more-or-less nice, if not a little neurotic—but Bastian was still determined to keep an emotional distance. He would work with him if he had to, but that was it. And working with people meant keeping them supplied with the same things he had.

"Here. It's your share."

Bastian held a stick he'd used as a skewer toward the smaller boy, the knots of roots steaming, even in the evening heat. When Cole didn't answer, he finally looked at him and he could tell immediately that he was unsure what to do with his offer. He sighed, then continued in a gentler tone.

"Please. Just take it."

That seemed to be enough, because his black-eyed companion finally left his rock to come and retrieve it. From the corner of his eye he watched Cole pinch at the roots, probably realizing that they were a bit like tiny potatoes now that they were cooked. Bastian blew on his own for a few seconds before popping one into his mouth. It was still too hot to eat comfortably, so he puffed air through his lips to cool it off before chewing. It was bland, but not bad-tasting, and when the mass hit his stomach he groaned just a little in satisfaction.

"Bastian?"

It was a little strange hearing the other boy say his name somehow, but he looked at him all the same and could instantly read the guilt on his face.

"Look, I'm sorry I pushed us so hard. We should have taken a break sooner."

"It's fine." He moved to sit on his backside, his legs tired from crouching by the fire. "Just eat, and we'll get moving again soon."

"Right."

They were quiet again as Bastian ate his little wild potatoes ones at a time, but no matter how long he watched Cole, the other boy never actually put the food in his mouth. He smelled it and prodded it, but never ate.

"Are you going to eat, or not? I thought you were in a hurry."

He watched uncertainty pass back and forth across his comrade's face before Cole finally sighed and walked the skewer back over to him.

"No, I'm not going to eat it," he said quietly as Bastian took the food from him. He walked back to his rock.

"We've never seen you eat." Bastian said, not pausing to question him as he started on the second helping. "Are you anorexic or something?"

"No." He actually chuckled a little. "I'm not anorexic. But I do have a, um... condition."

Bastian felt a half lie in his words.

"So you're sick?"

His mouth scrunched to one side and he shrugged. "Something like that."

Another half lie.

"There's just a very specific diet I have to keep to or I get sick." Cole continued, seeming to side step the heart of the matter.

"Is it serious? This condition?"

"Serious? Yeah, I suppose so. Not really life threatening, though, if that's what you mean."

Bastian felt a bit guilty about the food in his hand now.

"Are you actually hungry? But just can't eat these? Is that why you were in such a hurry?"

He looked at Cole this time, and just like in the hallway, found himself drawn into the tiny black holes in his eyes. Even from a distance, for a split second, he thought he saw stars going out at their centers. Something akin to pain, but deeper and slower than that, showed in those dark spots. Then a branch snapped somewhere in the brush that lined the river and the moment was gone.

Cole was on his feet immediately. "What was that?"

"Squirrels probably." Bastian didn't stand, but he didn't really believe his own answer.

There was another crunching sound—wood splintering—and they both knew that it was too loud a noise to be made by any squirrel.

"I think we should go." Cole's voice was low now, almost a whisper and Bastian was moving to his feet.

"I think that's a good idea."

He considered kicking dirt over the small fire that was still smoldering, but the moment he moved his feet, a red glow passed through the leaves—eyes. Then a snarl matched with a deep whirring sound. Whatever was watching them, it wasn't anything that belonged in those woods.

"Running now!" Cole shouted and both boys ran for the path they'd left inland.

Even with a full stomach and rested legs, Bastian felt his muscles shake a little as he ran, though he was sure it was the dump of adrenaline he was still trying to process. Even over their loud breathing, they could hear the fast, dense footfalls of their predator, punctuated by snarling and the demolition of the brush around it. It hung to their right, moving back and forth to keep them from predicting its pattern.

It was fast, and before they could make it back to the main path, Cole stopped abruptly in front of him and Bastian had to grab hold of the smaller boy's arms to keep from toppling them both over.

"It's in front of us, turn back, turn back!"

Bastian turned immediately, keeping one hand on Cole's wrist as he pulled him along behind him.

"Faster, I can hear it!"

They had been running at full speed, and yet this creature, which he could only assume was Marla's bluff, had been able to cut them off with ease. They wouldn't be able to out run it. Going on the assumption that this crazy woman really *had* set a monster dog on the loose, Bastian began scanning the trees.

"Here!" He deviated from the tiny trail and pushed through the tangled vines that lay on the ground, making a path to the base of a large tree. "Climb." He turned toward Cole, grabbing him around the waist and lifting him toward the lowest branch.

"What?"

"Shut up and climb!"

Cole was light, just as he'd expected from the boy's slight frame, and once he was high enough, Bastian put a hand under his foot to give him one last push into the branches.

"What about you?"

Without answering, Bastian took a few steps back, toward the rustling that was coming in fast from the direction of the trail. He was tall, with long legs, so as he ran for the trunk he was able to jump, kick off the thick base and just manage to catch the lowest branch. Cole's hands were on him immediately, hoisting him up. Then the creature erupted from the brush and crashed into the base of the tree, making the leaves shudder.

Both boys sat on the lowest branch that still hung a good ten feet in the air, staring at the beast that had cornered them. It had a black, sleek and muscular body, shaped like a massive dog, but as Bastian looked closer, he saw no fur. There was no flesh either. The muscles shone like oiled skin, but between them, he saw wires and pistons, and as the dog turned its head up to them, he saw lenses flash in the creature's eyes.

"Is that a fucking robot?" Bastian was about to say more when the creature leapt up onto the trunk, its claws holding it in place for a second before it had to jump away. Its teeth snapped only a foot below their branch. "Second thought, keep climbing."

Without any questions, Cole turned and climbed further into the foliage of the tree, both boys moving until the branches became too thin to support their weight. They shifted and settled as best they could, turning their attention back to their pursuer. The mechanical dog snarled and circled the tree, watching them as it did.

"Do you think we can wait it out?"

"My guess would be no." Cole was catching his breath, but didn't sound as shocked as Bastian felt. "Marla doesn't usually program giving up into these sorts of things."

"Is this normal for you guys?" Bastian didn't mean to sound so incredulous.

"Normal is maybe too strong a word. But it's definitely not a surprise."

"Ich hasse Amerikaner! What is *wrong* with you people?"

"Well if nothing else, we can catch our breath for a second and figure out what to do next."

Both boys were quiet after that, panting and watching the animal—if they could call it that—continue its slow pacing around the base of the tree. It was beautifully designed and Bastian was strangely impressed by this thing Marla had made, even if she had set it out to "kill" him. He wondered whether she'd installed some secret fail-safe that would keep the machine from actually succeeding. If she had, he didn't want to figure out how serious it had to get to kick in.

"So," Cole said, smiling in a way he probably thought was hopeful. "We're all special agents, right? People who work with Haven usually have some pretty cool powers. What about you? Anything useful? Laser vision? Telekinesis? Anything like that?"

Bastian swallowed. "Not really. How about you?"

"...not really."

Bastian nodded and took a deep breath, then an ear-piercing roar broke the silence of the forest. For a second, Bastian thought the creature really was screaming, then his brain placed the constant, deafening buzz. Looking back to the beast, he saw it had grown still, its stance wide as it faced the trunk of the tree, its upper jaw pulled back as its mouth gaped, leaving room for the spinning blade of a chainsaw to extend from its gullet. The tree shook as the chained blade began eating through the flesh of their tower.

"Are you fucking kidding me!"

"God, we're gonna have to jump." Cole squirmed on the branch beside him, and Bastian knew he was right.

41

"When we hit the ground, let's head back to the river. Maybe water will short it out."

"Sure."

Bastian could hear the nervousness in Cole's voice, but the other boy didn't question his choice, simply held on and waited as the tree began to sway and then eventually snap. The slow arc the tree began to fall in promised them an easy landing, then their mechanical assailant rammed itself hard into the splintering base of the tree and the whole thing jerked and gave. Cole faltered, and with nothing more than a gasp, started to fall.

Sitting inside of their underground base, Bastian would not have considered a future in which he would put himself at risk to save a person like Cole—a person with such a dark quality about him—but now he jumped from his own perch in an automated reaction, grabbing hold of the other boy, coiling around him and breaking his fall. They held still as the branches fell and shook around them, and for a second they remained still, Bastian's arms wrapped around Cole's slight shoulders, his body cushioning the smaller boy from the hardness of the forest floor.

Then the branches rustled as the creature began rooting for them.

"Go, hurry—I'll be right behind you."

Tearing themselves out of the leafy wreckage, they both made for the path that would lead them back to the river. Immediately, Bastian knew he'd damaged something in his leg. He didn't think it was broken, but pain shot from his ankle up through his knee to his hip. As the wild machine snarled and pushed through the branches of the fallen tree, though, his body dumped enough adrenaline into his system that he was able to ignore the pain, and kept only a few feet behind his partner.

It was hard not to feel useless as they splashed into the river, stumbling as the water came up around their thighs, then their waists. They slowed and grabbed onto each other for stability as they turned to watch their pursuer slide to a stop at the edge of the water. It looked like his guess had been right, and Bastian barked a triumphant laugh.

"Das ist richtig, du verdammter Taschenuhr!"

Cole laughed beside him until a slit opened up in the dog's

shoulder, revealing a small muzzle. A gunshot sounded and echoed as Cole's body jerked away from Bastian and fell back hard into the water. For a second, Bastian felt like the bullet had passed through him to get to the other boy. Air was forced out of his lungs, his stomach twisting and his mind blanking as he blindly reached from the dark hair that was floating just under the surface of the water. He pulled him above the surface.

"Cole!"

The panic of this boy's name on his lips struck something horrific inside him, though it was something he couldn't mold into any coherent thought. Then the pale boy coughed and flailed in his arms, bringing a hand to his chest that was now sopping wet, but blood free.

"R-rubber." Cole's voice was strained and just a little raspy. "Rubber bullets. Fuck that hurt." He staggered and grabbed at Bastian's bare shoulders for support as he maneuvered his feet back under him in the fast moving water.

Another gunshot sounded and the bullet pierced the water just beside them. Turning their attention back to their enemy they watched as panels slid open on either side. Buoys began inflating like some kind of comical doggie life vest. When they were full, the beast stepped into the water and began motoring toward them.

"Oh, come on!"

Cole kept hold of his chest as he groaned, turned and pulled Bastian toward the other side of the river. The deep water slowed them down and by the time they had their footing on the shifting river stones again, their pursuer was close behind them. Bastian pushed the smaller boy ahead of him, hurrying him into the shallows.

"Run as soon as you hit shore. Don't wait for me." It was hard to tell why he was suddenly so intent on keeping Cole safe. He barely knew him, barely *liked* him, and yet now, in the heat of the moment, all he could think about was keeping him unharmed.

The water splashed around their knees and Cole did as he was told, taking off at a sprint toward the tree line. Bastian stumbled on his sprained ankle, but said nothing, not wanting to give his partner any reason to slow down. He was glad that he saw the black of Cole's body suit, and the black of his hair, disappearing behind the leaves of the forest when the dog's teeth sunk into his calf. He'd barely heard the slosh of the creature hitting shore, and he growled to keep from shouting, not wanting to alert the other boy and draw him away from his temporary safety.

Luckily, the dog had caught him by his already injured leg, leaving his good foot to strike the beast straight in the face. It worked, pushing it off, but made the sharp teeth pull and tear at his flesh. He rolled onto his back in an attempt to get up, but the weight of the monster's body pushed him into the damp stones as it leapt onto him. His hands caught the cords of the dog's neck, which he realized were pipes, funneling what he could only imagine was fuel to the creatures bionic brain. He braced a knee between himself and the creature's chest and tried to pull the cords loose, hoping to short circuit the creature somehow, but it only snarled and snapped its jaws at him.

With a clicking sound that reminded him of a ratchet, the monster's jaw began unhinging like a snake preparing to swallow him whole, and he heard the beginning whirrs of the blade that had sliced through their tree minutes earlier. He felt his face drain of heat.

A kaleidoscope of lights had just begun shine off the tiny, spinning blades within the dog's mouth when Cole appeared. The creature shook as he struck it hard in the head with a rock the so large he struggled just to hold it. The black, shining body of the creature toppled off him, and Cole moved with it, pinning it down with his own body, lifting the stone over his head and bringing down over and over against the collapsing metal skull. He didn't stop until the body was still and the whirring had disappeared.

Cole panted, his hands still gripped tight on the rock that now sat in a mess of gears and brown liquid that used to be the beast's brains. Neither boy spoke for a while, then as Cole released his weapon and slid off the creature's body they finally looked at each other. Another intense silence passed between them and then Cole smiled.

"S'what he gets for shooting me."

Bastian laughed, louder and longer than he'd meant as he laid back, arms sprawled to either side of him as the tension left his body.

9

Bastian was heavier than he looked, and smelled much better than Cole expected. Not that he'd expected him to smell *bad*—he was almost at his limit after all, and just about anyone would smell mouthwatering. But Bastian smelled perfect, and Cole was starting to worry that he'd lose control if they were left alone much longer.

He tried to think of the ache in his legs as he helped the too-tall boy over the uneven terrain instead of the firmness of the arm that was draped over his shoulder. He tried to think of the bruise the rubber bullet had left on his chest instead of the line of muscles that rippled down the blond's side where Cole's hand was gripping him. He tried reminding himself that the tight fabric of his jumpsuit would *not* be able to hide his erection if he let it get that far.

Bastian's leg had stopped bleeding quickly, and even though Cole had cut the sleeve off the other boy's jump suit to use as a tourniquet, he thought it should have been a little harder to rein the injury in. He figured he shouldn't complain, and when Bastian grunted in his ear, he stopped thinking about the injury all together.

He was hungry.

Very hungry.

"I'm going to write a letter to your president." Bastian complained as they shuffled down a steep hill. "Complain about your boss's horrible judgement."

Cole laughed at how childish that sounded. Like a little kid who writes a letter to Santa to complain about the gifts he got that year. "Have fun with that. I doubt he even knows about us."

Neither of them talked much, too exhausted to do more than puff and complain every now and then. Cole was okay with that, though. Bastian's voice was deep, and the gruffness the pain in his leg added to it went straight to his dick.

This is fine. Just don't think about it, Cole. He tried to talk himself down. *Don't think about how amazing he smells...or whether he would notice if I licked that little bit of sweat off his chin. Or what he might smell like down where it counts. What he might taste like coming in my mout—*

"Fuck!" Cole actually shouted out loud to still that train of thought.

"What?" Bastian jerked and looked behind them. "Another one?"

"No, sorry." Cole pulled his partner's arm further onto his shoulders. "I just hate this place. I want to be home." He'd gotten good at lying over the years.

"Are we close?" Bastian asked after giving him the slow look he did sometimes. "I can probably make it without help now."

"No, we're close. And we'll just take longer if you're hobbling along."

They were quiet again for a while.

"You're different than I expected, you know." Bastian's voice sounded soft, even around the general gruffness it had taken on.

"Most people are."

"I mean, you're tougher. What happened to the meekness at the dinner table that first night?"

Cole knew exactly what had snuffed out his urge to please everyone else. Hunger. He considered his options. They were very close, and hopefully Milo would be waiting there for him. But Bastian was also injured. Cole could use the boy's other sleeve to tie his hands. His half removed jumpsuit would be easy enough to pull off. Then, after the shortest struggle, the sexual poison his body made would quiet any further resistance he might have.

"Being stuck in a shitty forest with a monster robot chasing you would ruin anyone's mood," is what he said instead of raping the other boy.

He hated himself.

"I feel like there's more to it than that." Bastian pressed after a moment.

"You're imagining things."

They didn't speak again until the bunker came into sight through the trees. It was built into the forest floor, with moss and shrubs growing over its domed top, leaving only a half moon face of concrete marking it as a man-made shelter. The door was unlocked, and the air inside was cool, though not air conditioned like their compounds. It had an earthy sort of chill to it created by the meters of dirt that lay over the top. It was dimly lit inside, though behind stacks of unmarked crates they saw the glow of an electric lantern.

"Did those losers finally get here?" Berlin's voice echoed through the low, wide space.

Milo was the first to come around the corner of crates. He looked like he'd spent the day strolling in a garden. "Jesus, what happened to you two?"

The tone of his voice caught the attention of the others who started filing into the space, none of them looking much worse for wear, save for Berlin who had a nasty rash creeping up his neck and onto his face.

"Somebody take him from me." Cole snapped, even more irritated now that he knew they were the only ones who had so much trouble with their little day trip.

Berlin came and immediately took Bastian's weight from him, and before Cole could process the questions that were starting to come, he took Milo by the arm. "I need to talk to you."

He knew he wasn't being subtle, but his heart was already racing and his vision was blurring. Behind them, he heard Berlin ask where they were going but didn't stop, leading Milo toward the back of the bunker where he remembered seeing a smaller store closet the last time they'd been there. As he closed the door behind them, sealing them in the dark, he heard Sabin cover for them, though he didn't quite hear his excuse.

"Cole, what's going on? Are you hurt?"

47

Cole could see the worry on his friend's face, his eyes built for seeing in the dark, but he knew Milo could barely make out his shape. He took the brunette's hands and moved them to the neck of his own jumpsuit where the snap opened up to release the zipper.

"Please, Milo, help me." Cole barely recognized his own voice. He was panting already, the erection he'd been fighting for the past three hours straining against the smooth fabric of his jumpsuit. He could hear the desperation in his own voice, but the hunger he felt dulled the shame.

Milo's breath shuttered and he paused, like he always did when Cole came to him trembling and desperate. Cole knew it was hard on him, that he wanted to be something more than a guaranteed meal. He also knew that no matter what, he wouldn't let Cole starve.

Cole's heart ached as the other boy paused, then he moved to his toes and breathed across the other boy's lips, extending his tongue to lap at the inside of his panting mouth. He never liked kissing Milo, knowing that the toxin in his saliva would cloud the other boy's mind, but the strength was draining from him.

"I need you," he breathed his poisoned breath into him as he spoke, and then Milo's hand was in the hair at the back of his neck and his mouth was on his.

Hands tore at jumpsuits, and now that Milo had been dosed, he refused to release Cole's mouth. The haze of arousal kept either of them from worrying about the mistakes they kept making, about the feelings they kept hurting, and soon they were both bare from shoulders to thighs.

Milo pressed himself hard against Cole's yielding body, his hand wrapping around both of them as their dicks strained against one another. Cole broke the kiss, his head dropping back against the equipment on the shelves behind him. His body rolled and pushed into Milo's hand, the friction of their members pressed so tightly together making him gasp and whimper.

"Hurry. Please, Milo, hurry."

Drugged by the aphrodisiac Cole had pumped into him, Milo turned and pushed him against the opposite wall where a small table sat. With a hand at the back of his neck he forced the smaller boy's chest down against the cold top of the metal workbench. Cole knew that Milo would regret being so rough with him, but now the force only spiked his arousal and he had to bite his lip around the moan that rumbled in his throat as the taller boy yanked the back of his jump suit down over his ass.

"You do this on purpose." Milo's breath was hot against the shell of his ear as he used his body weight to hold Cole in place. "God, you make me want to do horrible things…" he brought several fingers up to his own mouth, wetting them before moving them to Cole's opening.

There was no pain as Milo's fingers pushed into him, Cole's body buzzing with a need that masked any discomfort. His back bowed and his hands slid across the tabletop in an attempt to find something to hold onto.

"I'm sorry, Milo. I'm sorry. Please." He knew he was babbling, as he always did when his mind was plunged into this back hole of desire, but his legs spread and his hips pushed back against his friend's fingers as they thrust to the hilt and brushed all of his sweet spots. "Do it."

He was barely prepared, but Milo did as he was asked. Yanking his own jumpsuit down, he pressed into Cole's back, bringing a free hand to his mouth and panting against his ear. "Shh. When you make that sound, I can't control myself."

Tears stung Cole's eyes and rolled down his nose as he felt the hard heat press against him, his body surrendering immediately and letting Milo push inside him. He shuddered and moaned into his hand, reaching up to hold onto his friend's forearm. They were tears of relief, mostly, but the guilty ache in his chest made them feel a little sadder.

Then he felt the rush of Milo's ecstasy flood his body from where they were connected. This was what he needed; this was what would satisfy his hunger. His body shuddered and bowed. He wanted to tell him to go faster, to go deeper, but his hands were too weak to free his mouth. Instead he whimpered and grabbed blindly for the fabric at Milo's hip. He pulled and thrust back against his friend, forcing the taller boy to fill him completely. Milo staggered and had to brace himself on the table. Knowing that he was able to make Milo feel as good as he did was always a consolation prize.

"You're trying to make this hard to do in secret, aren't you?" Even through the whisper, Cole could hear the raw lust in his voice.

Cole gasped for air as Milo's hand moved from his mouth, but a moment later, he'd grabbed the sleeve of the horned boy's jumpsuit and stuffed it into his mouth. Cole's senses blurred as he inhaled a scent through the fabric that was not his or Milo's. Bastian's smell and taste filled Cole's brain—the other boy's sweat had saturated his sleeve when he'd been supporting him—and suddenly he found himself teetering on his own orgasm.

"God, Cole." Milo bit the side of the smaller boy's neck, his hands gripping his hips and pulling him back into every thrust. "I've never felt you squeeze me so hard. Are you that hot right now?"

It was almost scary how aroused he was, but it made his whole body come alive, and he cupped the fabric so it covered his nose as well and breathed deep.

"More," was all he managed to whisper before burying his face back into the fabric that smelled like a scandalous mixture of him and Bastian.

Neither of them could last long, and when Cole jerked and came against the side of the metal bench he was bent over, Milo had no choice but to fall over the edge right after him. The taller boy slumped over Cole's body, pressing him further into the now-warmed steel tabletop. He didn't pull out, knowing that Cole's body needed time to pull everything it needed from his release.

Cole could hear in his friend's panting breath that the high he'd been on was wearing off. Even the way he breathed was beginning to sound sad. And as Cole felt his mind wind down off the rush of feeding, his own regret moved in to take its place.

"I'm sorry." He had said those words so many times to Milo, but he never really thought they conveyed his true feelings.

Cole knew that going to Milo every time he lost his fight with hunger hurt the other boy, and yet, despite that hurt, his friend eased out of him with such care that it make Cole's heart ache.

"Are you okay?" Milo's voice was small as he moved his weight off him, the hand that had been gripping his hip so tightly, now moving to help him stand. "Did I hurt you?"

Cole didn't turn to look at his friend as he pulled his jumpsuit back up around himself. "No," he said quietly. "You helped me. Thank you."

Milo didn't move for a long time, his hands resting on the table on either side of the smaller boy's body, and for a second, Cole thought he was going to confess again. It happened sometimes after he drugged him in desperation. The toxins left the other boy's emotions raw, and even though they had talked about their relationship many times, it would sometimes bubble to the surface in the afterglow.

The small supply closet was silent for a few moments and Cole could see the uncertainty waver back and forth on his friend's face. Then Milo stood up straight and rearranged his own jumpsuit.

"We should get back," he said as he zipped himself up. "The new guys are going to be suspicious. We'll tell them I was checking an injury for you."

"Okay."

10

Typically, Berlin wasn't very sympathetic, but now he'd gotten Bastian settled down quite comfortably. Even Sabin had helped get him situated, fetching some blankets from a back corner of the bunker to help prop his injured leg up. This must be what Marla and Venja wanted.

Once they were satisfied, he got a better look at the tattooed boy's face. Dark red patches had spread over his cheek and across the bridge of his nose. It looked itchy and swollen.

"What the hell happened to you?" He said in English since Sabin was there and would probably have a more honest answer than Berlin was likely to provide.

"I hexed him," Sabin said offhandedly as he opened an antiseptic towelette.

Bastian looked back and forth between the pale, pierced boy and his friend. Berlin said nothing, but Bastian could tell he was pouting and probably embarrassed. Silencing Berlin was definitely a feat.

"What do you mean 'hexed'? Like magic? Is that real?" He'd seen plenty of other unbelievable things since he'd joined Haven, magic shouldn't be so surprising.

"Didn't they used to burn people like you?" Berlin sneered as he snatched the first aid towelette from the other boy's hands before he could begin cleaning Bastian's leg.

Sabin raised an eyebrow at him in a way that made Bastian think it was a threat. Whatever it was that Sabin was promising seemed to work because Berlin, despite being twice the other boy's size, ducked his head as he started wiping the dried blood away from the bite on Bastian's leg. He was still scowling, but Bastian could see the worry, and it made him smile.

"Cozy, aren't they?" Alistair laughed. "They've been like that since they got back."

"We haven't been like anything," Berlin snapped back in German, obviously wanting to rebuild the walls between himself and the American boys.

"He's whipped and it took less than a day," Alistair said as he twisted his strawberry blond hair up off his neck.

"How about you and Milo? Any surprise powers from him?"

"I couldn't tell you, honestly. But he seems to have his shit in order."

"It's called being a genius, boys." Sabin smiled as he handed Berlin a clean bandage, not giving him the satisfaction of snatching it out of his hands. "I'm assuming he made short work of your predator?"

"You mean those robot dogs? Did you guys have them?" Berlin was somehow relieved and appalled at the same time.

"We did," Alistair said, crossing his narrow, soft-looking legs and planting his hands in his lap. "And he did. I didn't even lay a hand on it, actually."

Sabin seemed proud of his compatriot, even though he'd not shown any affection for the other boys he lived with. "Let me guess, he pulled a cord out or something and the whole thing just fell apart?"

"Pretty much. He used a knife and cut some kind of fuel line while I distracted it. No idea how he knew what he was doing."

"You get used to not knowing how he figures things out. It's best to not ask though; he'll talk your ear off if you let him."

Yesterday, Bastian never would have thought he wanted this—to be friends with these American boys that they'd been forced to live with. Now he was thinking it would be a relief. Even with the pain that was thumping up his leg, he was content. He liked listening to the others conversation. He liked that it was easy.

"Why is Cole here?" he asked since the atmosphere seemed better now. "I didn't notice any sort of special power from him while we were out."

"Why are *you* here?" Sabin countered, not smiling anymore, but not seeming angry either. He watched him steadily for a second. When the other boy didn't answer, he continued repacking the first aid kit. "You'll find out when he's ready to tell you. And we'll find out about you when you're ready to tell us. Milo's brain isn't a secret, though."

As though on cue, the door at the back of the bunker clicked open and Cole and Milo joined the group. Sabin didn't bat an eyelash, but Bastian thought something was off between the two boys. They were very quiet and sat on opposite sides of the circle that they had all created.

"Alright?" Sabin glanced at Cole, and once the other boy nodded, they didn't talk about their absence again.

That evening, as everyone was settling down on the blankets they'd found to sleep on, Bastian realized he'd been watching the horned boy more closely than was probably normal. He was different than he had been out in the forest. He was quiet again, the feistiness he'd seen in him earlier gone. And when he unzipped the neck of his jumpsuit against the heat of the bunker, Bastian thought he saw a bite mark at the base of his neck.

Marla and Venja came and retrieved them the next morning and everything fell back into order once they returned to the compound. If anything, Marla had proven her point, because the invisible walls that had been put up around each of the groups were gone. Meals were often eaten together, and once Bastian told his friends that Cole had a condition that limited his diet, they stopped quizzing him and he stopped keeping fake plates in front of him.

Late each afternoon, Marla had the boys train together in the gym, working on their agility, strength and endurance. Bastian liked the familiarity of training—it was something they'd done back home. He also liked the opportunity it gave him to test himself, to push himself and explore what it might be that makes him special. He could tell no lies, and in return could detect them in others, but he didn't know what that meant, or why he could do it. He healed faster than others—the wound on his leg had closed up by the end of the second day without any complications—and he may have been stronger than some, but working out the way Haven expected would make anyone strong. He envied the others who knew exactly what made them special.

The door to Bastian's room had clicked open very quietly, and given his exhaustion after their afternoon of rope climbing and combat training, he was surprised it had woken him at all. He didn't bother moving when Berlin slid into the bed behind him and molded his body to his.

"Don't rub your rash on me," he murmured into his pillow.

"Don't be an asshole," Berlin complained as he slid a hand up the front of his friend's shirt. "You know it's already healed."

"Well I still don't know what you're trying to accomplish." He'd not even bothered opening his eyes. "I'm way too tired for this right now. And my ass still hurts from last night."

Berlin chuckled deep in his chest as he bit the edge of the blond boy's ear and pressed his persistent erection into the curve of Bastian's ass. "I'm sorry, Bastian," he purred. "Was I a little too rough on you?"

"I'm serious," Bastian said, finally opening his eyes and grabbing the dark-skinned hand that was inching its way down his body toward the waistband of his boxers. "It's not happening tonight." He turned over to look up at his friend who was still smiling at him where he was perched on his elbow.

"Come on." Giving up, he moved his hand away from the other boy's more sensitive areas and brushed fingers over his jaw. "I'll be extra gentle tonight to make up for it." He brushed a kiss across Bastian's lips that the other boy returned, though not enthusiastically.

"If you want to fuck that badly, then swap places with me."

Berlin rolled his eyes and leaned in to kiss a path down the front of Bastian's throat, spreading his hand over his chest again. "Are you getting caught up on that again?"

"I never stopped being caught up on it."

"I make you feel good, though. Don't I?" He smiled when Bastian let his hand slide into his shorts this time. He outlined the slowly growing length with his fingers. "Why fix what's not broken?"

"Because you're not the only one who wants to top. Isn't it unfair if I'm always stuck on bottom if I don't want to be?" Despite his frustration, he couldn't ignore the heat that was starting to pool in his stomach.

"You're so cute when you're all whimpery and begging, though." Berlin chuckled against his lips before sucking the other boy's bottom lip into his mouth.

Bastian didn't like thinking about himself that way. He didn't like feeling helpless—like he was just there as a tool to help Berlin get off. He knew that wasn't what he was, but he spoke before he could think more clearly about it.

"What if I don't like it, though?"

Berlin paused and looked at him but, the serious expression only lasted a few moments, then he chuckled like he was being teased. "Have you seen how cute you get?" He ran his teeth over the edge of Bastian's jaw. "How sexy you sound when you moan."

Bastian shouldn't do this. He knew he shouldn't, but he was too tired and too frustrated to stop himself.

"I don't like it."

This time Berlin went very still, the weight of those words coming from Bastian, who was incapable of lying, probably taking a few moments to sink in. He propped himself back up on his elbow.

"What do you mean?"

Bastian wasn't sure what to say now. Berlin moved to sit up on the bed, his brows creased as he looked down at him.

"You can't say something like that and then not explain yourself!"

It wasn't surprising that he was already angry, and Bastian moved to sit up as well so they were looking at each other as equals—Bastian hated when the other boy was looking down at him.

"I just...don't really like bottoming." He tried to keep his voice as unaggressive as possible.

"Well you could have told me that sooner!" Berlin was more bothered by the news than Bastian had expected.

He'd never thought it was a secret. He never went to Berlin wanting to be fucked. He would go for a quick hand job or even some shared blowjobs, but he never asked Berlin to fuck him. He only did it when the other boy pressed.

"I thought it was kind of obvious."

"Well it wasn't. Here I've been thinking that I'd actually made you feel good."

Bastian sighed. "It's not that it never feels good. It's just... not something I would do usually."

"Why let me do it then?"

"Because I care about you." He'd thought it was an obvious

answer. "Because I know you like it."

Berlin's face was a little funny.

"It's a trust thing," Bastian continued. "I'm sorry I didn't tell you sooner, but if you want to sort it out just…switch spots with me sometimes." He shrugged, not wanting this to blow up any more than it already had.

"No way!" Berlin's face twisted in something that could only be described as disgust.

"What the hell, Berlin?" It was hard not to be offended. It felt like he was saying, in the clearest way he could, that he was better than Bastian.

"I'm sorry! But it's not gonna happen."

"Why not? I do it for you. Why can't you do it for me every now and then?"

"Because it's gross!"

Bastian didn't want to admit that it was pain he felt in the icy spear that stung in his chest, but he was sure it showed on his face.

"So you're saying that I'm gross for doing this for you."

"Will you stop saying things like 'for you'? You make this sound like we're in love with each other. It's awkward."

The pain that Bastian had felt quickly boiled into anger.

He wondered how hard it would be to hide the other boy's body once he murdered him.

11

It was late, and Cole knew he should have been in bed. Instead, he sat in the smallest of the three TV rooms, the one that was usually used for videogames only because of the proximity of the couch to the television. Sabin and Milo were both whizzes at any game they tried, but Cole had never been very good. On nights like this, when he was having a hard time sleeping, he would try to get some practice in. Smash Brothers was their recent favorite, so there he was, being hammered by the computer, hoping he would somehow get better, even though he never really did.

He'd been there for nearly an hour, and just as he thought he should give up for the night, he heard a door slam down the hall. It was distant, but he could feel the anger in the sound. He sat still, trying to hear voices. Instead, he heard bare feet just outside the open doorway to the TV room. He wasn't sure why he felt heat rise to his cheeks when Bastian came around the corner, but the other boy's bare chest and the outrageously low ride of his pajama pants might have had something to do with it. He gave the V at the base of his stomach only a momentary glance before looking back at the other boy's face. It was a good thing he didn't let himself stare, because Bastian looked pissed.

"Oh, sorry," was all he said before turning around to leave.

"Wait!" What was he saying? He'd gone to that room to be alone in the first place; shouldn't he *want* Bastian to move on?

For a second, Cole thought the blond was going to ignore him, then he paused in the doorway and looked back at the couch Cole sat on.

"You wanna play?" He held up his controller, like he needed to specify what he was talking about.

Bastian was quiet for a second as his pale eyes flicked to the screen. Then, against Cole's expectations, he walked to the couch. He didn't say anything as he took up the second controller and they selected their characters. Bastian chose Samus, a character neither Milo nor Sabin ever played. Cole chose Ganondorf, hoping the character's power-heavy stats would give him an advantage. Maybe he'd get lucky and Bastian would be even worse at it than he was. Maybe that's what Cole needed to help his confidence—an actual victory.

Bastian decimated him.

If anything, he beat him harder than Milo usually did. It took less than a minute, then they sat in silence, Bastian refusing to move on past the victory screen.

"You're pretty terrible at this," he said after a moment, his voice surprisingly neutral.

"Yeah. Sorry."

"Was this your first time playing?"

That was an inevitable question, he supposed. "No. I play pretty often with the others. I've just never gotten the hang of it."

"What made you choose Ganon?"

"Um. I don't know. Milo's really good with him, so I just figured I'd use him too?"

Bastian finally looked at him, one eyebrow raised in a way that made Cole feel foolish.

"Well that's your first problem. Don't pick characters just because other people are good with them. Pick someone that *you're* good with."

"That would be great. If I was *actually* good with anyone."

Bastian snorted, and for the first time since he showed up in the TV room door, he looked *not* angry. "Here, try playing with a lightweight character like Pit or something. Let me see how you do with him."

Cole did as he was told and chose the small, angelic character. He'd be lying if he said the speed of the character's moves didn't make things a little easier, but even when he was trying to help him, Bastian didn't hold any punches. The match lasted longer than the last, but was still only a few minutes. Cole was okay with that, though—he was starting to feel embarrassed as Bastian sat grinning beside him.

"I think you like watching me lose more than Sabin does," Cole accused when they'd landed on the victory screen again.

"Some people just aren't good at games." He shrugged, even while he smiled. "Does it bother you that you're bad at them?"

"Not really, I guess. I mean, I practice sometimes because I think the others get tired of playing with me."

"So you don't care if you lose? You just want to entertain them?"

"I guess."

"Perfect. Let me show you something you can do next time. Just pick anyone."

It felt a little strange to have Bastian acting so friendly toward him, especially after the furious expression he'd had on his face when he'd come through the door. What was stranger, though, was seeing him choose Kirby for their next round. Cole couldn't stop his quiet snort. The idea of someone like Bastian—tall, broad shouldered, and masculine—choosing a tiny pink fluff-ball made Cole want to laugh.

"You think my choice is funny?" Bastian was smiling as he talked, and the beauty of it rolled off him like waves, making Cole's heart race just enough that he felt giddy.

"I just think it's surprising."

The match went on longer than the one before and Cole thought that Bastian was going easy on him. In fact, Cole thought he might be winning. He wanted to call the blond on giving him such a big handicap, but he didn't want to lose his opportunity to finally win a match. When Bastian's character was at nearly 200% damage, he went in for the kill. Then Kirby inhaled him. That was the main draw of the pink ball of goo, though, and Cole reminded himself that he would have to watch out for the arrow attack he would gain. Then, instead of spitting him out, Bastian turned his character around and jumped off the side, sending both of them to their death.

"Wh-what? That's cheating!"

Bastian laughed. "The next time you play, just keep swallowing them and jumping off the side. You'll still lose, but it'll make things interesting."

"That's horrible." He glanced at Bastian who was watching him with a casual smile. "Really, really perfectly horrible. Can I try?"

"Sure."

Bastian played several more rounds with him, helping him perfect the art of sneaking up on characters and then ruining them. A few times, the blond had to shush Cole because he was getting too excited when he successfully managed to drag someone to their death.

"So, do you stay up late like this often?" Bastian had finally set his controller down, letting Cole practice on the computer-played characters who wouldn't give him a leg up.

"Sometimes."

"Does it have to do with the eating thing? The condition you have?"

Cole shrugged one shoulder. He supposed it might. On occasion he stayed up simply because he was hungry and couldn't' sleep. He'd begun to feel the prickling at the back of his mind, but that wasn't the reason this time, so it was hard to answer simply.

"I guess? Sometimes?"

Bastian didn't ask any more questions about it, leaning back into the couch with his arms stretched casually across the back. It was becoming hard to focus on the game with the expanse of his bare torso coloring the periphery of his vision.

"What about you?" Cole watched Bastian's feet prop up on the table in front of them.

"I don't know. I'm usually fine. I just needed to blow off some steam tonight."

"Did you fight with Berlin?" The question was out of his mouth before he could really think about it, and from the corner of his eye he saw the other boy look at him.

"Yes."

Cole was surprised that he answered so honestly at first, then he remembered the others saying that he couldn't tell any lies. Berlin had mentioned it to him when they'd crossed paths by accident after they'd returned from the bunker in the woods. The information had come hidden in an insult, but Cole had gotten gook at ignoring a lot of those. He wasn't sure if he believed them or not, but he'd run into stranger things at Haven. And if it was true, he wondered if he should ask him anything at all, worried that it would be going against some sort of consent. He didn't want to force him into saying things he would rather keep to himself. Then again, he figured the other boy could always choose silence if he didn't want to say something.

"Was it a lover's quarrel?"

Bastian was quiet for a second and Cole kept his eyes on the screen as he pulled Ike off the platform to his destruction.

"So you knew?" He didn't really sound upset, so Cole just shrugged.

"It didn't seem like you were hiding it, really. And I did catch you sneaking out of his room in the middle of the night." He glanced at him and smiled.

Bastian let out a puff of air. "I guess that's true. And I suppose it would be easy for you to spot, too. You and Milo are a thing, aren't you?"

Cole's stomach twisted and his fingers paused on the controller, giving the computer players a chance to put him out of his misery.

"Sort of."

Bastian actually laughed. It was quiet and breathy—maybe a little annoyed. "Your whole life seems like one big *sort of.*" He watched Cole's profile for a while, and the smaller, horned boy could feel his eyes on him. "You're in love with him?"

Cole felt sick now, and he squeezed the controller hard for a moment before setting it on the table in front of him, accepting his game-fate. "No," he finally said after a long pause.

"But you sleep with him." It wasn't so much a question as an observation, and Cole felt his face flash with heat.

He always tried so hard not to be ashamed of it, but it was always hard to say out loud. Especially to Bastian, who had started taking up real-estate in his brain. He could feel a ghost of the shame he'd felt before joining Haven—before Milo had begun helping him—and suddenly found it hard to look at his new comrade.

"Yeah."

"I can tell by the way he looks at you sometimes that he probably doesn't feel the same way you do."

"I know."

He looked like he wanted to ask, "and you're okay with that?" But he never did. Instead he sighed and said in a quieter voice.

"I guess I just feel for him. I think he and I have a lot in common there."

Cole wasn't sure why he was so shocked that Bastian was confiding in him, but he was happy to move the focus off himself. "What do you mean?"

"Well, I've been trying to talk Berlin into swapping positions with me for months. But tonight he said that bottoming was 'disgusting.' Then he told me to stop acting like we were in love or something."

"Ouch," was all Cole could manage to say around the new and suddenly graphic image of Bastian spread across a bed with the dark-skinned boy plundering his body. He was definitely going to have a hard time sleeping now.

Bastian shrugged. "I'm not that surprised. Berlin's a good guy, but he's stupid and bad with emotions."

"You're in love with him?" Cole figured it was a fair question since Bastian had already posed it to him.

"I don't know," he said after a pause. "Sometimes I think I am, but...it's hard to tell when we're stuck down here without anyone else, you know? Our options have become very limited. Sometimes I think we just want someone to love, so we make exceptions."

Cole was speechless. He'd not expected someone who, less than two weeks ago, had disliked him so much to now be speaking so honestly with him. Bastian seemed to notice too, because he chuckled and scratched his bare chest.

"I guess Marla was right about getting chased around in the woods. Somehow, it's easier to talk to you now."

"Funny what falling out of a tree together will do, huh?" Cole thought his laugh seemed a little nervous as he tried to not watch the other boy's fingers rake across the hard expanse of his chest. He wanted to put his hand right there and find out exactly how warm that skin was.

No. Now that Bastian was starting to trust him, he couldn't do anything to mess that up. He would pay attention to what Bastian was saying about him and Berlin. He would listen to him and try to help him. He would do all the things a friend should do. A friend definitely wouldn't grope the solid looking abs that lead down to the waistband of his sleeping pants…

"Were you born with these?" Bastian's voice was quiet in the private room, and as his fingers brushed down the curve of Cole's horn, the smaller boy jumped in his seat. "Sorry. Are they painful?"

"No!" His face burned at the volume of his own voice. "I mean, no, they aren't painful. But yes, I was born with them." He froze when he felt the taller boy's fingers move from his horn into his hair, making his scalp prickle and his bones turn to jelly. He wet his lips, confused—he wasn't hungry enough to be *that* sensitive.

"I never thanked you for helping me while we were in the field." Bastian didn't move his hand, his fingertips coiling the downy strands of black hair. "I hadn't said anything because my ego was bruised. But you really helped me. Thank you."

Cole took a deep breath, doing everything he could to keep it from shaking. "W-we're teammates now. Of course I would help you." He saw the other boy smile from the corner of his eye. "And you know, I can try to help with other things too, not just missions. So, if you need to talk about anything—like if you keep having trouble with Berlin— or if you think I can help you sort things out with him, you can ask me."

"I'll keep that in mind." His voice seemed very gentle, and Cole found it hard to remember the cold way he'd spoken to him when they had first arrived. The warmth seemed to ease everything. "We should both sleep, though."

Cole felt his lungs seize for a second when the other boy's hand moved down to grip the back of his neck. It was a soft pressure, but firm enough to suggest how strong his hands could be.

"Thank you, Cole."

It almost sounded like the other boy was whispering, then he stood up and made his way for the door. "Don't stay up too late!"

His neck still felt hot where Bastian had touched his skin. He did sleep shortly after that—more comfortably than he had in a long time—and he wondered how the other boy made him feel so jittery and yet so calm at the same time.

12

It was hard to explain why, but the dark aura Bastian had once felt around Cole now felt soft and warm. He could still sense something black there, but now when he looked into the smaller boy's eyes they looked like star fields rather than black holes. They had seemed empty before; now they seemed infinite. He scoffed at himself. What was he thinking?

Berlin had returned to his own room by the time Bastian had gotten back, and by the next morning the other boy had been back to normal. He didn't bring up their argument, and so Bastian didn't either. Somehow, after talking to Cole, his feelings felt less hurt. When he got to the dining room for breakfast, he thought the horned boy looked a little more bushy-tailed than he had the night before. He was sat at the table beside Milo, listening as his friend chattered at him. Bastian had gotten used to listening to Milo talk about whatever research he'd been doing with Marla during breakfast. Cole was the only one who always listened to every word.

He'd not meant to sneak up on him, but when he put his hands on Cole's shoulders, his small frame jerked and he craned his neck to give him a wide eyed look.

"Did you go to bed like I told you to last night?" He smiled when the other boy's face reddened just a little.

"Oh! Good morning. Yes, I did."

Bastian could tell he made the other boy nervous, but he got the impression it wasn't caused by fear, and his jittery disposition was somehow endearing.

"What do you mean 'last night?'" Milo's brows had drawn into a straight line over his glasses. "I was the last one to see you last night. You went to your room straight from mine."

Bastian squeezed his new friend's shoulders as he felt him go just a little stiff, then he released him and went around the table to sit next to Alistair, who was flipping through a magazine that sat open beside his breakfast plate. He could hear the soft sound of music from his earbuds, so he didn't bother saying 'good morning.'

"I was having trouble sleeping, so I spent some time in the TV room. I ran into Bastian there." He glanced at Berlin, who suddenly seemed interested in the conversation, mid bite of toast. "We played Smash Brothers," he added.

Things were quiet for a second, both Milo and Berlin looking just a little put out, then Sabin chimed in. "I think it's great that you guys are getting along," he said as he pulled two more pancakes onto his plate.

"If I remember correctly, you weren't very interested in mingling when we got here," Berlin sneered as he scooped eggs onto his toast.

"It's called being mature and changing your mind when you realize you're wrong." Sabin cocked his head just enough to get the other boy's blood boiling.

Bastian glanced at his friend, wondering how he was going to handle his temper. He'd just thought he saw a slither of black at the neck of his shirt when Milo spoke up.

"I agree. I think it's good that you're getting along. We should all try to be friends."

Bastian was impressed by Milo's answer, because he knew he wasn't being honest. The half-truth probably came from the struggle between the boy's rational mind and jealous heart.

Bastian tried to keep the smile from his face as he felt Berlin seething beside him. He fixed his plate, enjoying his friend's just punishment until he heard him whisper, "What happened to him being evil? Weren't you the one who told us to keep away?"

Cole looked at him, obviously curious about Berlin's swap back to German.

"Evil or not, he's been kinder to me than you have recently." He didn't bother looking at his friend as he spoke, keeping the conversation private in their native tongue.

Milo had gone back to telling Cole about his work, but as Bastian looked at the black-haired boy he could tell he wasn't listening any more—his head cocked just slightly to keep an ear pointed in his direction. He thought the other boy was probably listening for any hints that Berlin was trying to hurt him again. It was sweet of him, but he chose to keep things private, and they both continued to avoid English.

"Are you serious?" Berlin asked. "I hurt your feelings once and now you'd rather hang out with the devil?"

"He's not the devil."

"You *said* he was evil."

"I think I was wrong."

Berlin scoffed, pushing himself into his chair's backrest.

"This is ridiculous. What happened while you were out in the woods? Did you fuck him? Are you *so* upset that I won't swap with you that you cheated on me?"

"Cheated?" Bastian didn't realize how loud he'd gotten, or how much attention he was drawing from his American teammates. They didn't need to know German to know that they were fighting. "If I remember correctly, it was *you* who said we weren't a couple. I didn't think it was possible to cheat on a fuck buddy."

Standing up, Bastian snatched his plate of food off the table, then took his cup of coffee and marched out of the room. From behind him, he heard a chair scrape on the ground like someone was about to come after him, then he heard Milo's voice saying "please don't," and no one followed him.

If he'd been a little less angry, he would have noticed Alistair grinning to himself, one earbud removed and hanging down onto his magazine.

For the next several days Bastian refused to speak to Berlin, though the other boy didn't seem very interested in ending the silent treatment either. In the evenings, after everyone went to bed, he would go to the TV room, where Cole was always waiting for him. They never did anything out of the ordinary. They spent a few hours each night sitting side-by-side on the couch playing games. Bastian learned that Cole was much better at co-op games and was talented at puzzle solving, and so often spent time back-seat gaming instead of playing. He would grab onto Bastian's arm when he realized what they needed to do and would wave his free hand around as he gave him directions. It was a good feeling having him huddled so close to his side.

They spent little time talking about anything of consequence. They told stories about missions they'd done and talked about movies they liked. Neither of them asked personal questions about powers or pasts, and neither of them seemed interested in changing that. Bastian found that he didn't even care anymore who or what the other boy was. He felt good being near him, and that was all he cared about.

During the day they had less time to spend together. Cole spent most of his day with Milo, who had started watching Bastian with uncertain glances. He could tell the brunette was jealous, and Bastian *did* feel sorry for him, but he refused to apologize for being friends with anyone. He wasn't trying to steal Cole from him. If he wanted to be angry with him, then he could knock himself out.

As for Berlin, Bastian wanted to force him to apologize. He knew he couldn't make the other boy feel differently about him, but he thought he at least deserved an "I'm sorry" and an admission that he'd been a complete ass. Despite his anger, he really did miss his friend. They'd come to Haven:Germany at nearly the same time. They'd been close ever sense. No matter what, though, he wouldn't give in first.

Then came their first real mission as a group, and for the second time since he'd arrived, Bastian found himself parachuting into a forest he didn't want to be in. This time there were no games, no secret bunkers they had to find, and no forced pairings. Instead, they were chasing a white stag, spreading themselves out in an attempt to herd the creature away from the town it had wandered dangerously close to.

Bastian's lungs burned in his chest, and despite the sweat that dripped from his chin, he didn't pull down the top of his jumpsuit this time. The material was thin, but it kept the branches and leaves from scraping him as he ran through the underbrush of a forest very much like the one he'd been in with Cole.

A flash of white caught his attention to his left and he aimed the small dart gun he'd been given.

"It's heading north-east!" He heard a quick 'roger' in his ear piece as he fired, the little red-tailed dart sticking into the massive stag's round hindquarter next to the three other darts his teammates had tagged him with.

The creature keened and swung his massive horns, breaking branches as thick as Bastian's leg like they were twigs. He hung back, not wanting to get within striking distance.

"How many of these darts is this gonna take?" he shouted into his radio.

"We have to keep the dose as low as possible." Marla's voice was steady in his ear and he had just opened his mouth to shout at her when Cole cut across his path, appearing out of the brush like a ghost.

Bastian toppled into the other boy, both of them falling to the forest floor. Neither of them moved for a few moments, disoriented and exhausted. When Bastian realized he was laying with his full weight on the smaller boy he finally moved up onto his elbow.

"Sorry," he panted.

Cole just shook his head, seeming happy to be lying down for a minute. They'd been sprinting for hours and everyone seemed to be at their limit.

"I never want to chase this thing again," Cole panted, his hand moving to hold onto Bastian's bicep.

It was hard to tell if the tingling in his limbs was from his exertion or from the feeling of having this boy underneath him. It was like a stiff wind had blown the exhausted haze from his mind as he looked down at Cole's panting, sweat slicked face. He seemed small underneath him, and for a second, he wanted to wipe the hair that stuck to his forehead away to get a better look at his face.

"Bastian."

His hammering heart skipped for just a second at the breathless sound of his name, and for a second, he thought he was going to breathe the other boy's name in response.

"We're going to lose the others if we don't go," Cole continued, and whatever spell had fogged Bastian's mind evaporated.

"Sorry," he said, and he moved to his feet, then pulled Cole up as well.

He shook his head as they started running again, following the wide path the stag had made through the forest. He wasn't sure what had come over him, but there was something comfortable about Cole's body beneath his. He almost wanted to say "familiar," but knew that was too dramatic a word. It just felt pleasant.

He needed to make up with Berlin quickly. It wasn't normal for him to become aroused so easily. He must be pent up.

They didn't see the stag again until they came across the animal's fallen body, the four others standing around it. Eight darts protruded from the white fur and its chest rose and fell heavily. Its legs kicked and shuddered as it continued its fall into a drugged sleep.

"You made it," Alistair said, his hair tied into a knot at the top of his head, small wisps of his red hair clinging to his high cheekbones.

"Sorry. We fell behind."

Milo and Berlin both shot them glances—probably tired of seeing them 'accidentally' ending up together—but Bastian paid no attention to them. Instead, he approached the fallen stag. Up close, the creature was even larger than he'd imagined. Bastian stood just at six feet, but if the stag were upright, he was certain his head wouldn't even reach the beast's back. He wanted to touch it, but somehow that felt wrong, like his hands would leave some sort of stain on the animal's pure coat.

Sabin was not bothered, though, and knelt quickly beside the animal, pulling a small kit out of his bag he'd had slung across his back. From it he pulled some small bottles, a knife and something that looked like a syringe.

"What are you doing?" Bastian asked, and immediately Marla's voice came over everyone's radio, her volume high enough that they all flinched.

"Sabin, don't you dare hurt that animal! I'm serious!"

Sabin tore his own earpiece out and quickly unscrewed one bottle.

Bastian's heart stopped a second as the pale boy grabbed the knife and moved it toward the stag's still-heaving flank. He was about to knock the other boy away, but before he could do anything, Berlin caught Sabin's wrist, pulling the knife away from the animal's hide.

"Are you out of your mind? White stags are symbols of purity; killing them is forbidden!"

Bastian wasn't the only one who was shocked. Everyone had grown still, including Sabin.

"Do you seriously think I could kill this massive thing with a three inch knife?"

"You're still pulling a knife on an innocent creature."

Sabin yanked his hand away. "You might think three inches is a lot to work with because you don't know any better, but trust me, this thing would do zero damage."

Bastian snorted despite his effort to ignore the shots fired. Berlin shot him an ice cold look and he shrugged.

"Relax, Jane Goodall." Sabin said after a sigh. "I'm not going to hurt it. I'm collecting some fur. Alright?"

"Fur?" Berlin sounded too incredulous.

"You know, this white hairy stuff?" Sabin sassed back, bringing the wide mouthed bottle to the animal's side. Keeping the flat of the blade against the creature's side he razored some hair into the jar, never once drawing blood.

"What the hell do you need fur for?"

"White stags are hard to come by, and their parts can be used in some pretty fantastic spells."

"Parts?" Alistair finally made a face.

"Trust me, if I was anything like the Wicked Witch of the West, I would take this thing apart piece by piece. White stag *heart* is especially powerful. Don't make that face," he said as he saw Berlin getting angry again. "I already told you, I'm not going to hurt it. Not badly, anyway." As he spoke, he pressed his syringe into a large vein along the stag's neck. It was drugged enough now that it didn't even flinch.

When the phial was full he dug out what looked like a massive nail file. Then they heard the sound of helicopter rotors and he cussed and moved toward the stag's head, placing a hand between the two massive horns, as though to sooth the already sedated creature.

"Somebody hold this." Milo moved in to hold the jar under the file as Sabin began filing bits of horn into powder. He never stayed in one place long, as though avoiding going deep enough to hurt the animal. Instead he took tiny samples from a dozen different places, the sound of their ride home getting louder every second.

He scrambled to put everything back into his bag as the helicopter landed in a nearby clearing. By the time Marla came thrashing through the brush, they were all standing around the deer as though nothing had happened.

"I swear to God, Sabin, if you've done anything to that stag—" she stopped when she saw them all standing so innocently around the still-breathing body.

"Don't be so mean," Sabin said innocently. "You know I wouldn't hurt a fly."

Marla narrowed her eyes at him, then paced around the stag's body, looking for evidence against Sabin's reassurance. "Alright. Go get the straps from the chopper. We're going to have to airlift this thing out of here."

Flying a stag that was ten feet tall at the top of its head with a six foot antler span two states away ended up being more difficult than they'd expected. On several occasions they had to re-sedate the thing. Finally, they released it on the side of a mountain that was at least a hundred miles from any town in any direction. Milo had asked about attaching a tracker, but Marla had sided with Berlin, agreeing that a creature as pure as a white stag should not be sullied by things like trackers.

She also said they may have to chase it down again in the next year or two.

Bastian was not looking forward to it.

13

Cole didn't go to the TV room the night after their chase with the stag. He was too exhausted. And he didn't go the night after either, but that had nothing to do with exhaustion. He'd been too hungry—the exertion shaving almost two days off the time he could spend between feeding. Now, instead of sitting beside Bastian where he felt as normal as he ever would, he was tangled together with Milo in a bed that smelled too familiar to him.

Milo was being particularly gentle with him this time, and through the haze of arousal, Cole knew it was because he felt threatened by his sudden closeness to Bastian. Cole's heart ached, even as he wrapped his legs around the other boy's hip, his body rising to meet his friend's every thrust. Milo kissed his cheeks and his brow, but never touched his lips.

"Please, Cole. Please don't go to anyone else for this." He panted into his ear, holding him as tightly as he could without hindering his movement. "Please, only me."

Cole shook his head where he had it buried against the hot skin of his neck, not sure what his answer meant, but hoping Milo would take it in whatever way would hurt him the least.

It was hard to tell if he'd noticed at all as Milo gasped for breath and came hard inside Cole's still shivering body. He collapsed atop his friend and for the first time in what seemed like ages, he didn't get up to take notes or graph data. Instead, he just lay there, recovering.

The weight of another person felt good, and Cole was in no hurry to be released, but his eyes stung as he realized what he really wanted was the weight he'd felt in the forest when Bastian and toppled into him. He didn't know how it was different, but at that time, even exhausted, he'd felt warmth flood his body—a warmth unlike the starving arousal he would feel when he'd not fed. It was a gentle heat. It was what he thought Milo might be feeling right now. Cole swallowed and managed to wipe the tears out of his eyes before Milo lifted his head. To hide the gesture, Cole placed a hand in Milo's hair and smiled softly at him.

"Thank you," he said, thinking that his smile had looked sadder than he'd meant, because Milo frowned and pushed himself up.

"I'm sorry," Milo murmured as he moved to sit at the edge of the mattress, halfheartedly looking for his clothes. "I know this sort of thing makes it harder for you when I get clingy like this."

Talk like this was rare for Milo, and Cole thought that maybe he was feeling more threatened than he'd originally thought. He tried to deny what Milo was saying—knew he should tell him that his feelings didn't make anything harder for him—but he would have been lying. Knowing that Milo cared for him in a way he couldn't reciprocate felt like a knife slowly peeling away layers of his heart. It made him hate himself even more.

"Please don't apologize, Milo." He tried to hide the warble in his voice but failed. "I'm the one that's causing you all this trouble." He knew he should say 'pain' instead of 'trouble' but it was the agreed upon language that kept them from having to face their real issues.

"It's not your fault, Cole." Milo had found his pants, but was just holding them, turning them over in his hands. "I agreed to do this to help you. I agreed already knowing how you felt. I just don't want to see you beating yourself up like you used to. I don't want to see you starving yourself anymore."

"This isn't fair though." Cole's whisper was so low that he wondered if Milo would be able to hear him at all. "I shouldn't be doing this to you. It's wrong."

"Cole..." The way he sighed his name made the smaller boy feel even guiltier. "You know I would do this for you no matter what."

"I know, but..." He tightened his shaking hands into fists. "This is hurting you." He wanted to say that it was hurting him as well, but he couldn't bring himself to do it. He deserved to hurt.

The smile that softened Milo's face was sadder than any other expression he could have shown him. "As long as I get to stay close to you, and as long as I can keep you healthy, it's all worth it."

"I wish I could fix this." Cole could tell that his words stung just a little, because Milo puffed air through his nose and started pulling his pants on. "If I could fall in love with someone, I know it would be you."

Milo wasn't smiling any more, his face falling into something so neutral that it felt unsettling. "We don't know for sure that you can't. You shouldn't write yourself off yet."

"I know I can't."

Milo was quiet for a second as he pulled his shirt on over his head, then, in a voice that was too even to be natural, he said "What about Bastian?"

"What?" Cole felt his face heat instantly and his heart begin to race.

"I'm asking if you're in love with Bastian." Even in the stony calmness of his voice, Cole could hear the weight of the accusation. He could tell that Milo had already decided on an answer.

"Of course I'm not." A strange urge to cover his naked body washed over him and he wondered how just the thought could embarrass him so intensely. "It would be you if I could. I know it."

Milo's sigh shook just a little and he looked away from his friend. "Love doesn't work that way, Cole. You don't get to pick who you fall for. It's instinctual. Hormonal. You can't just choose the person who's done the most for you."

"There's nothing between me and Bastian, Milo. I promise." He was telling the truth. Nothing had happened between him and Bastian. All they had done was play games together. And yet, somewhere in his gut he felt a jab of dishonesty. His heart hurt a little as he admitted, "He just... smells good. He makes me hungry sometimes. Even after I've fed." He felt like garbage admitting this, but thought that Milo of all people deserved the truth. Both because he'd done so much for him—sacrificed so much—but also because he'd asked him about this sort of thing before, insisting that it would be important for his research and the development of the medicine he'd been making him.

He didn't look at his friend, not wanting to see the pain he was sure he was causing.

"I think it would be best if you didn't spend time alone with him," Milo finally said after a long pause.

"What?" Cole didn't expect to sound so disappointed, but his voice squeaked out like a child's.

"If you feel drawn to him even when you're not hungry, I think it could be dangerous."

A wave of self-loathing crashed onto him. He'd not thought about it, not objectively anyway. He'd felt the draw toward Bastian, but he'd ignored it, he'd indulged. But Milo was right. If he knew that the other boy stirred the hunger inside him, but continued to put himself in a position where he could cave...

He would be responsible if anything happened.

"I can't force you to do anything, Cole, but please... Let me make this one selfish request." He was looking at him now, his brown eyes swimming with something Cole thought might be love or pain. "Please don't see him anymore."

The thought of not seeing Bastian again made something squirm inside him, but Cole's heart ached under his friend's gaze, and after a moment he nodded. "Alright."

Staying away from Bastian proved harder than Cole had anticipated. During meals he tried to look at anyone but him. He kept his attention trained on Milo for the most part, and when he saw Bastian in the hall, he tried ducking down a different corridor. He wasn't sure if the other boy knew just how much he was doing to avoid him, but he felt like any choice he made would betray someone. His loyalty had to lie with Milo, though, so he continued for the better part of a week.

Then he found him in the gym.

That wasn't so unusual, but from the far end of the hall that lead to the gym, Cole had heard the sound of music. Music wasn't so unusual either, whether it was the fast-paced punk that leaked out of Sabin's room, or the dance music that had started to fill the hall since Alistair had moved in, but this time it was something much gentler. A classical, string-heavy song floated down the hall and before Cole knew what he was doing, he'd followed it down to the open room they used most often for martial arts practice. A mirror covered one wall, but the mats they used to cushion falls and take-downs had been moved and stacked to the side, revealing a wooden floor Cole didn't even know was there.

Bastian was there, but more surprisingly, he was with Alistair.

And they were dancing.

Cole wasn't sure why it was so surprising to see the two men *waltzing*, but it struck him as being particularly strange. Maybe because he'd not seen those two interact much, or maybe it was because Bastian hadn't struck him as being the type to *want* to waltz. Either way, Cole found himself transfixed.

He wasn't very familiar with classical music, but Cole thought the song might be Blue Danube, and he was definitely more interested in it now as he watched Bastian's arm cradle Alistair. The thinner, willowy boy bowed back into a gorgeous arc. Even with his flexibility and dexterity in fighting, Cole knew he could never look so graceful. Bastian, on the other hand, looked taller and broader with his posture pulled to its full height, and it was hard not to feel a little breathless.

They spun and traveled across the gym-turned-dance-floor, their feet sliding effortlessly into the spaces created with each movement. Alistair looked like he was an extension of Bastian's body, every move he made perfectly complimenting him and perfectly trusting the arms that kept him from falling as he dipped or spun. How long had they practiced this? *Why* had they practiced this?

"Ow!"

Cole jumped as Alistair's voice broke the trans all three of them seemed to be in.

"Tut mir Leid..." Bastian wasn't panting, but he did sound just a little out of breath.

"Warum Schritt Sie auf meinem Fuß?" Alistair slid his foot out of his shoes and bent down to rub it, like he was trying to make sure he wasn't seriously injured.

Cole hadn't even seen Bastian step on the other boy, but their legs had been such a tangle he was surprised it hadn't happened sooner.

"Es ist immer das gleiche verdammte Fuß."

"Ich weiß. Es tut mir leid , aber ich kann in diesem Zug nicht Recht bekommen." Bastian put his hands on his hips, his stature relaxing into something Cole was more accostomed to seeing.

The two bickered for a while longer, Alistair looking like he wanted to shake his finger at him. It was more than he'd ever heard the tall, slender redhead say. Cole couldn't see Bastian's face since his back was almost fully turned toward him, but he could see in the way he rolled his head back just a little that he was used to these lectures.

Then Alistair's eyes fell on Cole and he froze.

"Wir haben ein Publikum."

Bastian turned around faster than Cole was expecting, leaving him no time to flee.

"Cole." The blond man seemed surprised, but not unhappy about the intrusion. "What are you doing here?"

"I heard music."

"Well come on then." Alistair waved him into the room, smiling wider than he'd ever seen his usually aloof teammate manage.

There was still something mischievous in his eyes, but Cole did as he was told, inching into the room. This wasn't going against what he'd promised to Milo, not technically. He'd promised not to spend time *alone* with Bastian. He wasn't alone with him. Alistair was there.

"Have you ever danced before?" The redhead asked as Cole approached them.

"Hör auf." Bastian's voice was a bit hard as he looked at his friend.

"Entspannen Sie Sich. Sie haben Spaß." Alistair's tone was very dismissive, and he continued in english immediately. "Have you ever danced?" he asked again.

"No, I haven't," Cole admitted, only glancing at Bastian for a second.

"Come on. We'll teach you." Alistair had grabbed Cole's arm before he could say anything, and even as he tried to scramble away when he was pushed toward Bastian, the thin arms behind him wouldn't budge.

"He didn't say he *wanted* to learn, Alistair. Leave him be."

The tone in Bastian's voice reminded him a little of the first time they'd arrived at Haven. It hurt to hear it, but Cole knew he probably deserved the cold shoulder. He'd not been that secretive in his avoidance. Despite his words, though, he still opened his arms to receive Cole as Alistair pushed them together.

"Now, now. I bet he's a natural."

Cole's heart felt like it was trying to break his ribs out from the inside. He'd never felt the same pheromonal draw to Alistair that he seemed to feel toward Bastian, but there was no way he could deny that the redhead was beautiful. He was the type of beautiful that made other people uncomfortable. And as he stepped up behind him, sandwiching him between his slender figure and Bastian's broad chest, Cole thought his head might explode.

Bastian sighed, but did as he was told as Alistair moved Cole's arms like some sort of puppet master, murmuring directions in his ear as he did.

"Keep your hand on his shoulder like this. Bow your back so that his hand sits in the curve it makes here." He pressed Bastian's hand firmly into the soft place just below his ribs and Cole could feel strong fingers splay out across his back, promising support. "Eventually you'll have to keep your head up, but for now watch your feet."

Bastian didn't hesitate as Alistair used his own body to press Cole into the moves.

"One. Two. Three. Four. Just like that, over and over." His voice was soft as he spoke near his ear, but the only thing Cole could focus on was the heat of Bastian's hands on him.

What was he doing? He'd promised Milo to keep away from Bastian less than a week ago, and now he was dancing with him? Alistair was still there, though. That counted. It had to count.

"Okay. Keep going."

The slender body behind him dropped away, stepping back to watch as the other two boys continued in the motion he'd started them in. Their movements were much slower than what Cole had seen from the doorway, and he was sure his limbs jerked awkwardly every time he moved them. When he finally dared a glance up at his partner's face he felt a weight drop into his stomach. He looked so cold.

"I'm sorry you got stuck teaching me this." Cole muttered as he looked back down at his feet.

"Do you really think that's the apology I want to hear?"

Cole's breath paused a second, and he thought the other boy might be able to feel just how fast his heart was beating where his hand was pressed into his back.

"Are you still fighting with Berlin?"

"He's been happy that you've been ignoring me." The bite was obvious.

"Fahren Sie weiter, und er wird Sie in kürzester Zeit zu lieben!"

"Halt den Mund!!" Bastian snapped at his friend, though it only made the other boy chuckle. "Berlin is an idiot. I don't care if he's angry with me. We've always fought, even before anything happened between us."

"I just don't want to cause you problems."

"You're lying."

Cole swallowed. Bastian had never called him on a lie like that before, not so directly. He wanted to throw Milo under the bus, wanted to tell him that it wasn't his fault, Milo had *made* him promise, but he couldn't betray his friend like that. He said nothing at all instead. They were both silent as they continued, neither of them counting, even as their movements slowed and got off beat. Finally, as though he were imagining it, Cole heard Bastian whisper.

"I've missed you."

Like his words had been a flame cast too closely to him, Cole jerked away from him, feeling more breathless now than he had even while they'd chased the stag. The flood of happiness he felt hurt him, made him feel like he was drowning in his own betrayal.

"I need to go. Thanks for teaching me." His words stumbled out of his mouth before he hurried to the door.

Just as he took the corner into the hallway, though, he felt a now-familiar hand catch his wrist. For a moment, Cole thought Bastian's olive skin was tinted just slightly in the cheeks. He spoke quickly before Cole could protest.

"If you really don't want to be friends with me anymore, that's fine. But if you do, please..." He swallowed like he might be nervous. "Come to the TV room tonight?"

Before Cole could decide what his answer *should* be, or what it was *going* to be, Bastian let him go and turned back into the gym.

14

It was almost 2am, and Cole still hadn't come. Bastian tried to tell himself that he didn't care, that the annoyance he was feeling came from the Needler that kept killing him as he wandered through the sewers of Silent Hill. He told himself he wasn't even waiting on Cole anymore, but every chance he had to look away from the screen, he found himself glancing at the door.

It was hard to explain why he wanted to see the other boy so badly. They didn't even know each other well, but there was something about the feel of him being close. It calmed him. It made him smile, even if he didn't quite understand why. Alistair had been harassing him relentlessly since he told the other boy how unhappy Cole's absence had made him. He should have never confided in him, knowing what a nosy, pushy personality he had.

"Are you sure *this* isn't why you can't sleep?"

Cole's voice startled him, and Bastian just managed to pause the game before his character was cut to ribbons. Throwing an arm over the back of the couch, Bastian felt a small swell of relief when he saw the other boy standing in the doorway. He was smiling, but it was a tight expression. He felt guilty for being there.

"Does this sort of thing scare you?" He tilted his head toward the screen.

Cole shook his head, but said nothing.

"Do you want to sit down?"

Bastian thought he saw the barely defined Adams apple on the other boy's throat dip as he swallowed, but he nodded and moved around to take the spot that Bastian opened up for him.

"Have you played this before?" Bastian asked as he un-paused his game, barely managing to escape death as he did so.

"No."

They were both quiet for a long time as Bastian played. Even with the slightly awkward silence, being close to Cole was still comfortable. He'd been playing for nearly thirty minutes when Cole finally spoke up.

"I'm sorry I've been avoiding you."

Bastian took a deep breath, trying to keep focused on his game to keep the conversation from becoming too stressful for either of them.

"Did I do something to make you uncomfortable?"

"No. You didn't do anything wrong."

"Did Milo tell you to stop seeing me?"

"Yes," Cole admitted after a moment of hesitation, and for the first time, Bastian thought he disliked the brunette. "But it's not why think. It doesn't have to do with jealousy."

Bastian could tell that Cole at least partially believed his own words, but he could still sense shards of a lie in them. He tried not to bristle, but he found it frustrating to see the other boy defend his friend even after he made such a selfish request.

"Then why *did* he tell you not to see me?"

Cole sighed in a way that Bastian had come to understand. It meant he was bumping up against information about whatever condition he claimed to have. Next he would say that it was complicated or that it was hard to explain.

"It's a safety thing."

Bastian couldn't help but look over at him now.

"Safety? Whose?"

Cole watched his fingers as they drummed on his own knees, his feet perched on the edge of the couch. "Yours." His voice was soft as he spoke.

"Mine? We're teammates. Marla obviously thought it was safe enough to drop us into the woods together. How could I be in danger hanging out playing video games with you?"

"It's hard to explain."

There it was. One of the typical answers Bastian got when their conversations got close to the heart of whatever was causing Cole so many of his problems. He'd been okay with letting the horned boy keep his secrets, but the longer they spent together, the more he wanted to know—the less he wanted to see his friend suffer on his own.

"Are you contagious?"

"No."

"Do you think you're going to hurt me or something?"

The pinholes to the night sky that made up Cole's eyes seemed to grow darker, if that was even possible, and his fingers grew still. For a second, Bastian thought he saw the other boy's shoulders quiver.

"Cole? Do you really think you might hurt me?"

"I don't *want* that to happen." His voice was so small, and shook so delicately that Bastian wanted to hold onto him until the tremors stopped.

Instead, he placed one hand over his cold fingers where they still sat on his knees.

"If you don't want it to happen, then why would it?" He seemed to just shake harder. "What is it that's wrong with you? I know you don't want to talk about it, but if I know, I might be able to help."

"No!" Cole pulled his hands away from him. "No helping. You can't help."

"What? Why not?"

Cole held onto his own arms, his knees pulling just a little closer to himself. "People suffer when they help me. That's why you can't."

Something prickled at the back of Bastian's mind, like some sort of knowledge that he couldn't quite remember, and for a second he thought he understood Cole's affliction, but it was gone in the next moment. Like a habit he didn't know he'd developed, he carefully brushed a soft piece of hair out of Cole's face.

"Alright," he said, his chest aching when Cole turned his eyes to him. "You don't have to tell me anything. Just please, don't avoid me anymore. We don't have to tell Milo if you don't want."

Cole nodded, and Bastian was happy to see some color come back to his face, even if it was a pink that flooded his cheeks.

Just as they'd agreed, the next morning Cole said nothing to Bastian at breakfast, and during their morning workout they both avoided partnering together. Cole stuck close to Milo, and Berlin seemed back to normal, chattering in his ear about some trip into the city he was trying to talk Venja into. An outing sounded nice, but the longer he stayed near Cole—the longer he had to pretend they hadn't seen each other just the night before—the harder it became for him to think of much else. He couldn't explain what it was that drew him so powerfully to this cimmerian boy, but the distance they were forced to keep between them seemed to only make his draw stronger.

It was the mystery of him, Bastian decided, though he wasn't fully convinced he was right. It was curious, though. Being told he suffered from some unnamed illness, the half-lies he kept detecting from the otherwise straight forward boy, being told that those who helped him suffered. Was Milo suffering? He seemed healthy enough, save for the lovesickness he seemed to suffer from. The more he thought about it, the more he wanted to know. Then he would remember the way Cole had shivered at the thought of telling him, and he knew he couldn't press him for information. That meant he would have to get his answers from somewhere else.

Getting Milo alone had been harder than he'd expected. He had met with Cole two more times, their meeting time pushing back later and later so they could do it in secret. He didn't press him anymore for information, and Cole seemed to settle back into the relaxed nature of their nights in the TV room. They would play games, or Cole would insist on watching Bastian play. He'd developed a new appreciation for the horror games he'd already enjoyed, because with the lights out and the room filled with the low, ominous music, Cole tended to huddle in close to Bastian's side in the dark. They never embraced, but the smaller boy would lean his weight against him, and

Bastian thought that felt better than anything he'd done with Berlin. Maybe spending time alone with him *was* dangerous in its own way.

Finally, Bastian got his chance. Cole had been looking pale at lunch, so Milo talked him into going back to his room to rest. It was hard to not watch Milo press his hands to the other boy's face, and it was stupid to feel jealous of a relationship that had gone on years just because he'd spent a few secret nights together with the smaller boy. He wanted to be the one to take care of him, but he also realized that he may be part of the problem. He'd not been getting enough sleep either. Cole going to bed early meant that Milo would be on his own, though, and when he left the dining room a half hour later, Bastian hurried after him.

"Milo!"

The brunette stopped a second to look over his shoulder. He didn't seem thrilled, but he still said, "Yes?"

"I was wondering if we could talk for a minute."

As though he could sense what the subject might be, Milo turned and continued down the hall. "I'm kind of busy right now," he said.

"I'm sure." It was hard to not let the annoyance he felt seep into those two words. "But this is kind of important."

"If it's about Cole, then we have nothing to talk about."

Bastian felt his face flush just a little, though whether it was from anger or from embarrassment at his transparency, he couldn't tell.

"Will you stop acting like you're the only one who gets to care about him?"

The suddenness with which Milo stopped and turned back toward him made Bastian realize immediately that he had said more than he should.

"Excuse me, but the last time I checked, you've known Cole for less than a month."

"So I'm not allowed to be worried about him because I've not been around as long as you?" Bastian tried to keep his stance loose, fighting the urge to square his shoulders.

"You can care all you want, but you don't get to just *decide* that you have the right to snoop around for information about him. And don't you dare tell me that you're wanting anything else."

Bastian stuffed his hands into his pockets, irritated that he'd been found out so easily.

"I'm worried. I want to help him."

"You don't *get* to help him!" The anger that rose in Milo shocked Bastian for a second and he was reminded of the strong reaction he'd gotten from Cole when he'd offered to help. "You don't have the *right!*"

"Look, calm down, okay?" Bastian had raised his hands in surrender, too shocked by the seething boy to really feel angry about it. "I'm not trying to get between whatever it is that's going on between you can Cole, alright? I'm not trying to steal him or whatever it is you think I'm planning, but you seriously need to take a step back and look at how you're treating him."

"How *I'm* treating him? I give him everything. I do nothing but help him."

"You told him to stop seeing me. You're using the guilt he feels to manipulate him and keep him tethered to you!"

Bastian could tell that he'd stepped on a landmine, or at the very least that he'd given away the closeness of his relationship with Cole. Milo watched him in silence for a long time, the realization that he'd probably been betrayed already sinking in. When he continued his voice was much quieter.

"You have no idea what you're talking about, or what you're getting into. I told him to stay away from you because you bring out the worst in him. You are going to make him hate himself more than he already does."

"There is nothing bad *to* bring out in him." He was shocked by the sincerity he heard in his own voice. "There isn't anything wrong with him."

Milo scoffed, a sound that seemed too crass for someone as poised as him. "You have no idea what he is."

Bastian opened his mouth, prepared to defend Cole from whatever slander he was sure Milo was raising against him, but the words never got out. Just before the pressure between the two boys in the hallway could hit its breaking point, a shriek echoed down the hall, followed by a clattering. They exchanged a glance, both knowing they would have to come back to their conversation later, then hurried down the corridor that lead to only one place—the showers.

15

Even from the distance and muffled as it was, Bastian had instantly recognized Alistair's voice. Bastian called for his teammate as soon as they entered the locker room, but got no answer in return. Something was wrong. The space was humid, still hanging thick with steam, and from the back of the snaking walkway they heard a shower head still running.

"Alistair?" Bastian glanced toward the empty locker area before taking the corner that lead back to the shower room. "Antworte mir!"

He thought he may find his friend laid out on the floor with blood pooling around his head, and as he turned the final corner he saw that he'd been half right. Alistair's slim, pale body lay sprawled across the wet tile, his strawberry blond hair imitating the blood he'd imagined, spread out in a sopping halo. But he wasn't alone. It took a second for Bastian to understand what was actually happening, but he recognized the familiar black, feathery hair and small body that was nestled between the other boy's legs.

Cole rested on one hip, his arm draped over Alistair's thigh, his fingers digging into the soft skin of his lower stomach, his head bowed as he swallowed the other boy's dick deep into the back of his throat. Bastian had never seen the black-haired boy naked before—had never actually seen him in the locker room at all. His whole body was pale save for the pink head of his erection that kept peeking through the fingers that formed a fist around himself.

Bastian didn't realize he'd frozen so completely until Milo pushed past him. The brunette snatched the other boy away, but for a second, all Bastian could focus on was the string of saliva that pulled between his swollen lips and the head of Alistair's cock. Then Cole's hands grabbed at the unconscious boy's body, making his head lull and his limbs drag lifelessly on the ground.

"No!" Cole's voice was shrill and sent a tremor all the way down to Bastian's feet; he wondered if he'd ever heard such a desperate sound as that one word.

"Let him go!" Milo took hold of the smaller boy's wrists, wresting his hands from Alistair's skin and from the red marks left from the ferocity of his grip. "You don't want this!"

"No, he's mine!" Cole's legs thrashed against the tile floor as Milo dragged him several feet away, twisting and struggling to get loose.

Finally, Bastian felt blood rush back into his head and he surged forward, bending to collect his friend's limp body, pulling him that much further away from Cole's grasping hands. His skin was cold, and while his eyes were open, his head lulled and flopped as he moved him. Bastian tried to rouse him, but all he could hear was the inhuman shouting and screeching as Cole struggled against Milo's stilling hands.

"Alistair. Alistair! Wach auf. Hören Sie mich?"

"Bastian!"

The sound of Milo's voice drew him away from his unconscious friend. He was losing the fight now, Cole having turned on him, forcing him onto the ground with a strength that betrayed the slender shape of his arms.

"Grab him!"

Pausing a second to lower Alistair's head back to the floor, Bastian hurried to his new teammate's aid, his hands closing around Cole's upper arms and hauling him to his feet. He was light, and for a second he wondered at how delicate he felt. Then Cole turned his impossibly dark eyes on him, and Bastian felt cold. The anger on his face seemed to soften as he passed his gaze over his face and then down his body.

"Bastian..."

Goosebumps broke out across Bastian's body, the hum of the other boy's voice vibrating his spine like a cello string. Fingers brushed Bastian's cheek as another hand snaked behind his neck, pulling him closer to the sweet-smelling breath that brushed pasted those reddened lips.

"I want you." The shiver that crawled over his skin broke out into a heat that clouded his judgment, and for a second, all he could think about was how soft those lips might be. "Please, Bastian. I want you to fuck me." He was whispering so quietly that Bastian wondered for a moment if he'd imagined those words.

"Don't let him kiss you!" Milo wrenched the smaller boy away by the horn, toppling him onto the floor.

Cole screamed as he was forced down onto the unforgiving tile, his hand reaching over the brunette's shoulder, begging Bastian for help. But before the blond could finish clearing the fog from his head, Milo had pulled a small glass phial from his pocket, pried the top open with his teeth and forced it into Cole's mouth. Blood spotted the other boy's lip where the soft flesh was caught between glass and tooth, but Milo didn't ease up, moving to straddle the other boy's chest, his free hand stationed on the boy's forehead to hold him still.

"Swallow it!"

Cole sputtered and choked, but eventually swallowed the opaque liquid. His body shuddered, and his legs slowed and then stilled where they had been thrashing under his friend's weight.

"Shhhhh." Milo's hand softened and then brushed the hair back from Cole's forehead as he shushed the slowly unwinding boy. "You're okay now. I've got you."

Cole's mouth worked around the liquid residue in his mouth once Cole removed the now-empty phial, and when he managed to speak, his voice was cracked and pathetic.

"Help me..." A shiver had started in his hands and feet and by the time Milo had maneuvered off him, he trembled down to his core. "Please, help me."

"I've got you. You're okay." He repeated over and over as he returned the glass container to his pocket.

Bastian thought he should say something, but he was still trying to process whatever it was he'd just seen.

"Take Alistair to Marla." Milo said, turning his head over his shoulder slightly, but never looking away from his friend. "The toxins should wear off in an hour or so. She'll make sure he's alright."

"What about Cole?"

"Bastian..." The name breathed past the shivering boy's lips, beckoning him, and before he could explain why, he'd taken a step toward him.

"Stop!" Milo was standing again, moving between Bastian and Cole. He put a hand on his shoulder, pushing slightly. "You take your friend and leave. *I'll* help Cole. I know what he needs. You need to go." He moved to block his line of sight again, seeming to notice how Bastian shifted just slightly to catch sight of Cole's pale body one more time. "Go!"

Bastian's feet felt like they'd been filled with cement, but after another shove from Milo, he moved back to Alistair's body, lifting him off the ground. It felt wrong to leave, and even as he made his way through the locker room, he could hear Milo shushing the smaller boy who still whimpered and begged for help.

Alistair was totally unresponsive, and yet some dark corner of Bastian's mind wanted to drop him in the hallway and go back to Cole's side. His mind had been preoccupied with the mysterious black-haired boy for a while, but now it overflowed with him. He knew that Alistair was the one who needed his attention now, who was the victim, and yet, he wanted to be cradling his attacker instead.

"What the fuck?" Berlin's voice jolted Bastian out of his head and he realized he'd been wandering back toward the dorms instead of toward the health center.

"Take him." Bastian wasn't sure what he was doing, but he passed Alistair into his friend's unprepared arms anyway. "Take him to Marla. Tell her something about toxins. I don't know. I have to go."

His heart was hammering in his chest, his body feeling alive at the thought that he'd get to return to Cole, and before Berlin could ask any other questions, he'd turned to sprint back to the shower room.

When he entered the locker room again, he thought that maybe they had left, though the shower was still hissing in the distance. Had Milo taken Cole somewhere? What had he given him that quieted him so instantly? And what had incited the change in the usually gentle boy in the first place? He didn't have any answers, but when he heard Milo's voice he thought he'd have the chance for some.

"You're okay now, Cole. I've got you. Just hold onto me."

"No..." His voice was weak, almost tearful, and for a second, Bastian thought he shouldn't interrupt such a sad sounding moment. Then he heard Cole's shaking voice continue. "I want Bastian."

Bastian's heart leapt into his throat, and he couldn't stop himself from peeking around the corner, no matter how private their conversation might be. Then he wondered how he'd ever mistaken the atmosphere. Laid out, right where he'd left him, was Cole, but now Milo was with him, the smaller boy's hips lifted into his lap, his hands gripping his hips, holding him still as he pushed his way inside his body.

Despite his words, Cole gasped and his back arched, pressing his shoulders down into the cold tile. Milo paused to catch his breath, his head bowing until his forehead almost touched the other boy's chest. Bastian could see a tremor start from where their bodies were connected and move up Cole's back, his hands reaching down to hold onto Milo's wrists.

As he caught his breath, Milo looked up at Cole's face, a hand moving up to brush his cheek. "You don't need him. I'm going to take care of you like I always do. You don't need anyone else."

"Please. Please, I want Bastian."

The pain on Milo's face was obvious, even from a distance, even from an angle, and for a moment, Bastian felt his stomach twist with guilt. Then Milo's hand moved to cover the smaller boy's mouth. "Stop saying that." His voice shook, and before Cole could say anything else, he pushed his body forward, wringing a muffled groan from the body underneath him.

As though he were trying to convince Cole's body, he picked up a solid pace, keeping one hand pressed tight over his friend's mouth, the other wrapping around his lower back to keep his hips off the floor. Cole held onto his wrist, though he didn't struggle against the silencing hand, his body shuddering and his legs wrapping around Milo's waist.

Heat washed over Bastian's body. He'd been asking for him. Cole had said he wanted *him*, not Milo. Was *this* what he meant? Did he want him for *this?* Bastian brought a fist up to his mouth to silence a groan as he slipped out of sight again, his back pressing hard against the wall, but he couldn't escape the suppressed sounds that Cole made and that seemed to vibrate the whole room. He could measure the speed of Milo's thrusts by the whimper that seeped from Cole's throat with each stroke, and all Bastian could think of was how tightly he must be squeezing around him. Despite the confusion that spun in his head, his body was much more honest, and the sounds left his dick straining against his zipper.

He should leave. He knew that even as he pressed one hand against the pressure at the front of his jeans, willing it to go away even as he reveled in the pleasure it gave him. He shouldn't be seeing this, but he told himself that one more look wouldn't do any more damage than he'd already done.

Bastian had never been into voyeurism, though Berlin had tried to talk him into it once or twice. Now, however, as he looked around the corner again, he felt his heart hammering with adrenaline. He wanted to see the flushed look on Cole's face one more time before he left. Bastian held his breath, not that his seized lungs would have done him much good as he saw Cole's body arch and roll against Milo's. Cole turned his head and Milo's hand slipped off his mouth, moving instead to the back of his neck where he held him for leverage. Bastian's eyes were fixed on the soft pink tongue that showed as Cole's mouth opened in a continued gasp.

Then he tore his eyes away from Cole's mouth and saw that he was watching him. He froze, certain for whatever reason that Cole would blow his cover. Then he brought two fingertips to his own lips. With the black pools of his eyes locked on his, he thrust those two digits into his mouth, massaging them into the wet, pink muscle that had caught Bastian's attention a moment before. The straining in Bastian's pants throbbed, and when Cole used those two wet fingers to trace the outline of his still-swollen lips, he had to look away.

This time, Bastian left for real. He bolted from the locker room and went straight for his own, not even thinking to check in on Alistair. In the silence of his own bedroom he struggled to get the image of Cole pinned under Milo out of his head. Bracing himself with one hand on his dresser, his free hand made short work of his zipper. He pressed his lips together against the groan he felt stirring in his throat and only grunted as he wrapped a fist around himself. Panting hard through his nose, it only took him a dozen strokes before he shot hot shame across the top of his dresser. How was he supposed to face Cole again after this?

* * *

That evening, Marla called for a group meeting—Cole was the only one who wasn't there. Just as Milo had said, Alistair had come around without any side effects or injuries, save for a few bruises and a small bump on the back of his head. He'd not said much about the incident. They met in the largest of the three TV rooms, and Bastian realized he was relieved that it wasn't the one he'd been meeting Cole in. There was something about that room he didn't want to see tainted. Marla leaned against the massive TV cabinet and Venja stood to the side while the five boys sat split between two couches and an arm chair.

"So you all know that our normal policy is to keep each of your files private. We do this because it's not our place to force any of you to discuss things you may be uncomfortable with, but given today's events we'll be breaking that rule." This was the first time Bastian had seen Marla speak without smiling. "We can't say for sure what Cole really *is*..." She folded her hands in front of herself. "But what we can tell you is that he sustains himself on sexual energy."

At this point, Berlin was the only one whose back straightened at the sound of those words. Bastian was surprised, but after seeing what happened in the locker room he couldn't say that he was terribly shocked.

"I'm sure you've all noticed by now that he doesn't consume food the way we do, and that's because his body can't process it. What you saw today is what happens when he goes too long without acquiring the energy he needs."

"Like an incubus?" Berlin's voice was already hard, and Bastian could tell this conversation was going to be a long one.

"It does seem similar." Marla had a look on her face like she was tired of hearing people say those words. "But we have no reason to believe that incubi are real. And we certainly have no reason to believe that 'demons' are real either." She used her fingers to make air quotes. "Because of that, we've chosen not to place a label on him."

"You're in this line of work and you don't think demons exist? Have you been sleeping through some of the missions you've had?"

"There are dangerous things out there, and unexplainable things. But there are certainly not demons in a biblical sense. There will be no labels of good and evil here."

Berlin's voice got a little louder. "You have someone living with us who might rape us if he gets a bit peckish, and you're saying that's not evil?"

"No, it's not. Ordinary humans have been known to eat each other if starved long enough. That doesn't make them intrinsically evil. When hungry enough, he's not in his right mind. He's ill, not bad."

"Tell that to *him*." Berlin swept a hand toward Alistair who sat in the recliner, his feet pulled up onto the cushion with him. He pulled his arms a little more closely to his stomach, but said nothing. He didn't look particularly traumatized, but anyone could tell he was bothered.

"This is *very* unfortunate. And we'll be doing what we can to make it right, but this was also very out of the ordinary. We don't know all the details yet."

"So now it's Alistair's fault? You think he did something to make him deserve this?"

"What I'm saying is that unforeseen things may have happened that turned a safe situation into a dangerous one. And while that may bring our choice to keep the information from you into question, it does *not* mean that Cole is dangerous. I just want you all to know that."

"Ficken Sie das. Dies ist Blödsinn."

"Watch your mouth." Venja interrupted, her hardened 'mommy' voice in perfect order.

Then Berlin started yelling. Marla yelled back. Venja tried to keep things civil. Bastian wasn't surprised by any of this. He'd expected Berlin to shout. He'd expected Marla to shout. They were acting just as they always did. The only one who seemed off was Milo. Given what Bastian knew about the brunette, he was sure Milo would be the first to jump to Cole's defense, but he didn't. He sat quietly, his elbows resting on his knees, watching his fingers twisting each other. Sabin was quiet too, but in a way that suggested they'd had to sit through this conversation before.

It was a relief to finally be released, though the subject carried on as Berlin followed him back to the dorms.

"That woman is out of her mind if she thinks there isn't something evil going on in that kid."

The way Milo glanced at them as they all shuffled toward their rooms made Bastian wonder if the other boy knew German. He was supposed to be a super genius, wasn't he? He supposed it wouldn't be surprising if he did. Bastian didn't answer, still not sure how he felt about the whole thing. He was glad once they'd made it to the privacy of his bedroom, though he pointedly avoided looking at his dresser, not wanting to remember how shamefully he'd had to clean his own semen from the top of it just an hour before.

"So?" Berlin said as he plopped himself onto the bed.

"So, what?"

"Tell me the details. You saw the whole thing, didn't you? Tell me about it. Was he frothing at the mouth or something?"

Bastian sighed. He regretted telling him that he'd seen anything at all.

"He wasn't frothing. He was pretty pathetic actually. I feel kind of bad for him." He sat on the bed as well, leaning back against the headboard.

"No, no, no. Don't let them get that sappy 'everyone's a victim' bullshit stuck in your head." Berlin folded one leg under himself as he turned to look at his friend full on. "Alistair is the victim. No one gets to try raping someone and then cry about it. That's not how it works. Besides, you said from the beginning that you sensed evil in him, right?"

Bastian picked at nonexistent dirt under his thumb nail. He *had* felt something dark inside Cole from the very beginning. And even after the boy had enchanted him, he'd still felt it—he'd just chosen to ignore it.

"He seems so innocent most of the time, though." He'd not expected his voice to come out sounding so small.

"Look, whether they refuse to say it or not, this kid's an incubus. I'm sure of it. Which means he's hell-spawn." Berlin got surprisingly serious when it came to his religious beliefs, and Bastian supposed it was the years he'd spent living in a Catholic orphanage that did it. "He's probably got you under some sort of spell. He obviously did something to Alistair, so we know he has that sort of power."

Bastian let his head fall back against the wall behind him. That would explain the draw he felt toward Cole, considering the nasty vibe he'd gotten from him that first week. He didn't want that to be the case, though. He liked Cole.

"Don't let him do any sort of black magic bullshit on you. He's tricking you. Manipulating you. Don't let him do it. We've seen his true colors now, so his charm shouldn't have such a strong effect on us anymore. Just stand your ground."

Bastian still wasn't sure if what Berlin was saying was true, but he nodded, trying to convince himself that he agreed.

16

Cole turned over in his bed for what felt like the hundredth time. He ached all over, but not from any physical excursion. The shame he felt twisting inside him made everything hurt. The worst part about losing his struggle against the hunger he almost always felt was that he could always remember everything he did. Everything he said. Despite his embarrassment, his face went cold, and he knew the blood had drained from it. He'd said those words to Bastian of all people.

I want you to fuck me...

He pulled his pillow around his face, hoping that it would just suffocate him and put him out of his misery. He could hear his own voice saying those words over and over in his head and wondered how he would ever manage to face Bastian or any of the others again. It had been two days since the incident in the showers, and he was still struggling to leave his bed, let alone his room.

A soft knock at the door startled Cole, and he lifted his head from his pillow in time to see Milo come in. He managed a weak smile for his friend, but didn't sit up, staying planted on his stomach in the safe cocoon of his blankets.

"How're you feeling?" Milo asked as he moved to sit on the bed beside him.

"'Bout the same," Cole admitted. "But I'm alright. I think I'm almost done pouting. I'll apologize to everyone tomorrow." He didn't want to tell Milo just how horrible he was feeling. And anyway, he knew that apologizing was the right thing to do, and all he really *could* do to try and make things right again.

Milo nodded, but looked uncertain. "You know, even if they don't forgive you, Sabin and I are always going to be on your side. You don't need them. Not any of them. They might be living here, but they're not part of our family."

Cole finally pushed himself up onto his knees, folding them under himself as he sat facing his friend. He could tell by his reaction that things were still tense outside his room. He smiled, though, not wanting to make Milo worry any more than he had.

"They aren't family, but this is their home now too. I'd be upset and uncomfortable if I was in their position. And whether they forgive me or not, I *have* to apologize. Especially to Alistair. And to Bastian. They're both kind; I think they'll understand."

A small warmth formed in Cole's chest as he recalled the short time he'd spent in the gym with Bastian and Alistair—when they'd taught him how to waltz. Things had been tense at the time between himself and Bastian, but both men were good to him. Milo's face hardened a little at the mention of Bastian though, and after a second he stood up.

"I just want you to know that you don't need their validation. I'm always going to stand with you. Okay?"

"You don't have to remind me." Cole smiled again, though it didn't seem to have the effect he'd hoped.

Milo's face looked pained as he left the room with a quiet "Goodnight."

The room felt quieter now than it had before Milo had come in to check on him, and he knew that it was the guilt that was slowly burying him, blocking any sound or light from reaching him. Maybe this incident was a good thing. Maybe this is what he needed to stop whatever feelings he'd felt stirring inside him for Bastian. Maybe the blond man would just stop speaking to him all together. That would solve a lot of his problems.

Cole pressed a palm against his sternum to try and alleviate the pain in his chest. He didn't want Bastian to hate him. He didn't want to be separated from him. Maybe he would apologize, but remind the other boy not to get *too* close. Maybe some healthy caution was exactly what they needed.

He wanted to see Bastian.

Needing the comfort, Cole pulled a hoodie from his closet on, zipped it up in a hurry, and left his room. No light came from the sliver under Milo's door, and Cole shut his as quietly as he could, knowing that his friend would be upset if he knew where he was going. It was stupid to think that Bastian might be waiting for him in the TV room, but if he was, it would mean he didn't hate him. It would mean that Cole still had a chance to apologize and make things right again.

His heart raced and as he navigated the dividing corridors, and he prepared himself for an empty room. That would be expected. Bastian, after all, had every reason to hate him now.

No. Bastian's too kind for that. He'll understand once I explain it.

The pounding in Cole's chest turned into a fluttering for just a moment, the warmth he felt when he thought of Bastian banishing the anxiety that had been pressing down on him.

Even when he is frustrated, he's not hateful.

He would definitely understand—if he was waiting for him at all.

Then he turned the last corner that would lead him to their secret meeting place. At the end of the hall, as though he'd just left the TV room, Bastian paused, clad in his grey sleeping pants and black tank top. Both boys held still a moment, several yards separating them. Cole thought the blond looked shocked, maybe even embarrassed that he'd been caught out of bed, then his face hardened a little and he closed the distance between them.

Cole hoped he'd been waiting on him, and after a few awkward moments of silence he smiled just a little.

"I was hoping you'd be here."

"I was just collecting something I forgot." His voice was cold in a way that started a small tremor in Cole's hands.

"I, um…" Cole swallowed and pulled the sleeves of his hoodie down over his hands. "I wanted to find you so I could…explain."

"Marla already explained everything to us."

It was hard to remember why Cole had wanted to see Bastian now.

He was angry—of course he was angry. He knew he shouldn't be surprised, but somehow he'd let his feelings for the other boy cloud his judgement, and now he wished he could just disappear back into his room.

"Then, I guess all that's left is for me to apologize to you. I never wanted you to see me like that."

"I hardly think I'm the person you should be apologizing too. Shouldn't you be saying that to your *actual* victim?"

The word 'victim' hit Cole in the stomach like a fist.

"I will apologize to him, I just—" His voice cracked and he had to try again. "I just want you to know that I never meant for anything like that to happen. I don't want to hurt anyone, I just...lost my head and—"

"Stop."

Cole felt so tiny under that one word.

"You don't get to call attempted rape 'losing your head.' And you don't get to say you weren't trying to hurt anyone *after* what you did. You *did* hurt someone." He paused and his jaw tightened, like he was chewing on his words, then he added, "and I have a feeling Alistair's not the only one you've hurt."

"No, I don't hurt anyone. That's why Milo always helps me. I don't want anyone to have to go through this. I just—" His words sputtered out when he realized he really couldn't say anything that would make what he did okay. There was no real excuse.

"What about before you met Milo? How many people had you attacked?"

Cole never liked to think about those months he'd spent in the New York underground before Marla had found him. He wasn't sure how he'd even gotten there, or who he was before that time. All he remembered were the abandoned tunnels he lived in and the way he would sneak into the subway terminals when he needed to feed. He hated thinking of that time in his life.

"I never meant to hurt anyone..." he finally said in a voice that was so small he wondered if Bastian would hear him at all. "But I didn't have a choice."

"You always have a choice. You *always* have a choice to do what's right." Bastian shook his head as he looked down at him, his body seeming taller and broader than Cole remembered it. Or maybe it was just that Cole felt so very tiny right that minute. "I should have trusted my gut from the beginning. There's evil inside you."

Cole stumbled as Bastian brushed past him, his shoulder clipping his as he left, and from the far end of the hall—

"We'd probably all be safer without you around."

The corridor around Cole seemed to white out, and even the clicking of Bastian's bedroom door was blocked by the pounding in Cole's ears. It shouldn't have been so shocking to hear Bastian say those words. Cole had known from the beginning that he did nothing but put people in danger. He hid behind Milo, saying that he wasn't hurting anyone, but he knew that was a lie. He noticed it every time Milo fed him—the ache in his chest, the sadness in Milo's eyes. They did what they could to keep the toxins his body made from effecting Milo, but Cole knew he wasn't going unscathed. Milo was caught in a web he'd never intended to spin, and Cole was sucking him dry even while pretending to cut him loose.

He thought he should be crying, but he was too numb to manage even that. Instead he walked back to his room, slid inside and locked the door. His first order of business would be to find every drop of medicine that Milo had left for him—little glass tubes he found hidden in dresser drawers and resting on tabletops—and flush the contents down the toilet. Then he would decide if he had the courage to do the right thing himself or if he would just have to wait until he wasted away for good.

17

Bastian had told himself over and over that he shouldn't feel guilty for what he'd said to Cole. It wasn't really a lie, after all—they really would be safer without him there. But the way he'd looked standing in that hallway still haunted him. He was glad he hadn't glanced back to see his face as he'd walked away. He wanted to talk to someone about the guilt that had been rising inside him, but Berlin was out of the question. He knew the other boy would just tell him to stick to his guns—tell him that Cole was just manipulating him.

But no one had seen Cole in days.

The other boy seemed to like his privacy, and it wasn't the first time he'd ducked away for a period of time, but it had been nearly three days, and Bastian couldn't keep himself from worrying. He also couldn't keep himself from noticing how much Milo was worrying.

Bastian wiped the sweat form his face as he made his way toward his dorm room after his mid-morning workout. The exertion had provided him a small break from the turmoil, and he felt cleansed for the time being. As he approached the cluster of dorm rooms, though, the reprieve he felt disappeared. Milo was stationed outside Cole's room, his head bowed until it almost touched the door. Bastian hung back, not really interested in being alone with the brunette.

HUNGRY FOR YOU

"Cole?" Milo knocked lightly on the door again. "Please. You don't have to talk about it, just... let me at least bring you some more medicine."

There was silence for a second, then Bastian heard a soft murmur from inside the room. He was too far away to make out the words though.

"I know you said that already, but I just want to give you more. Just in case. Please. Open the door."

Bastian watched Milo try the handle again, though it didn't budge, and neither did Cole. Milo put both hands on the door and pressed his forehead into his knuckles. It was hard for Bastian to guess why Cole would lock himself in his room, not even letting his best friend in to see him. The softer part of him felt like it might be guilt. He had looked so sad about what he'd done, but then he remembered Berlin's warning, that Cole wanted people to keep viewing him as a victim so he would have a continued food source.

But if he wanted a continued food source, why lock Milo of all people out?

He wanted to ask more questions—wanted to see if Cole was really alright in there on his own. But he didn't. He had to stay strong and fight the draw the demon seemed to have on all of them. Bastian turned away from their rooms. He would skip changing. Instead, he went to meet Berlin and Alistair for lunch. They would just have to deal with his sweat.

Marla and Venja often had dinner cooked for them, but let them fend for themselves at lunch time. There was a small kitchen attached to the dining room with a fridge that stayed stocked with drinks, snacks and simple cooking ingredients. If ever they had a craving for anything, all they had to do was request it and it would appear in the fridge the next day. Sometimes Bastian thought they bent to their every whim in an attempt to keep them from noticing that they had about as much freedom as a state prisoner. He didn't have much interest in leaving, though, so he never dwelled on it much. He hadn't left anyone on the outside. There wasn't anything waiting for him out there.

Alistair and Berlin were already there when Bastian arrived, pulling out what they needed to make sandwiches.

105

"So guess who got caught on the upper levels of the compound last night?" Berlin announced with a grin the moment Bastian entered the room.

Alistair seemed unbothered, but Bastian caught the subtle raising of his brows that said he was tired of hearing Bastian talk about it.

"No luck sneaking out yet?" Bastian said easily, not wanting to cause Alistair any more stress than he'd already been placed under.

Bastian my not have had any interest in escaping the facility, but Alistair didn't feel the same way.

"Security is a bit tighter here than it was at home. I'll figure it out though. It's only a matter of time."

The other boys laughed, mostly because they knew it was true. Veja had gone out of her way to try and keep the redhead from escaping, and had failed every time.

"Well if you're looking for inside information, you might want to try Milo," Bastian said as he pulled some plates out of the cabinets for the three of them. "He seems to be on the inside with all that stuff."

"Given recent events, I don't think relying on any of them is a good idea." Berlin said, the atmosphere of the room going a little frigid.

"Well blaming all of them isn't going to help us much."

Before Berlin could say anything else, their privacy was interrupted. Sabin walked into the room with his usual air of disinterest. They paused as the black-haired boy moved to the fridge, then Berlin continued anyway, as if he'd just remembered that they were speaking in German and had little to worry about.

"All I'm saying is that we shouldn't rely on someone who enables that kind of behavior. It's obvious that he's on *his* side, and not ours." He was at least smart enough to avoid saying Cole's name.

"I just—" Bastian glanced at Alistair, who had grown quiet again, as he usually did when the subject was brought up. He felt bad making him talk about it since it must have been a very traumatic experience, but he needed to say how he felt. "I saw him this morning." He paused, trying to think of a way to say it without giving their conversation away to Sabin. "The *criminal* wouldn't come out of his room. It seems strange that he won't even let his best friend in. I mean, isn't that something to worry about?"

"No. Let him sit in there and rot. Like you said, he's a criminal."

"Wow." Sabin shut the door to the fridge and opened the can of soda he'd fished out. "You guys are a bunch of grade-A assholes, aren't you?" He was speaking English, but they all got the impression he knew exactly what they'd been talking about.

"And what makes you think that?" Berlin put his hands on the top of the small island that separated them from where Sabin stood, his stance set and challenging.

"I'm here because I can do magic," Sabin said with a grin. "And you think I can't sort out a spell that lets me understand German? That's cute." He looked at Bastian now. "And if you're actually worried about Cole, you probably shouldn't call him a criminal. It's a bit rude."

"So you've been spying on our conversations?" Berlin's body seemed to puff up, like a cat trying to intimidate his opponent.

"You're the one who assumed that no one here knew German, *fotze*."

"Du Hurensohn!" Berlin made a motion like he was about to jump over the island and break Sabin in half, but as Bastian caught his friend by the arm, the slighter boy didn't even flinch.

"Stop it. Both of you." Bastian wasn't sure why he had to be the one playing referee, but he knew their team couldn't handle any more divisions. They might get dropped in the woods again if that happened. "I am worried."

Bastian rarely wished that he could lie, but it would have made things a bit easier at that moment, because Berlin looked at him like he was a traitor.

"I think it's strange for someone who is intentionally taking advantage of others to react this way." He felt like he was defending himself more than anything.

"That's because he's not trying to take advantage of anyone." Sabin sighed and set his drink on the counter. "That kid hates himself. He gets it in his head sometimes that he's a monster and then he locks himself up for a while. Milo will talk him out sooner or later. He always does."

"He *should* feel like a monster." Berlin said before Bastian could ask how often things like this happened.

"I am seriously shocked every time by what a raging asshole you are."

"He attacked our friend. Unprovoked!"

"That's not *completely* true, actually." For some reason, Alistair's voice seemed out of place, but as they all stopped and looked at him they realized it was because it was the first time he'd said anything about the incident.

"What do you mean?" Bastian let go of Berlin, turning his full attention to his red-haired friend.

"I may have been teasing him a bit." It was rare to see Alistair looking guilty, but his hand moved up to muss his own hair and Bastian recognized it immediately.

"What did you do?" He'd not meant to sound quite so stern.

"I thought it was cute the other day when we came in on our dance lesson. I could tell he liked you, so I was just teasing him a little."

"What did you *do?*" His voice was louder this time.

"I went in to get a shower and he was already there. I told him I could tell he wanted you. I said I could show him some pointers since I figured he was a virgin. He was *acting* like one!" He added the last part as though that were the thing he had to defend himself about the most.

"He goes out of his way to not shower with anyone else so he doesn't get tempted." Sabin didn't sound as angry as Bastian felt. If anything he sounded tired.

"Well that would have been good to know."

"Did you touch him?"

"Come on Bastian, I'm the victim, remember?"

"Did you touch him!"

Alistair huffed and shifted his weight between his hips, knowing he couldn't get away with lying.

"I might have grabbed his dick." He finally said, his arms making a floppy attempt at a shrug.

"What?" Berlin, of all people, seemed the most shocked.

"What? He's adorable. I couldn't help it."

Guilt wrenched Bastian's stomach as he recalled the things he'd said to Cole. Why hadn't Cole told him that he'd been provoked?

"To be honest, though, I don't even remember it. I was holding onto him and sort of laughed at him when he got hard, like as *soon* as I touched him. Then he kissed me and I sort of blacked out after that. You guys were the ones who decided I was traumatized. I guess it just felt good to be seen as the innocent one for a change."

"Christ, Alistair." Berlin looked more disgusted than was necessary. "Have you seriously gotten that desperate?"

"Why do you think I was trying to sneak out? Not all of us have fuck buddies hanging around down here." He swept a hand toward Bastian.

"Oh, I'm learning *so* much." Sabin raised an eyebrow as the three of them looked his way, as though they'd forgotten he was there. He sipped his drink.

"You're going to apologize as *soon* as he's out. You understand." Bastian jabbed a finger in Alistair's direction, ignoring Sabin for the time being. "I'm going to talk to Milo about it. And we're going to tell Venja and Marla too." Alistair groaned behind him, but Bastian was already out the door, not interested in lunch anymore.

18

Bastian had known that the facility in the US, as well as the one he'd lived in back in Germany, was much larger than what he saw on a day-to-day basis, but he'd never really understood *how* much larger it was. Milo had not been in his room, and Bastian had been too nervous to knock on Cole's door himself, so he'd asked to be taken to wherever it was that Milo did his research. It was always an annoying reminder of their prison-like circumstances when he had to buzz someone in. There were panels set throughout the facility and if they ever needed to get in touch with Marla or someone else in charge, they just hit a button. In this case, Bastian had gotten Venja, which he was happy for. He was closer to Venja and had to do less explaining with her. When he said he wanted to see Milo, she agreed immediately and sent a guard to escort him.

Doors opened from walls that seemed perfectly solid, and soon an armed guard appeared and escorted him through one of those hidden corridors. The lighting was different in these halls. It was more artificial, more bleak. It felt like an office building that eventually gave way to a hospital as they arrived on the research level. Bastian was asked to put on a jump suit before he could enter the small facility, and when he saw Milo's face planted in a microscope he thought the other boy looked much better in the flimsy jumpsuit than he did. He felt awkward and too large for the space. Milo looked sleek, even with the baggy suit covering his clothes.

Milo only looked up when the door hissed shut behind Bastian, and even through the facemask he wore he looked surprised to see him.

"What are you doing down here?" he asked as he pulled the mask down to his chin.

"I wanted a chat." Berlin's tongue felt heavy around those words, his body warning him that he was straying too near a lie. Milo seemed to notice, because he kept watching him, as if he was waiting for the real reason. "I'm worried about Cole."

Milo sighed and wheeled his chair away from the microscope where he could talk without having to worry so much about contaminating his slide. Bastian had thought he might get angry with him for poking his nose where Milo seemed to think it didn't belong, but the brunette seemed a little too defeated for that.

"He tries very hard to keep people from seeing him like that. He's probably just embarrassed. I'm sure he'll come around soon. He always does."

"He's done this before? Lock himself up, I mean."

Milo nodded. "It happens on occasion. He gets it in his head that the rest of us would be better off without him around. He's threatened to starve himself to death a few times. But he always comes around. He just needs time."

"I didn't realize it was that serious."

"Well you would probably hate yourself too if you felt like a constant threat to the people you care about." The dislike he obviously held onto toward Bastian seemed dowsed now.

"So," Bastian thought he may be crossing a line, but his docile attitude provided him with a rare opportunity he couldn't pass up. "You feed Cole?"

Milo looked at him and for a second Bastian could see the defiance in his eyes again. When he saw that Bastian wasn't trying to be snide or disgusted, he softened a little. "Yeah. He doesn't want me to, though. He thinks he's hurting me somehow by doing it."

What Bastian wanted to say was, "isn't he, though?" But he stopped himself. He was sure that no one needed to tell Milo that his feelings were being torn into tinier pieces every time he fed Cole. Instead, Bastian nodded and said, "I'm sure that's because he cares about you."

The single puff of air that was a halfhearted chuckle made the situation very clear to Bastian. "True."

"But not the way you want him to care about you?"

Another pause. Bastian wasn't surprised. He knew Milo didn't particularly like him, and here he was asking him the most personal of questions.

Now the look that Milo gave him was a little harder and Bastian could only guess what it meant.

"What was it that you gave him? In the shower room?" Bastian knew when to change the subject.

"It's a medication I've been developing. It helps stave off his hunger, but it can't replace a feeding yet."

"Is that's what you're aiming for?"

"If I can find a way to feed him where nobody has to be his 'victim,' then I think he could live a much happier life. I've been adding more hormones to it, but it still doesn't quite do the job." He looked back toward his equipment.

"How do you do something like add hormones?" Bastian felt his face heat up just little bit, already guessing what the answer might be.

"Well I've tried a few things, but semen seems to be the most effective right now."

"Oh." Was all Bastian could say as he rubbed his nose in an attempt to hide the slight blush he felt on his cheeks.

"I'm thinking that different profiles might work better, like how we're attracted to different people for inexplicable reasons. But my pool of people who can donate is very limited. I'm hoping if I can find the right profile it will give the medicine a longer period of effectiveness."

Bastian tried not to think about the "pool of people who can donate." He was by no means shy when it came to the subject of sex, but he wondered how Milo managed to talk about all this in such a matter-of-fact way.

"Why all the questions, though?" Milo finally seemed to come out of the tiny research facility that must act as his brain, because the eyes that turned toward Bastian now were suspicious

"Well," Bastian said, knowing that he was going to have to confess sooner or later. "I just wanted to find some way to help. I feel... a little responsible."

"Why should you feel responsible?" His back straightened, though he didn't stand up.

"Well, I found out just today that Alistair had actually been teasing Cole when the incident occurred. Some inappropriate conduct may have been what triggered it."

Milo actually looked relieved, as though he had, somewhere at the very back of his mind, been questioning whether Cole was more dangerous than he thought.

"I also, um," Bastian swallowed around his confession. "I also may have said some things to Cole that exacerbated the situation."

"What did you say to him?" Milo stood up now, his face dead serious.

"At the time I still believed the attack to be unprovoked. I um—" He wet his lips. "I accused him of rape. And I told him that we'd all be safer without him here."

Bastian's heart was pounding hard against his sternum. Even though he *couldn't* lie, it didn't make telling the truth any easier. He tried to gauge which outraged response Milo might turn to, tried to prepare some sort of answer. Before he could formulate anything, though, Milo crossed the tiny space and punched him hard in the nose.

Bastian stumbled, blood erupting from his suddenly very broken nose. His arms flew out to his sides to catch himself and succeeded in clearing the countertops. Glass shattered as empty beakers and petri dishes fell to the ground, and before he could do much else, Milo's hand had him by the collar of his jumpsuit and he hit him again, this time on his cheekbone.

"You asshole! Do you know what you did?"

Bastian barely heard him as his body, for a moment, considered surrendering—taking the beating he deserved. That only lasted a second, though, before he reached out and grabbed the smaller boy by his jumpsuit and flung him onto the ground. He didn't hit him back, wanting to at least offer that much as his penance, but he did push his head against the floor a bit harder than he meant to.

"I wouldn't be in here apologizing if I didn't!"

By now, the guard who had escorted Bastian through the compound was in the room again, with two other men who looked like researchers close on his heels. Milo thrashed and grabbed for him as the soldier yanked Bastian away. He didn't resist as he was shoved out of the small research room, though he was surprised that the officer didn't say anything to him. At first he thought he was just lucky, that maybe the man had seen what happened—had seen that Milo had been the one to start the fight—but as he was lead through halls he didn't recognize, he realized he might be wrong.

Instead of being sent back to his room, the guard shoved him into a dimly lit office, the back wall lined with screens. He'd known from the beginning that they were monitored more closely than any of them liked to imagine, but it was still jarring to see exactly where all of the cameras were hidden. The kitchen, the gym, every TV room. He was a little embarrassed to know that someone could have been watching every meeting he'd had with Cole. Not that they'd done anything he should be ashamed of.

There was no one else in the room, so instead of sitting and waiting the way the guard had instructed him, he went to the monitors. He was happy to see that, at the very least there were no cameras in their bedrooms, or in the showers. He would never have suspected such improprieties from Venja, but Marla seemed too nosy for her own good.

"Are you worried we're gonna watch you tinkle?" As though she'd been summoned by his thoughts, Marla's shoes clacked into the office behind him.

He must have looked guilty, because Marla laughed at him as he spun in place, wiping the blood that still covered his nose and mouth. Then she waved a hand at him and moved around to her desk to sit in the large leather chair.

"Sit down, Bastian."

She didn't sound upset, though Bastian was still nervous as he took a seat across the desk from her. It was hard to explain what it was about Marla that intimidated him. Venja always felt like a mother figure, and while Marla seemed keen on wearing that image, there was something a little more diabolical about her.

"I didn't hit him back." Bastian said the moment his butt hit the chair. "He swung first."

"I'm not upset about you and Milo beating the crap out of each other. Well, I mean, I'd rather you didn't. But that's not what I wanted to talk to you about." She pulled a tissue from her drawer and handed it to him.

"Should I be worried?" Despite the unease he felt, Marla was still surprisingly easy to talk to, so instead of panicking, he wiped his nose and waited.

"Of course not. I'm your new mommy, why would you have to worry?"

"That's exactly the sort of thing that makes me worry."

Marla laughed and leaned back in her chair, looking like she wanted to prop her feet up on her own desk. "It seems like you've taken an interest in Cole. That's what you went to the labs to talk about, right?"

"Yes, Ma'am."

She smiled. "I'm glad. I've wanted the two of you to get along from the beginning. You really had me worried there at first. You took to each other like a cat to water."

"I'm sorry. It sounds like you're more interested in the two of us on our own rather than the team as a whole. Am I misunderstanding?"

"You know, I had heard of you before Venja came to me about Haven:Germany being shut down." She seemed disinterested in any part of this conversation that deviated from whatever she had planned.

"What did you hear?"

"A story about where you come from. About how you were found wandering around the catacombs in Paris with no memory of where you came from. Just of waking up in the dark. Do you mind telling me about it?"

It was hard for Bastian to guess what she might be trying to get at. His history was no secret. She could have asked him at any time, and he knew that any information he could give her would be available to her already in his records.

"I don't really know what there is to tell. I just sort of came to myself. It wasn't so much like waking up, since it didn't really feel like I'd been sleeping. It was like my brain had just been turned on. I was alone, but I knew my name and I knew how to speak. We did some tests to see if brain trauma had caused some sort of amnesia. Nothing ever came back. I was normal."

"Normal? Except that you can always tell when someone is lying to you. You can sense evil, also?"

A few weeks ago, he would have simply said "yes."

"I think that something like 'evil' may be a little more relative than we think. But I *can* sense ill intentions a few moments before someone can act."

Marla nodded her head slowly. "The reason I've taken an interest in you, Bastian, is because your story is very similar to Cole's. He was found in the New York underground. No memory of a childhood or family. Like you, he also suggested that he'd not woken up. That he'd just begun to exist."

Bastian swallowed. That was definitely not what he'd expected.

"What's more, according to our best approximations based on your two accounts, these events were concurrent. Some estimates suggest it they may happened on the same day. What do you think of that?"

What *did* he think of that?

"I…" He shook his head. "I think that would be a very unusual coincidence."

"I agree."

The room was silent for a few moments and Bastian felt like Marla was watching him as intently as Milo had been watching his mark through the magnifying glass.

"Why are you telling me this now?" he finally asked.

"No reason. I just thought it's something curious that you might have wanted to hear."

After that, Bastian had been ushered from the office. Marla had stood up, clapped her hands on her desk and smiled. She'd told him that she had an appointment, and as she'd passed him back off to the guard, she had asked him to please make sure that Cole came out of his room. She was tired of him sulking. Then he'd been dumped unceremoniously back into the hall that lead to his bedroom.

19

Ignoring Milo's soft knocking was becoming harder every time Cole heard it. He had to stay strong, though. He knew that he was making his friend hurt, but in the long run he would hurt less this way. Cole turned over in his bed for what seemed like the thousandth time. Who knew that starving to death would be so boring? He *was* hungry, but still nowhere close to dying. He'd done nothing to expend extra energy, so he knew he could still manage for several more days. He wished he could speed it up.

Maybe I should just do jumping jacks for the next six hours. It might help.

He closed his eyes, hoping to sleep a few more hours away, but as his body began to settle into his blankets he heard a faint hammering at his door. It seemed strange that Milo would be trying to talk to him again. It was still midday, which mean the other boy should be down in the labs. He didn't answer. He would just have to wait for him to give up again.

"Cole?"

The air from Cole's lungs rushed out of his body when he realized it wasn't Milo at his door—it was Bastian. He sat up in his bed, watching the sliver of light that outlined his door inside the dark room. He didn't want to talk to Bastian. He couldn't handle hearing him say such horrible things in the deep voice that usually made him feel so good. It hurt too much.

"Cole, are you awake?" The voice paused. "I'd like to talk to you."

It was hard not to leap out of bed right that instant and fling the door open. The other boy didn't sound angry, or exaggeratedly soft the way Milo's did. He sounded calm, steady. Gentle in a way that still felt powerful. Cole swallowed around the answer he was so tempted to give. He couldn't back out now, just because Bastian had come tapping at his door.

"Cole?" His voice was a little louder now. "Come on, I don't want to have to do this through the door."

Cole laced his own fingers together, pressing his thumbs into his mouth to keep himself from giving in. He wasn't sure if he was praying or just holding his breath, but he was begging someone, anyone who was listening, for a little bit of strength. Even if Bastian was regretting his words, they were still true. He was still dangerous and he still deserved to waste away inside that room where he couldn't hurt anyone.

"Alright. Make sure you're dressed."

Before Cole could even stop to guess why he would say something like that, a loud creaking came from the door, like the sound of metal bending. He looked back to the light that came in through cracks, which somehow seemed a little wider now.

"Bastian?"

Before the name was fully off his lips, a crashing shook the room, and the door was off its hinges. The massive metal slab that used to be his bedroom door toppled to the floor several feet from the opening, sliding to a stop at the foot of Cole's bed, one massive dent creasing the middle. Cole had to shield his eyes from the light that shown through the now open doorway, but he was surprised to see Alistair shaking the pain out of his hand.

"There, I opened it for you."

Cole didn't need a mirror to show him that his mouth was hanging open. It would have been hard to imagine Bastian being strong enough to break down a solid steel door, but *Alistair?* With his slim arms and delicate frame? Was Cole starting to hallucinate from hunger?

"You're not finished."

As though the other boy *hadn't* just proven he could snap any one of them in half if he really wanted, Bastian shoved the thinner boy through the doorway, guiding him into the dark room until he stood beside Cole's bed.

"Now apologize."

"I'm sorry I broke your door." Alistair sneered, looking at the pattern on the comforter.

"Apologize for real." Bastian's hand shoved the back of Alistair's head, making him look like he was bowing.

"Fine! Just stop pushing me." The redhead swatted Bastian's hand away, huffed, then turned back to Cole, looking at him properly this time. "I'm sorry I didn't tell the others that I had provoked you." He glanced at Bastian, rolling his eyes when he noticed that he didn't seem satisfied. After moving a hand to hold onto his other arm, as though he were showing just a hint of bashfulness, he said in a softer voice, "and I'm sorry for teasing you. And calling you a virgin." He shifted his weight to his other hip. "And for grabbing your dick."

Cole was about to say that it was okay, or at the very least that he accepted his apology. But then Alistair waved his hand again.

"There. I'm done. Now I'll stay out of... whatever this is you guys have going on."

Alistair was gone a moment later, and Cole found himself wanting to call him back. He was sure being alone with Bastian was going to be awkward. What was he going to say?

"Drink this." Bastian said once they were alone. In his hand was a small glass tube full of an opaque liquid Cole recognized as his medicine. "Milo doesn't lock his door. I found it on his dresser."

He'd still not been able to able to look Bastian in the eyes, but he couldn't stop the small chuckle that escaped him. "He's going to be pissed that you went in his room."

"Well, he broke my nose today, so he can get over it."

"What?" He finally looked at Bastian's face properly and saw that he was right. There was a big lump across the bridge of his nose, and bruises had started to seep into the corners of his eyes. "What happened?"

"Just drink that first."

119

It was impossible to not do as he was asked, but Cole's heart still beat wildly as he opened the phial and drank. He'd gone days without taking any of the medicine and now, in less than a minute, Bastian had talked him into it. He felt like he'd just thrown all his hard work away.

"Now come with me."

"No. Bastian, I really don't think I should—"

Anything else he was going to say died in his throat as strong hands caught him by his arms and pulled him up out of the bed like he weighed nothing at all. A pathetic, breathy half-question managed to squeeze past his lips as he was lifted and thrown over Bastian's shoulder.

"W-wait a second!" He was suddenly very aware of the fact that he'd not showered in several days.

Bastian didn't listen. Instead, he carried him out of the room and down the hall. No one else was around, which was at least one good thing that had happened in the past ten minutes. Cole tried to keep himself propped up so the blood wouldn't rush to his head, but that meant he had to keep his hands pressed hard against Bastian's back where he could feel his muscles flexing and stretching as he carried him. He wondered what that broad expanse would feel like without the shirt between his hands and the heat of his body. He wondered if his tanned skin would mark if he raked his nails across him.

I just took medicine! Why am I thinking this?

By the time Bastian deposited Cole on the couch in their little TV room, Cole was sure he was going to lose his mind. He shuffled his knees up close to his chest as he leaned into the corner of the cushions, afraid that if his body reacted any more than it had, Bastian would notice.

"What do you want to play? Smash Brothers? Do you want me to play Silent Hill? We still haven't beaten that one. Or we could do something new if you want. Something more laid back?"

Cole held onto his knees a little tighter, not sure what he should say. His chest still ached from his excited heart and from the residual pain of Bastian's words. The desperate look the blond had as he looked to him for an answer didn't help, either. Finally, the taller boy sighed and sat down beside him, running his hands over his face, then through his hair.

"Cole, I'm sorry." He watched the floor like a child who was being punished. "I should never have said those things to you. I spoke before I knew anything about you or your circumstances."

"It's fine. You didn't say anything that wasn't true." His stomach hurt to say those words out loud.

"No. That's not true. I *have* sensed something dark inside you, but it's the same darkness that you're already fighting. Having darkness in you doesn't make you a bad person. It makes you a better person than the rest of us because you don't give in to it. We should all strive to be as pure as you."

It was embarrassing for Cole to realize that the burning in his eyes was actually tears that had just begun to cloud his vision. Milo often talked about him like he had an illness. He called him strong because he fought, but never had he called him "pure."

"I think you need to look up the definition of 'pure' before you use it on someone like me."

Cole was surprised by the warm thumb that brushed the corner of his eye.

"The fact that you're trying not to cry over this proves my point, Cole." His hand moved from his cheek into his hair, his finger brushing the base of his horn. "The fact that you would hurt yourself before another person, that you do so much to keep everyone safe—these things prove it. No one here thinks you'd be better off locked up in that room."

To keep the warm feeling that was filling him up from drowning him completely, Cole raised one eyebrow. "No one?"

"Okay, well maybe Berlin thinks you'd be better off gone. But he's an asshole."

They both laughed, the sound tentative and soft. Then Bastian's arms circled him and pulled him close. When he spoke again, it was into the crook of Cole's neck.

"Please forgive me. I never meant to hurt you."

Finally giving in to the contentment he felt when he was so close to Bastian, Cole wrapped his arms around the other man's back. He breathed deep through his nose and thought the blond hair that tickled his face smelled like sunshine. It smelled like the forest they'd spent time in. He wondered how someone could smell so nice.

Smell? Shit!

Cole's arms straightened, pushing the taller boy as far away from him as he could. He could feel the heat in his face.

"What's wrong?"

"Oh my god, I haven't showered in days. I smell so bad right now."

Bastian only laughed. Taking hold of Cole's wrists, he moved his hands away and leaned in just long enough to whisper, "I like the way you smell."

Before Cole could reign in the wildfire that swept over his whole body, kindled by the deep sound of the other boy's whisper against his ear, Bastian had stood up and pulled him along for the ride.

"Come on. I'll keep an eye on the door while you shower. I won't even peek."

Just as he'd promised, Bastian stood guard in the hallway while Cole scrubbed the days of bed rest from his body. Then he'd helped him remove the broken door from his room, assuring him that Marla would definitely do something about a new door. Cole was more worried about Bastian getting into trouble for it than he was about his own privacy. The blond had told him that Marla asked that he help get him to leave his room, but refused to say anything else when Cole asked about the conversation. Once Milo got back from the labs, though, he didn't have time to ask. Bastian slid away while his best friend fawned over him.

20

"It's just a door, Milo. I really don't need to stay in your room." Cole wasn't sure what else he could say to stop his friend from stuffing the clothes from his dresser into a bag.

"No. This is ridiculous. You're not staying in a room where anyone could just walk in whenever they want."

"Nobody's going to come into my room. Especially not after what happened in the shower room." It didn't hurt him quite so much to mention it now that he'd talked with Alistair and Bastian.

"I'm *more* worried about you after what happened. What if someone comes in here to hurt you?"

"No one is going to hurt me." He knew that wasn't completely true. Berlin still seemed very uncomfortable with his presence, but Cole was sure that as long as Bastian was around, he wouldn't let his friend do anything. Given the bad feelings between Milo and Bastian, however, Cole kept that to himself.

Milo seemed to deflate, a puff of air signaling his inability to hide his real feelings. His voice was much quieter when he said, "Just... stay with me tonight. At least until the door is fixed. Please?"

It was impossible to say no to Milo when he begged like that. He had done so much for him. How could he say no?

"Alright," Cole said, defeated. "But stop packing. I don't need that much if it's just for one night."

Milo's room had always been a comfortable place for Cole, but recently he had started feeling uneasy there. Milo was caring and protective, but the jealousy Cole had seen growing in him was starting to frighten him. He wondered if it really was jealousy, though, or if it was the toxins they tried so hard to shield him from finally overtaking him. He watched his friend at his desk, wondering if there was any way that he could tell for sure. He knew that asking would only cause a fight, so after several minutes of silence he put on his best attempt at a casual tone and said:

"I'm kind of sad you missed it, actually. I never would have expected someone as delicate as Alistair to just knock a door off its hinges."

Milo hummed a half-answer. He didn't seem very surprised by it.

"Did you already know about it?"

"Yeah, I had glanced over his files with one of the head researchers when they got here."

"So you know why the others are here?" Cole knew he had sounded a little too eager because Milo looked at him instead of answering right away.

"You know that I usually do. You also know that it's not information I'm supposed to give out." He looked back to his screen.

Cole always admired how seriously Milo took his responsibilities, but sometimes he wished he would lighten up a little. Cole thought of the time he'd spent in the TV room with Bastian, of how much he laughed while he was with him. He tried to remember the last time he laughed like that with Milo.

"They all know my secrets now. I think I deserve to know theirs." His words were defiant, but he still looked down where his hands were wringing nervously in his lap.

"It's unlike you to be so nosy."

"I don't think it's such a bad thing."

"Well, I think the others have been a bad influence on you. But apparently asking you to stay away from them is pointless." No matter how casually he tried to say it, Cole still heard the intention of his words.

"Bastian hasn't done anything but play a few games with me. I had fun. I didn't think that was against the rules."

"You had so much fun with him that he was able to talk you out of your room in a few minutes when you completely ignored me for days? And that was *after* he was the one who hurt your feelings so much that you locked us out in the first place?"

"Why does it matter who talked me into coming out? Yes, I was really upset about what he said, but he explained it to me. He apologized and I forgave him. Why are you so angry about this?"

"Because I don't want him to take you from me!" The sound of Milo's fists on his keyboard dropped the room into silence.

The space felt smaller in the aftershock of Milo's voice. It was rare to hear the other boy yell, and somehow it was more frightening than Cole remembered it. He suddenly wondered if the door was locked—wondered how quickly he'd be able to escape if he needed to.

Escape? No, this is Milo. He would never do anything to hurt me.

"Just because I like spending time with him doesn't mean he's taking me away from you." Despite his effort to sound comforting, he could feel himself shivering just a little. "You're my best friend. You're always going to be important to me."

"That's not the *point*, Cole!" He pushed his hands hard through his hair as he stood up and moved toward the bed. "He's tricking you. He's trying to make you fall in love with him just so he can take you away."

"But I can't even fall in—"

"You don't know that!" His voice was so loud that Cole's ears rang. The wide, wild look in Milo's eyes shot tendrils of ice through Cole's body. "He's luring you away from me. He's confusing you. He's trying to make you forget that I'm the one who's done *everything* for you. I'm the one who's given you everything. I'm the one who's in love with you. You belong to me and he's trying to take you!"

Cole swallowed around the dry ache that had settled in his throat. He took a deep breath, hoping his face didn't show the fear that had his ribs vibrating. Raising his hands in the softest gesture he could manage, he stood up, whispering in an attempt to sooth Milo's raw nerves.

"You have done so much for me, Milo. And you're really important to me, but you're upset. Okay? I think we should talk about this later, so I'm going to leave for now."

Cole hoped he could just slip past him and leave before things got any worse. He had to give Milo a chance to cool his head so they could figure out what was happening to him. This was not who Milo was, and Cole was sure that he was the one causing this to happen. He had to put distance between them.

He was just about to clear the bed when Milo's hand caught his wrist.

"You're going? Where? To see Bastian?"

"No. I'm going so you can cool off." His voice shook just a little.

"You're lying. I bet you just want to leave me so you can go slink into his bed instead of mine. Have you even been *trying* to fight that urge, or is he just that much better than me?"

"Milo, you need to stop. This isn't like you. Something is very wrong, and I need to go. Now let go of me." Sounding stern was hard while his heart hammered so persistently in his ears.

Milo's face shifted into something much softer, but even more desperate somehow. He whispered Cole's name and his eyes shone just a little, like tears might be forming behind his glasses. He moved one hand to Cole's face, brushing his cheek so gently that, in any other circumstance, Cole's heart may have wavered, but the grip on his wrist was still painfully tight.

"Please, Cole. You can't leave me. I'm so worried about you." Fingers pushed into Cole's hair, petting him before hooking gently behind his skull where he tugged to bring their foreheads together in a gesture that felt artificial all of a sudden. "When's the last time you ate?"

Cole's fingers were shaking as he moved a hand to the other boy's chest, trying to push him back as gently as he could.

"I'm fine. I'm not hungry right now." His voice cracked around the words.

"You're not fine. You've been in that room for so long. You need to feed, Cole. I'm so worried for you. I don't want you to hurt anyone." His mouth moved across Cole's cheek as he spoke, and for a second, Cole felt his resolve waver. His fear of hurting those close to him squeezed his body almost as tightly as Milo's hand on his wrist. "Please, just let me help you."

Milo's hand moved from his hair down the curve of his body to his ass, his fingers dipping low between his legs.

"You feel so good." His voice was barely audible against his cheek. "No one else will do this for you. No one else cares."

This time the bite to his words hurt too much, and Cole pushed him away harder than last time.

"Stop it! I don't want this."

Even as he was forced away from him, Milo twisted Cole's arm hard to the side, sending waves of pain into Cole's shoulder. His legs buckled, and he heard himself begin to shout before he was pushed down hard into the mattress.

"You don't get to decide!" Milo's body felt heavier than Cole remembered it, though the crippling pain that came from Milo's perfect understanding of the human body didn't help. "I've never denied you. Not ever! No matter how sad it made me, I always gave you everything. It's your turn to give me what I want!"

Beneath the fear and the foreign feeling of Milo's hands on his body that used to feel so comfortable, Cole knew he was right. At least a little right. How many times had he gone to Milo, pathetic and pleading, begging for him to give in even while he knew how much it would hurt him? His excuse had always been that he couldn't help it, but that didn't make the pain he put Milo through forgivable. In that moment he thought he should give in. Maybe Milo did deserve to be given what he wanted. Then he felt Milo's hand reach beneath him, squeeze hard on his thigh, and heard his voice growling in his ear.

"Don't see him again. You belong to me."

Cole moved before he could decide what exactly he was doing, and blood gushed onto his skin the moment his elbow met the other boy's nose. This wasn't the Milo he had compassion and sympathy for. The blow did exactly what he'd hoped, and Milo reeled away from him, his hand moving up to cover his face which barely muffled the litany of curse words that came out of him as fast as his blood.

"You need to calm the fuck down!" Cole was surprised by his own words, but he didn't stop as he twisted and kicked the other boy off him. "When you've come back to your senses we'll talk!"

He left Milo lying face up on his bed, both hands clamped around his face, his legs squirming against the pain. He'd sounded tough as he left the room, slamming the door pointedly behind himself, but the moment he was in the hall his whole body felt weak and tears sprang to his eyes. Maybe this slow unwinding of those closest to him was what really made him so dangerous.

I can't feed from him again. I don't want to turn him into this.

It was shocking how quickly his resolve had come.

21

Bastian had waited in the TV room until very late the night after his talk with Cole, but the other boy hadn't shown up. He didn't have much of a right to be surprised, really. Just because Cole had forgiven him didn't mean things would go back to the way they'd been overnight. A simple "I'm sorry" didn't do much to pad out the hateful things he'd said. Milo was also probably doing everything he could to keep them apart. In the end, Bastian figured he would just have to keep waiting. Maybe with a bit of time things would settle down again.

The next morning, Marla and Venja woke the boys up with reports of a new mission, but unlike their punishment trip, or the emergency reconnaissance of the white stag, they were called to the briefing room. It looked like they would finally have a mission with proper preparations. Bastian was one of the first to arrive in the briefing room, and most of the others who filed in looked just as tired as he felt, then Milo showed up sporting two black eyes and a nose that looked as broken as his. He tried not to smile. His own injury would heal quickly, but he looked forward to seeing Milo's broken nose for the next few weeks. Then Cole arrived separately and sat himself between Sabin and Alistair, the seat farthest away from milo. It was becoming clear that things were maybe a little more mixed up than

Bastian thought. Something very serious must have happened between the two, and now he wondered if Cole wasn't the reason for his black eyes.

Venja and Marla seemed unsurprised and mostly unconcerned about it. Instead of asking about injuries or tensions between them, they only dimmed the lights.

"The Lechuguilla Cave system, in New Mexico, is over one hundred and thirty-six miles long, and as you can imagine, it's not one straight tunnel. You'll all be provided with both a digital map that you'll be able to access on your mini computers and a backup paper copy that will be placed in your bags in case of emergencies." Venja was standing in front of the long conference table, admiring the twisting spaghetti bowl that was supposed to be a cave map on the viewing screen at the front of the room. "It does still draw professional cavers, and new tunnels and caverns are still being discovered, so you'll need to stay in constant radio communication with us. We'll be able to track you from the surface and tell you if you've wandered off our map."

Bastian looked at the smaller version of the map they'd handed out, but only used it as an excuse to look away from the screen long enough to peek at Cole. He looked a little paler than usual, but seemed normal otherwise. Milo wasn't looking at his map, though. He was watching Cole, and there was something in his expression that suggested things their issues were more serious than even a few shiners would suggest.

"We'll be going through survival techniques this evening before your departure in the morning. But until then I'll pass this off to Marla." Venja took a seat at the front of the table as Marla replaced her by the viewing screen.

"Now that all the boring stuff is out of the way, let's talk about why we're really going."

Bastian got the impression that Marla was always excited about whichever horrible monster they would be facing off against. It was much easier to be excited, he supposed, when you weren't the one being put in danger.

"The national park that Lechuguilla Cave is on has been closed to tourists for the past week after several bodies were found inside the cave system. And by 'several,' I mean an entire tour group including three families and two tour guides." Several images of the wounds sustained by the victims passed across the screen: gashes, circular bite marks, chunks missing from fleshier parts of the bodies. "Suspecting it was an animal attack, a small team of park rangers were sent in with traps and tranquilizers. They thought perhaps a wild cat had wandered into the cave system. Two out of the six rangers came out of the cave alive. They had managed to take these photos, and that's when Haven was asked to handle the situation."

The room was quiet as Marla brought up several very dark images. They could just make out the shapes that she wanted them to see, but not well. Many of the photos were blurry, as they were images captured from the panicking rangers' shoulder cameras, but in the darkness beyond their flashlights inky shapes could be seen. Marla stopped on one of the steadier photos that seemed to have been taken from just before the attack. It showed an outcrop of dark, wet looking stone, but nothing else.

"The native people who lived near these caves before western settlers arrived called this creature Hi'iska Daaparu. It roughly translates to 'The Knife Shawl.' We've taken to just calling them Cloakers."

"We sure do love eloquence, don't we?" Sabin seemed to be talking to himself, but Alistair, at least, found it funny.

"I don't even see anything." Berlin said more bluntly.

"Well, kiddies. That would be exactly why we call them Cloakers." She walked to the screen, and with one hand she outlined one of the many lumps on the rock. "This right here is our little friend."

"I still don't see it," Berlin said after a small snort.

"Alright. How about now." The screen flipped to the next photo which must have been taken only seconds after the first. The lump of rock that had once been just that—a rock—now flashed a fleshy pink underbelly, with great, muscled wings peeling away from the stone wall as the thing prepared for its ambush.

No one else chuckled or snorted.

"Most descriptions suggest they resemble manta rays or sting rays, though they're probably more closely related to bats. They use their membrane covered fins to glide silently inside the caves. They have flawless night vision, but again, we don't know what sort for sure. It could be a literal vision or some sort of echo location."

"It sounds like we don't know very much at all."

It was the first time Bastian had heard Cole's voice since he apologized, and he was shocked to realize how reassuring it was to hear again.

It's only been a day... What's wrong with me?

"You're absolutely right." Marla smiled a little wider than the topic called for. "We hardly know anything at all. Which is why we'd like for you to bring at least one live specimen back with you."

Somehow, that wasn't surprising.

The hangar was hot with the fresh air of summer and the idling engines of the fuel trucks that serviced the plane they would be taking to New Mexico. As Bastian entered the noisy space, twisting the band that held the curved monitor on his forearm, he noticed Milo in the corner with Marla. As they spoke, the brunette waved one hand in a way that suggested the conversation was heated. He figured whatever argument they were having had to do with the partner assignments she'd announced on their way out of the briefing room. Milo had been paired with Sabin, and Bastian had been paired with Cole.

Bastian tried his best to avoid eavesdropping, but as he made his way toward the equipment rack where the others were, he couldn't ignore Marla's words.

"I'm done talking about this, Milo. I choose partners for a reason, and you need to accept that. Besides, you two could use some time apart if that shiner you've got is any gauge of your relationship right now."

Bastian didn't look at them, not wanting to advertise that he'd heard anything. Marla had said on their first mission, when they'd been airdropped just to be chased around by her mutant dogs, that she'd partnered him with Cole because of the poor start to their relationship as teammates. He didn't figure that was still the case. He thought back to what she'd told him in the office full of monitors— that he and Cole had a similar pasts, that they may have woken up at the same time. He didn't know what that meant, but he got the impression that was why she kept pairing them up.

"Nice suit." He said as he approached the others, happy for a distraction.

While they all wore the same pliable, armored suits they'd used on their last two missions, with their high collars and long sleeves, Berlin now wore one that was sleeveless and fitted like a tank top. Both of his muscular and heavily tattooed arms were left fully exposed, and the spiral of black that wrapped up his neck was visible as well, the high collar also gone from this new design.

"Well it won't do me any good if they're covered up when I need them."

"Don't lie. You just thought we wanted a gun show," Sabin said, his voice flat, but something in the tone suggesting this was his version of friendly banter.

"Well if you look too hard I'm going to charge you an admission fee." He grinned in a way that Bastian recognized immediately, even though Sabin hadn't been looking at all.

A few weeks ago Berlin's flirting would have sent fire bubbling through Bastian. He could still remember the sting of jealousy he used to feel when Berlin would flirt with other members who were passing through. Now he didn't feel anything other than vague annoyance. He wondered why he'd tried so hard to get Berlin to be more serious about their relationship—it seemed so unimportant now.

When Milo finally joined the others, he kept his distance even from Cole, and Bastian couldn't help but wonder what had happened between the two of them. Venja approached them a few moments later, ensuring no time for any issues to arise.

"Alright, everyone turn on your mini coms. I want to make sure all of your trackers are working properly." Venja and Marla both were probably only in their thirties, but dressed in the loose fitting jumpsuits they wore while in the field, they both looked younger. "I also want everyone to make sure their earpiece is working."

Like they had been choreographed to do it, each Haven member brought one hand up to their left ear, making sure the bud was secure. With a tap to the outside it opened the channel, and they each took turns testing the sensitive microphone that would keep them in touch with each other.

"Great. We'll be checking all of them again when we get there. For now I think everything checks out, so let's board up."

Their flight would take about three hours, but judging by the icy atmosphere between Cole and Milo, and with Berlin's suspicious glances toward his horned teammate added on as a bonus, Bastian was sure it would feel much, much longer.

22

Dawn was just breaking when they arrived at the cave entrance—an unimpressive dip in the ground—where a nervous-looking man was waiting for them. Marla had talked about him during the van ride that took them to the isolated entrance, and as they stood beside the giant metal valve at the bottom of the small sliver in the earth, he introduced himself as a geologist who specialized in Lechuguilla.

"I'm sure your director already introduced me, but I'm Dr. Hartford. And I'd like to take this moment to impress upon you one more time just how important and *delicate* this cave system is."

Bastian turned his head to watch two of the park rangers open the massive valve behind them. Air rushed out of it, filling the space with an eerie, hollow sound that reminded him of breathing. He could just make out a tiny row of ladder rungs that lead down into the darkness. The rangers began lowering their packs though the opening on rope.

"The formations in this cave took *millions* of years to become what they are, and the gypsum formations in particular are very rare. No other cave in the world is comparable. So I understand that you'll have... work... to do while you're down there, but please, *please* do what you can to spare the cave itself. It is a very delicately balanced system."

That explained their new boots, at least. The tread was smoother and more flexible than the ones they usually wore. Marla continued to reassure Dr. Hartford as Bastian and the other made their way to the opening, securing their rappelling harness as they went. Berlin had been chosen to go down first, and as he squeezed himself feet first into the pipe, Bastian thought the opening was much smaller than he had initially estimated. Then again, it may just seem extra small with the other boy's broad shoulders crammed into it.

"I swear to God, it better not be like this all the way through this damn cave." Berlin was griping as he made his way down the pipe, but he never stopped, and a moment later the rope that had been fluttering against the wind that howled out of the opening went tight. It was supporting all of Berlin's weight now.

Several minutes passed before they heard their companion over the radio in their ear.

"I'm in. Everything seems clear so far."

One at a time they each squeezed their way through the metal pipe into the cave. Bastian went down just after Sabin. The aperture was more claustrophobic than he'd expected. His shoulders brushed the sides of the pipe, and the rungs of the ladder were so close to him that he struggled to move his hands over each other to grab the next rail. Then the pipe opened up and he took two steps along stone before the rock gave way to nothing but air. Even after spending so much time jumping out of plains, it was difficult to give his weight up to the rope and harness that supported him. He was free hanging from the ceiling of a massive cavern, feeling a bit like a single bulb hanging in a ballroom. He'd already turned on the small light attached to the head gear they wore. The beam swiveled with his head as he peered in every direction his neck would let him.

Once Bastian hit the bottom, he stood aside as they waited for Cole and Alistair, who came down right behind him. He was relieved that any personal issues the other members had with each other seemed to be set aside. They each checked in on their radios and with their trackers.

"Alright, kiddies." Marla's voice was so clear she could have been standing next to them. "This cave is big enough that we'll never manage to get all of these critters, but we need to sweep out as many as we can. We'll collect the bodies, and with the live specimens you guys get we should be able to sort out some kind of fumigation plan to get rid of the stragglers. So remember. Try for the tranquilizers first. The more we get alive, the more quickly we can get rid of the others. Also, Bastian will be team lead. So no fighting."

Of course she waited until now to tell us that. I can't refuse now.

Immediately, Bastian noticed the glance Milo gave him. She was trying to make this boy hate him, wasn't she? He pulled the small bag onto his back and then went for the boxes they lowered down after them.

"Alright. Come on, guys." They opened one of the boxes and took turns strapping the pistols inside to the harnesses on their suits. One under each arm, one on each thigh—two with live ammunition, two with darts. Berlin and Alistair each carried a longer, rifle-like gun that could be switched between live ammunition and tranquilizers. "We're beginning. Following trail markers north."

"Proceed," the answer came back.

As they exited the massive cavern with their lights shifting over the dark stone, the whistling of the entrance began to fade. Soon, after climbing through tiny apertures of stone and sliding down steep rock faces, each one leading them deeper into the cave, all noise eventually disappeared. The only thing Bastian could hear was the sound of their boots scraping on stone and the breath of his companions. An hour passed in silence like that, the trail they followed leading them through wide open spaces like the one they'd initially entered, and through tiny openings they had to pass backpacks through before their bodies would fit. And every surface they passed shone with tiny flecks of crystal that bounced the light back to them. It seemed like too pretty a place for something so wicked to be living there.

Nobody spoke, which meant nobody fought, so Bastian was okay with the suffocating stillness in the air. On several occasions they paused so their teams of two could investigate smaller trails that split off. Every time they changed direction, or split, or reconvened, Bastian radioed their progress back to Marla. They'd been traveling for nearly four hours when they finally decided to break for water and something to eat. They'd made it to a sizable body of water, the surface still as glass, and decided to pause before tackling it. The habits of silence that had already formed seemed to persist for a while, until

Milo finally broke the silence.

"I think this place is called Lake Labarge," he said, his tone casual, though he still wouldn't look at Bastian.

"I wonder if these things can swim." Sabin said as he bit off another chunk of the meal bar they all had. "It would explain why we haven't seen a single one. Do you think they moved on since the last attack?"

"It's hard to tell without knowing anything about them. It's pretty cool though, isn't it? That we get to help learn about a creature that's more or less unknown?" Milo looked at Cole, a tentative excitement in his voice.

Bastian got the impression that he was trying to rekindle some shared interest they had, in an attempt to smooth over whatever had happened between the two of them.

Cole didn't answer; he seemed icier than normal.

"Well I don't know about you, but it's not interesting enough that I want to hang out down here in the cold and the dark." Alistair crumpled the wrapper of his snack and stuffed it back into his bag. "If I'm going to be sitting around a lake, I'd rather it be somewhere that I can get a tan."

Bastian thought it must be the darkness—the overwhelming feeling of isolation—that had the others so quiet and uneasy. It wasn't a good feeling for him either, but it was nostalgic at least. The cool, moist air and the gentle silence reminded him of the time he'd spent in the catacombs of Paris.

After their meal, they pressed on. The lake took up nearly the entire cavern, and they would have to shimmy along the wall to get around it. As they skirted the lake, Bastian looked back toward Cole, who was only a few paces behind him, pressed hard against the cave wall to keep out of the chilly water. Marla said he'd lived for a time underground, just like he had. He wondered if Cole felt the same calming nostalgia he did. And what were the chances they both would come to themselves at the same time, in underground tunnels on opposite sides of the planet?

In the dark, Cole's alabaster skin seemed to shine like the gypsum crystals in the stone around them. He looked more beautiful in the dark than he did under the harsh lights of their compound. Cold water splashed up Bastian's leg as his footing gave way, and he stumbled, nearly falling completely into the pool. Cole's hand caught his arm and helped to steady him.

"Careful," was all he said, but Bastian felt his face heat anyway.

He needed to focus on their mission. Not on Cole or the state of his skin.

Another hour passed, then two, and still they'd found nothing but more rocks, more crystals, and a few other tiny pools of water. The only change seemed to be in their path. Sinkholes began opening up, like the trap of an antlion, waiting for someone to just slide in. They spent some time trying to decide if they should rappel into the openings to search them. In the end, Bastian decided they would leave them for now, only going through the effort if their targets continued evading them on the main path. Bastian was starting to wonder if they would be spending the night in the cave when Marla's voice crackled into his ear, the massive amounts of dirt between them weakening the signal.

"You're coming up on the Grand Ballroom. Why don't you guys hang out there for a while? Venja and I are going to go over our options. I'd rather you lot not have to sleep down there."

"Roger. We'd rather not sleep down here either."

"Well take a break, put your feet up, and we'll get back to you."

"A grand ballroom huh?" Berlin chuckled to himself and nudged Alistair with his elbow, making him stumble a little. "You and Bastian will feel right at home."

Alistair didn't even wince as he stumbled, but he did turn around and give his teammate a shove back, but in an imitation of Cole's bedroom door, Berlin was pushed right off his feet. He toppled into a smattering of stone that stuck up like blunt spikes, sending an echo of German cusswords bouncing around the cavern.

Cole looked horrified, and even Sabin took a few steps back, but Bastian only laughed. Berlin had teased him and Alistair about their dance sessions for years. It was always satisfying to see his fat mouth put back in check.

"Oh, I'm sorry, Berlin." Alistair smiled sweetly as the other boy climbed his way out of the uneven rock bed. "It sounded like you were suggesting you were manly enough to take a little nudge from a dancing pansy."

"Verpiss dich…"

Berlin was still grumbling to himself when Milo seemed to realize this wasn't any serious sort of fight. "You guys need to stop goofing off. These are delicate formations. We'll be held responsible if you guys damage it because you're horsing around."

"Well I heard your boss say that Bastian was in charge," Alistair said, passively letting Berlin catch him in a head lock. He reached up and squeezed the larger boy's tattooed arm until he shouted and let him go. "So we don't have to take any orders from you."

Bastian sighed, rubbing the bridge of his nose. This was why he hated being in charge. The last thing he needed was for Milo to be even angrier with him than he already was.

"Milo's right," he said after minute. All three of them looked his way, each looking equally surprised. "No rough housing. No breaking anything. Let's just get to the rest spot Marla gave us and wait for our orders."

Berlin huffed and put his arm over Alistair's shoulders. "Sie sind kein Spaß. Was ist passiert?"

"Just go." Bastian waved his arm onward and the two did as they were told, even while Berlin grumbled. Alistair didn't seem to mind either way.

The Grand Ballroom, it turned out, was named more appropriately than any of them could have expected. Massive white crystals hung from the ceiling like tree branches bowing under the weight of snow. White covered every surface, including the ceiling that rose thirty or forty feet in places. The walls were lined in tiny spindles of white crystal that branched like sprout roots in a jar, tapering off until they were thin as hair. For a moment all of the unease between the team members vanished, and they stood beneath the crystal that fractured their light and sent it bouncing around the space in a smattering of what could only be described as underground starlight.

"Wow," Cole finally breathed, one hand reaching up to gently touch the lowest portion of one of the hanging ornaments.

"Normally gypsum structures aren't this intense," Milo said. "But Lechuguilla wasn't carved by water like most caves. It was carved by sulfuric acid. Gypsum is a byproduct of limestone that's eaten away by sulfuric acid."

"Nerd..."

"Shut up, Berlin." Bastian was beginning to wonder what had drawn him to the other boy in the first place. He could almost hear his friend's eye roll, but neither of them said anything else. "Let's rest here," he said as he pulled his own backpack off, his eyes never leaving the massive crystals. "Be careful not to touch them too much."

They remained quiet for the next twenty minutes, but it wasn't the same heavy sort of silence they'd fallen into around Lake Labarge. This was an awed silence. They each sat reclined, watching the light shatter through the crystals as if they were watching a meteor shower. Bastian had to push his eyes far to the right to see Cole's face, not wanting the light attached to his headgear to give away his staring.

He really was lovely underground. His face reflected light the crystals bounced back to them, the glowing, milky texture of his skin making his eyes look even darker than they already were. In his awe, Bastian thought they might be so deep that they could hide wonders as unexpected as the Grand Ballroom.

"Enjoying the view?" Milo's voice was only a whisper.

Bastian didn't jump, his body refusing to give up his fight to not be noticed, but he felt his heart rate increase. He glanced at Milo who was closer to him than he remembered.

"Yes," he said, hoping he could play his way out of this. "I've never seen anything like this place." A prickling broke out over Bastian's skin, reminding him that he was skirting to near the border between truth and lie.

"You know he's just fooling you, right?" Milo didn't even acknowledge his near-lie with an accusation. "I call tell that you're captivated by him, but it's all just pheromones. He's like a honey trap. He'll lure you in with beauty and the promise of sweet things...but you're just a meal to him."

"That's a funny way to talk about someone you're supposed to be in love with."

"I'm only telling the truth. Marla won't say it, but we all know what he is."

"An incubus?"

"You think that sounds farfetched?"

Bastian hadn't heard the incredulity in his own voice.

"Berlin thought that's what it is. But I have a hard time buying the 'demon' slant. Demons are just scare stories for the religious."

"You can believe what you want, but he is booby-trapped. Every cell in his body is made specifically to lure you in. I can fight it because I know about it. And it doesn't change the fact that I *do* love him. But you don't. What you're feeling is the kind of lust that he knows will secure him a meal."

Cole looked at them, and Bastian realized it was because he had accidentally turned his head more fully toward him, his beam of light flashing in Cole's eyes. He looked between Bastian and Milo and the line of his mouth seemed to thin, then this eyes met Bastian's, and for a second he looked like he wanted to ask him something. The soft humming Bastian felt in his chest when he locked gazes with Cole fuzzied his head for a second, then he heard Milo's whisper from behind him.

"He won't ever have real feelings for you. He's incapable of loving anyone. Don't let him trick you."

Bastian wondered why Milo was saying these things to him. He'd never even thought about the possibility of being in love with Cole, or wanting him to love him back. He barely knew him, after all. But hearing those words, and seeing Cole's brows crease ever so slightly as he tried to hear what Milo was whispering to him, made something in his chest constrict. It suddenly felt hard to breathe.

"I don't think you're supposed to touch those." Sabin's voice broke the stillness that had fallen around them, and Bastian looked toward him just in time to see Berlin's clumsy fingers break a spindle of crystal off of the wall he sat by.

"Oops," was all he said before holding it up in front of his flashlight.

"What are you doing, you idiot?" Milo's voice echoed and vibrated around each of them as he stood, his face red with anger. The volatility of his temper sent red flags up in Bastian's mind. "How many times do we have to tell you that this place is delicate before you get it through that fat fucking head of yours?"

Bastian had just opened his mouth to tell him not to shout, the noise making the sharp-looking crystals hanging over their heads feel like guillotines instead of chandeliers. Before he could say anything, though, a flash of white fell from the tangle of crystals above them, landing square on Berlin's face.

23

Everyone was on their feet instantly, and Bastian's brain began running through first aid procedures for concussions, sure that a chunk of rock had fallen and he would see blood pooling on the cave floor. In the next second, however, he realized that it wasn't rock that fell on him at all. An expanse of white, fleshy material had wrapped itself around Berlin's head, and it writhed against him as his friend flailed beneath it. Muffled shouting was the only thing they could hear from him.

The entire team descended on Berlin, hands grabbing the creature in an attempt to pry the long, fleshy wings from the back of his head. The animal was hard with muscle but velvety to touch, and so white that it was difficult to look at directly, its skin reflecting their lights right back into their eyes. Finally, Sabin stood and pulled a tranquilizer pistol from his thigh harness. Bastian turned to order him to hold fire, uncertain if the dart would be long enough to hit Berlin through the animal's narrow body. Sabin fired before he could say anything.

A high keening sounded from the animal and its whole body rippled as the dart plunged into its back. A few seconds later it's wings relaxed and, as a group, they tore the thing from Berlin's face.

A circle of red incisions marred Berlin's cheek, blood trickling down to his chin as he sat up, gasping for air.

"Are you okay?" Bastian's hand moved to staunch the bleeding from his face.

"Did it lay eggs in your throat?" Sabin sounded inappropriately excited. "Do you have a chest-burster? Please tell me you have a chest-burster."

"Of course it didn't fucking lay eggs in me, you ass! It bit the shit out of me!"

"Guys?" Cole's voice was soft, drowned out by Berlin's shouting.

"What the hell is this, even?" Berlin didn't get up as Bastian continued to press against his wound, though his boot kicked the limp creature further away from him. "I thought these monsters were supposed to be black."

"Marla said they used camouflage to blend in with their surroundings." Milo knelt beside it and ran a hand along the underside of one wing, his finger moving to the single claw along the edge that it likely used to hold onto the walls. "How much black do you see in this place right now?"

"So it's like a chameleon?" Sabin asked, bending to look over Milo's shoulder.

"Guys." Cole's voice was a little louder now, but even Bastian was having a hard time tearing his eyes away from the alien-like animal laying between them.

"It very well could be. The octopus can change its color in a matter of seconds. It has cells in its skin that expand and contract to spread color across its body. It could be something like that."

"Hey!" Cole's voice echoed when he finally shouted at them. "If you guys are that fascinated, you need to stop freaking out over that one and look up!"

Bastian's body went cold as his eyes moved toward the spectacle they had been admiring only minutes before. The beam of his flashlight passed over the ceiling that had been just like any other crystal-covered wall, but now it teemed and slithered. There had to be hundreds of them nestled between the pillars of crystals, like bats lining the mouth of any other cave. But these weren't bats, and Bastian knew his team didn't have enough bullets or darts to handle them. He swallowed and stood slowly. His voice was soft, just barely audible over the low sound of rubbing and scraping made by the mass of monsters above them.

"Let's not panic, okay? We're going to grab this one. Then, very quietly, we're going to go back the way we came. Alright?"

One by one, they each got to their feet, even Berlin, who seemed uninterested in his wound now. He let the blood ooze down his face until it soaked into his suit. Once Milo had collected the toddler-sized creature, they began shifting toward the path that had led them into the Grand Ballroom. Their boots shuffled over rock, but there were no other sounds—no shouting, no twigs to be snapped. There was no trigger at all. But even without one, as they reached their escape route, a chorus of screeching filled the room, and like a school of delicately savage fish, the Hi'iska Daaparu—the shawl of knives—descended, following one leader toward them like the head of a spear.

"Run!" Bastian finally turned his back to their enemy, shoving the others out of the cavern and back into the narrow corridor that had taken them there.

Nobody needed encouragement.

The space felt narrower than it had going in the other direction, and as the tunnel filled with the scraping of claws and the clicking and whooping of the teaming mass behind them, Bastian started feeling claustrophobic. More as a way to bolster his sense of control than anything else, he pulled one gun from the holster under his arm. He didn't have combat powers the way some of the others did, but he was a good shot. Pausing as they took turns scrambling over the sharp stones of an incline, he turned and unloaded a clip of live bullets into the school of death coming toward them. One creature fell for every bullet, but it did little to slow them down, and before he could load a new clip into his gun, it was his turn to climb.

He dropped the gun, and hands reached down to hurry him along as he reached the top.

"Go ahead of me." Berlin pushed him toward the others, the black tattoos on his arms twisting and swelling like great worms trying to break out from under his skin.

"You better be running while you're doing that," Bastian said, even while doing as he was told.

"You think too much of me if you think I'm sacrificing myself."

Like arrows bound with inky black cords, the squirming tattoos shot from Berlin's arm with one sweep of his hand—the places they once rested on his body left pale and scarred. He was running as best he could, following the others, even as he twisted his arm, pulling his hand into a fist. The motion carried down the tendrils of black and the whipping tentacles formed a crude net-shape between them and their pursuers.

"That's probably not a great choice!" Bastian didn't stop running, knowing that fussing over Berlin was a waste of time. No matter how badly he might hurt himself, the other boy never did let anyone talk him out of a decision once he'd made it.

"I don't see you coming up with anything better, Captain."

Bastian could see the little cuts opening up on his friend's skin, a matching mark on his body for every injury the living tattoos received. Berlin didn't even flinch, used to the cost of his powers now. Distantly, Bastian could hear Milo shouting into his radio, his voice and Marla's crackling in his earpiece, but he was too focused on their escape to worry much about it. He never was good as a leader. He *did* hear Marla order them to "get out of there," but that just annoyed him. Did she think they were going to take a detour? Chill out for a while with their new friends? He'd had enough of this cave and its "wonders."

Endurance was something they all trained for, and under normal circumstances, none of them would be struggling. But the Lechuguilla's terrain was unforgiving, and their pursuers were relentless. Then the corridors of limestone opened up into another massive chamber, and the Daaparu erupted into the space behind them, like sparks flying in every direction. The open space gave their constant trilling an eerie reverberation and only made Bastian and the others feel more surrounded.

In a straight line, they weaved around the pillars that acted as immense buttresses to hold the walls upright, dodging the small pits they had considered repelling into. The holes in the ground had been a minor inconvenience on their way in, but now they were gaping mouths, waiting for them to take that one miscalculated step. The white swath of peril filled the room, disseminating until Bastian felt like they were pushing through a blizzard of razorblades and teeth.

The black lines of Berlin's tattoos wrapped around the group like a cocoon, protecting them as their progress was dragged to a halt by the sheer number of enemies.

"Shit, there are too many of them." Berlin's voice was surprisingly stable, but his body shook, patches of blood soaking into his jump suit and forming tiny rivulets down the muscled lines of his arms.

To Bastian's surprise, it was Sabin who spoke up first.

"Just stop before you really get hurt," he said, one arm hooking over the crook of his shoulder and pulling, though the darker boy's strong body didn't even budge.

"We don't have much of a choice, do we? What are you going to do, give them all a nasty rash?"

"You're gonna kill yourself!"

It was the first time Bastian had heard the pierced boy raise his voice.

"Well then we better figure out how to get out of here before that happens!"

"Let's all calm down for a second," Bastian said, trying to reign the situation back in. "Berlin is right. Before we can do anything else, we have to figure out a plan."

"God, this is ridiculous." Taking a step back, the smaller boy swept one hand across Berlin's face. "Somno."

Instantly, the tension in Berlin's body disappeared, the thatch work of black above them falling like threads in the breeze as he crumpled under his own weight.

Sabin made an X with his forearms, his fingers straight as knives. "Dispersio!" In one sure motion he swept both hands away from himself, his forearms brushing together like a blade on a sharpening stone. What Bastian could only describe as a blast of heated air—a waving illusion like the mirage over a hot road—rushed out from around him. The sphere of magic expanded so rapidly that Bastian could only sense a subtle breeze before it had passed him and moved to fill the entire cavern.

Instantly the shrieking rose to a cacophony, the sounds high and broken as though in a panic. Their tight choreography broke, and the Daaparu scattered.

"Somebody grab him and let's get out of here." Sabin was already starting toward the next opening that would slowly lead them back toward the surface, obviously aware that he would never be able to lift Berlin's limp body himself.

Without arguing, Alistair hoisted Berlin's massive body off the floor by his jump suit, then flung him over his shoulders. The stick-thin, ballet-built redhead carrying the hulking figure of their friend would have been comical had the situation been any different. Sabin was in front now, leading the team between the pillars and around the sink holes. Milo was right behind him with the tranquilized Daaparu, and Bastian followed behind Alistair and Berlin, keeping an eye on them. Cole was a few paces behind him, expertly picking off any of the creatures that flew too close to their tiny caravan with his pistol. His aim was perfect, and built a sense of security in Bastian the he probably shouldn't have taken for granted.

Bastian couldn't hear the words Sabin used to cast his spells as they weaved through the room, but he could see the Daaparu shifting and shuttering around him as they went, the movement in the cavern becoming more and more frantic, the creatures flying higher, dropping around them as they slammed into the ceiling or walls in their confusion. As though trying to regain their unity, high in the chamber a mass of white coagulated, then shook like the static on a television screen before diving low as one great mass.

The ground shook all around them as the Daaparu broke against a massive pillar like a wave on a bulkhead. A crack appeared across the shaft of the massive stone column and the earth moaned around them.

"No," was the only word that slipped out of Bastian before the massive beam of stone splintered like a bone under too much pressure.

They could feel the weight of the stone above them disperse onto the other, smaller pillars, and everything around them quivered as stones the size of Bastian's fist began dropping around them, like some subterranean summer shower. The creatures around them seemed to sense the same impending annihilation that Bastian did because they appeared to come to themselves, bee-lining for exits, crossing each other's paths, knocking their compatriots out of the sky.

Bastian stumbled as one of the heavy creatures swooped low, clipping him with one wing. He raised his hands over his head as they began swooping down on them over and over, then from behind him he heard a gasp so faint that he wondered how it had reached him in the din that was shaking the entire cave. He should have kept a closer eye on Cole. He should have insisted he take up the rear.

As he turned, he saw the other boy's slight figure slip across the rounded edge of the sinkhole they'd just passed, the Daaparu that had swept him into it moving back toward the ceiling as if in slow motion.

24

Even with the ground shivering under Cole's feet, he'd felt so sure as he'd followed his friends. He'd felt aware. Then, in the matter of a single breath, he was gone. He'd not even had a chance to shout, the sudden weightlessness driving the air from his chest. Just as he slipped into the sliver that lead to the darkest part of the Earth, he'd seen Bastian's face turn over his shoulder. He'd seen what could only be pure horror in his eyes, and wondered if that was how his own eyes had looked in that moment.

Cole had been falling for what he knew had to be only a few seconds when he heard his name. Opening his eyes, he saw Bastian, his flashlight shining in his face, falling hands first toward him. Cole reached out for him, even knowing they were both rushing to their demise. He didn't even consider how far they may have to fall, but he needed to hold onto Bastian before he reached the bottom.

Hands grasped each other, and Cole pulled Bastian toward him, his arms hooking around him, wanting to tell him how happy he was to not be dying alone.

Then they stopped.

Or very nearly stopped. Bastian shouted in Cole's ear where they held each other in a tight hug, the sound pained as his arms wrapped even tighter around Cole's narrow frame. Behind them, Cole saw white and red flit across the stream of his flashlight, and as he realized they were still coiling toward whatever unseen floor lay beneath them, he recognized what had slowed them.

Immense white wings, marked with blood, unfurled behind them, awkwardly catching the air like the poorly controlled parachute of a novice jumper. A moment later, they hit ground hard enough that their legs buckled under them and they toppled into a heap, stones falling around them from the cave-in that still rumbled high above them.

Bastian lay collapsed atop him as Cole tried to catch his breath. He was alive, something he'd not anticipated moments before. Slowly, he reached a hand over the other boy's shoulder and pressed his fingers into the bend of one great wing. It was hot under his touch and quivered, just like the rest of Bastian's body that pressed him into the smooth stone of the floor.

Shaking the confusion from his head, his hand moved to Bastian's hair, trying to pull it away from his face.

"Bastian? Are you okay?" He didn't answer at all. "Wake up!" He tried pushing the other boy off him, but his arms and legs still shook from adrenaline and terror. He couldn't budge him at all.

Letting his head fall back against the hard ground, he took a few deep breaths, trying to calm himself. He could feel the other boy breathing against him, could feel his heart pounding where their chests pressed together. He was alive, and at that moment it was more than enough.

Above them, the rumbling began to quiet, then there was silence again. He tried to look around but could see very little with the other boy pinning him to the floor. The best he could figure, they were in another large cavern. He thought he heard the soft lapping of water but could tell little else.

Wriggling one arm out from under Bastian's unconscious body, Cole pressed the tiny button attached to his ear piece, opening the communication line.

"This is Cole, can anyone read me?" There was no answer. "Repeat. Bastian and I are uninjured, is anyone there?" Nothing.

He took a deep breath, tears stinging his eyes. How had he fallen toward his own death without a single *thought* of tears, yet now, faced with the possibility that his teammates had been caught in the landslide he had just escaped, he felt like bawling. Over the next few minutes, as he rested, waiting for Bastian to regain consciousness, he heard several crackles from his earpiece, like a signal trying to come through but failing. He tried responding every time he heard it, but eventually gave up.

Finally, after what must have been fifteen minutes, but felt like fifteen hours, Bastian shifted and grunted.

"Hey." Cole moved his hands to the other boy's hair again, pushing it away from his face. "Are you okay?"

"Shit, what happened?" Bastian shifted his arms to push off of Cole, but as his back muscles flexed he gasped and collapsed again.

Cole caught him as best he could, giving the other boy a cradle to bury his face in as pain shook his body. Petting the sweat from his face, Cole shushed him until he stopped trembling.

"I didn't know you had wings." Cole's voice was soft; he was too afraid that his echo might tell him just how big the abyss they were in might be.

"Is that was this horrible pain is?"

"You don't sound very surprised."

"I just jumped off a cliff without any actual plans. I guess there isn't much left that could surprise me about myself."

Cole managed to chuckle.

"What do they look like?" Bastian's breath puffed across his neck and a familiar prickling washed over Cole's body.

"Well, bloody right now."

"Great."

"But they're white, and really big."

"Big is good. Always nice to hear those words."

Cole blushed, then immediately felt like an idiot for it. Sucking dick could be considered an appetizer for him. Why was he suddenly embarrassed by a little size joke?

"I don't think that now's really the time for jokes like that. Also, my bag is starting to hurt me."

"How mean." The wings that rested out to either side of them shuddered, and then Bastian pushed himself up to his hands and knees.

Lying beneath him, Cole could see the sweat across his face as he grit his teeth against the pain. Maybe he shouldn't have told him to get up. Not sure what he was trying to accomplish, his hands moved to Bastian's ribcage as though he could help steady him.

"Take it easy. As soon as you're up I'll have a closer look at them."

Bastian barely nodded as he maneuvered himself off the ground, not doing anything more than rocking himself back to sit and crossing his legs underneath him.

"These things feel like they weigh a ton." They were still splayed out to either side and as Bastian turned his head, his light caught the tip of one of them. "Jesus, they really are real." Moving as little as possible, he reached toward the tip of one wing and brushed his fingers down one of the long, rigid feathers. He gasped just a little, then smiled. "I felt that."

Cole had to smile as well. It was comforting to see Bastian taking this in stride. Seeing him smile made the tiny storm of panic that waited to rage through him fizzle then dissipate.

"Can you move them?"

He shifted and winced a little and the wings quivered and shifted like they wanted to lift off the ground.

"A little, I guess. But I don't think I want to right now. They hurt."

"Fair enough." Cole smiled and squeeze the other boy's shoulder. "We have first aid stuff in our packs. I'm going to see if I can do anything."

Cole's body ached from their fall as well, and he was stiff as he got to his feet, taking a wide path around the wings that covered a good three feet of ground on either side of Bastian's figure. The amount of blood covering them made his throat feel dry.

"We may need to get wider doors for you now," he said in an attempt to hide his worry.

The fabric of Bastian's jumpsuit was torn from one shoulder blade to the other, and his backpack was missing. Glancing around the cavern, his flashlight fell upon the other boy's bag laying several yards from where they'd landed. He would collect it later. Settling down behind him, Cole pulled his own bag from his bruised back. The skin around the base of Bastian's new, mysterious wings was torn, the downy feathers around the wounds matted with blood. He would need to clean the blood away before he could do much else. How had such massive things burst from wounds that, in comparison, seemed so small? Keeping his touch as soft as he could, he peeled the jumpsuit off of Bastian's shoulders, pushing the thin fabric down over the swell of his biceps.

Not a time to think about those...

Kneeling behind his teammate, Cole opened his bag, trying to remember what first aid Marla had included in it. He knew there was gauze, but he wasn't sure if there would be enough to handle a situation like this. As he reached into the pack, his fingers touched something wet and his heart dropped to the pit of his stomach. He found two broken vials—shattered from his fall, no doubt—the medicine he'd stored in them gone, soaked into the lining of the backpack. Cole took a deep breath and pressed the broken tubes into the very bottom of his bag. The last thing he wanted was for Bastian to have anything else to worry about. He would figure out what to do after he was done tending to the other boy's wounds.

Taking a few moments to explore the cavern they were now trapped in, Cole found a small body of water, which meant they at least wouldn't need to worry about that. Collecting it in a spare canteen, he used a wad of gauze to slowly pat the blood away from the wounds left around Bastian's new wings. They looked painful, but given the strange circumstances and the amount of blood, they were not as severe as he'd expected. Combining the supplies from both of their first aid kits, Cole managed to pack gauze around the bases of each wing, then he secured them with bandages wrapped crudely around Bastian's chest.

As he worked, the blond tried over and over to reach someone through the radio, even after Cole told him that he'd already tried.

"Is this too tight?" he asked as he tied off the last bandage.

"No, it's perfect."

Cole moved back around Bastian so he could sit facing him. It was silent for a few minutes.

"Now what?" he finally asked, his fear showing in his voice a little more than he'd hoped.

"I don't know." Bastian looked up, his light not even reaching the ceiling. "I wish I could say I'd just fly us back up there, but I don't think I can."

"I don't think there are any openings left anyway."

"Well once I've rested a bit we can check more thoroughly."

Cole swallowed, trying to keep the panic that twisted in his gut from taking over.

"I can explore the cavern we're in a bit more while you rest too. Maybe we'll get lucky and there'll be a path that will take us back." He tapped the small screen on his forearm, pulling up the map. "Who knows, maybe we're still on the map and we just took a short cut."

Bastian leaned over him to look at the small 3D map. Their GPS signal was faint, but still visible on the screen.

"There, see? We're still on the map."

They took several minutes to survey the model and seemed to come to the unfortunate realization at the same time—the only way out of their cavern was straight back the way they'd come.

Cole swallowed and reminded himself that he needed to stay positive so that Bastian could heal properly. "That specialist guy said there are a lot of uncharted tunnels in here. I'll look around myself so we can be sure. What's important right now is that you rest and heal up a bit. Who knows, by the time you're feeling better, I'll probably have found a way out for us."

Neither of them talked about the possible fate their friends had met above them. Neither talked about the possibility of starvation. Instead, Cole helped Bastian ease onto his side, lifting and moving his wings for him so they could lay out flat behind him. Cole would focus on getting Bastian comfortable for now; after all, he owed the other boy his life now.

"What about you?" Bastian asked as he settled his head on his backpack that just barely replicated a pillow.

"I'll stay up for a bit. I want to look around a little. At the very least I want to make sure there aren't any of those creatures down here."

"You sure know how to tell a bedtime story."

He was joking, but Cole could hear the shadow of worry in his voice.

"Relax, you big baby. I'm not going to go far." He left out the fact that he didn't have far to go.

Cole stood up, ready to leave, needing a few minutes alone to figure out what he should do. Before he could take his first step, though, Bastian's hand caught his ankle.

"Could you at least wait until I'm asleep?" His voice was quiet, and Cole thought he heard a hint of embarrassment. "I'll worry about you if you're not here. I won't be able to settle down."

Cole hoped it was dark enough that Bastian couldn't see the blush that heated his face and chest.

"Alright. If you need me to, I'll wait." He sat right where he stood, which meant he was within arm's reach of Bastian, who was still holding onto the other boy's ankle.

"I'm sorry I can't do more." Bastian's voice was so soft that it made Cole ache.

Reaching toward the other boy, Cole placed a hand in his hair, then down over his eyes, like he was trying to block some nonexistent light from him. Mostly he wanted to keep the other boy from seeing whatever shameful expression he knew he was wearing at that moment.

"You saved my life, Bastian. I don't want you apologizing for anything."

Bastian's hand released his ankle and moved to the narrow fingers that laid across his eyes. He squeezed them so softly that Cole thought his heart might stop all together. At the forefront was the question he'd considered since he'd first met this boy. Why, when they could only measure their time together in weeks or months, did Cole feel so drawn to him? He'd always believed that Milo was the one who would own his heart if he had one to give, but even when things were at their best between him and his friend, he'd never felt the tender overflowing of adoration he felt when he looked at Bastian. He felt like a traitor.

Minutes passed, and Bastian's fingers laid across Cole's relaxed, then slipped off his hand all together. Slowly, Cole sat back to look at him properly. It was the first time he'd gotten to see the other boy's sleeping face, and now, with the wings laid out behind him, Cole thought he really did look angelic. He snorted at himself, then switched off his flashlight. He would be able to see better without it.

Leaving his bag and his light behind, Cole walked first to the small lake. It seemed to glow the palest blue in the dark. This is what his eyes were built for, though he never liked to admit it. He'd always felt like he'd been cast from some wicked mold, and the ability to thrive in the darkness, to see through the deepest shadow, seemed to only bolster that belief. Only evil things thrived in the dark.

25

Using the minicomputer on his arm, he kept track of the time and the areas he'd already searched. He kept to the outer wall, skirting the entire cavern. He shimmied between stones and climbed small inclines that seemed to lead somewhere, only to find more rock. Hours passed, and eventually he had to give up.

He stopped at the lake again on his way back to where he'd left Bastian. His body felt weak. It had been too long since his last feeding for him to be scurrying around on rocks. He thought of the broken vials in his bag. He'd meant to take one of them just before they'd been ambushed. He should have done it faster. Then he wouldn't be so scared of being trapped there with Bastian. He guessed he had a day before he lost what strength was left in his limbs. He would have to find a way to keep the deterioration from Bastian if they didn't get out soon.

"You aren't planning to get in there, are you?"

Cole jumped. He'd been too lost in his head to hear the other boy's footsteps, or see the beam of his flashlight.

"No. I thought about it, though. There could be a tunnel under there."

"I don't think it's a good idea. Not until we hear back from someone."

Cole didn't want to tell him that he'd lost hope in hearing from anyone. Maybe it wasn't that the others had been hurt at all. Maybe *their* gear had been broken during the fall. If that was the case, then they were out of luck.

"What are you doing standing here in the dark, anyway? I was worried when I saw your light left behind."

"I was just looking around. But look at you, on your feet again already. You sure do bounce back fast."

Bastian looked over his shoulder were his wings were folded neatly against his back. "They still hurt, but I don't know. They seem to know what to do on their own."

"So this has really never happened to you?"

"Not that I can remember." He betrayed the strength he'd been showing as he winced and sat down.

"You really shouldn't push yourself," Cole said as he moved to kneel behind him. There was a bit of bleed-through on the bandages, but it wasn't as bad as he'd expected.

"I never realized you were such a worrier," Bastian said as he twisted and caught the smaller boy by his arm. With a few firm tugs, the blond managed to pull the other boy in front of him and into his lap.

"What are you doing?" Cole struggled a little, but did little else, not wanting to accidentally hurt him.

"I'm cold. Just help warm me up for a second."

Cole's body felt hot from his climbing, but now that he considered it, the air around them was chilly. He recalled Venja saying that the caverns remained a steady sixty-eight degrees. Bastian's hands were icy on his skin and he figured settling down in his lap wouldn't be too bad.

"I didn't know you could see in the dark." Bastian's voice was quiet against the shell of Cole's ear.

It was worrisome how perfectly Cole seemed to fit in the taller boy's lap. Bastian's legs sat folded under them, making a perfect seat for Cole's slighter body. His chest pressed into Cole's back, and his arms wrapped around him in a perfect cocoon, his chin resting on his shoulder.

"It's not something I usually flaunt," Cole said, trying to focus on their conversation and not every curve of the blond's body that pressed into him.

"Why not? It seems like it would be pretty useful."

"People already think I'm some kind of demon. It would just be another thing for them to add to their list of evidence."

"Not everything that sees in the dark is bad. Kittens can see in the dark, and they're adorable."

Cole couldn't help but chuckle. Why were they talking about kittens and seeing in the dark while they sat stranded underground, no immediate hope of rescue to be seen? Maybe it would have been better if they'd just fallen to their death.

Before Cole could tell him that he was anything but adorable, a crackle sounded in his ear again. He knew Bastian heard it too, because the other boy stiffened beneath him. They both went silent as they listened to the static come and go. After a minute or so, Marla's voice came in, broken and quiet, but there.

"Cole... -tian... copy... you..."

Cole's hand flew to his earpiece. "Marla? Marla, this is Cole, we can hear you, but just barely!"

More static. Then her voice came in clearer.

"How's this? We're having to... manually... hear me?"

"It's better."

"Alright. Here, I think we've got you now. Can you hear me alright?"

"Yes. You're clear now." Cole's hands shook in excitement.

"Good. What's your status?"

"We're both alright, more or less. We're trapped though. I've already searched the area and I didn't see any way out."

"Alright. If your GPS markers aren't malfunctioning then I can tell you there probably isn't any way out."

Cole leaned back against Bastian's chest, his whole body feeling deflated.

"But we already have a team of excavators in, so you're just going to have to sit tight, okay? They said it should be forty-eight to seventy-two hours to get you out. The cave in wasn't as severe as it could have been."

Cole's stomach twisted. He'd never make it that long.

"You should both have rations that'll last you that long. So you just need to wait on us, alright?"

"Right." He hoped his despair hadn't seeped into his voice.

"Everyone else got out uninjured, but the cave in put too much material between us for our usual short wave radios, so we had to bring in something stronger. Now that we've got your frequency, though, communication should stay open. You'll want to conserve your battery power, though. Keep them turned off. Check in every hour. The others will be taking turns manning the channel."

Cole bit down on his own lips, knowing that Marla was waiting for his response, but all he could think of were the broken vials at the bottom of his pack.

"Copy, Marla. We'll keep them off."

"You take care of my boy down there." Marla said, her smile evident in her voice.

"Will do. Just get us out of here."

"Alright, boys. I'll talk to you again in an hour."

Bastian pulled his ear piece out and flipped the tiny switch that turned it off. A few seconds later, Cole felt the other boy's fingers pull his earpiece out for him as well.

"You okay? It's good news, right?"

"Yeah," he lied.

They built what could be very loosely called a camp right there beside the lake. Of course it only consisted of their open bags that they used as pillows and their canteens that they were able to easily keep full being so close to the water. At least they had no weather they had to shelter themselves from. The only struggle they faced was with the chill in the air.

It had been about twenty hours since their first conversation with Marla, and just as she'd promised, one of their friends was always on the other side of the radio when they checked in. Bastian chose not to tell any of them about his wings, and Cole kept quiet as well, figuring it wasn't his business to tell anyone. Bastian said he didn't want to worry them, and that it would be easier to explain once they could see the wings for themselves.

During the short time they'd had to talk to each of their

teammates, Cole and Bastian learned that no one had been injured during the cave in. Not severely anyway. There were the general scrapes and bruises, but they were alright. They'd also managed to get out with the Daaparu they'd tranquilized.

"Well at least there's that," Bastian had joked over the line to Berlin, who seemed unwilling to get off the line. "You should have seen yourself thrown over Alistair's shoulder, though. It was a pretty funny sight."

Cole's body squirmed with the possessiveness he felt when he got hungry. He didn't want Bastian looking so happy while talking to someone else. He wanted to yank the radio from his ear and throw it in the pool. He wanted to straddle the lap he'd been relying on for warmth and make the other boy drown in the pleasure he knew his body was built to provide.

"You've not been jumped yet, have you? Are you safe trapped down there with him?"

Cole snapped back to his senses as he heard Berlin's words finally get through to him.

"You know he can hear what you say too, right?" Bastian rubbed the bridge of his nose, obviously embarrassed that his friend had said something so rude.

"Whatever. He already knows that he's dangerous."

"I'm signing out." Bastian said, turning off his earpiece before the other boy could get another word in.

Cole heard Berlin go on once Bastian had turned his radio off, presumably to Alistair, because he was speaking in German again. That meant that he wanted Cole to hear what he'd said. If he hadn't, he would have just avoided English. He turned his own earpiece off, tossing it into his bag.

"I'm sorry Berlin can be such an asshole," Bastian said after a few moments of silence.

"It's fine. He's not saying anything that isn't true."

Bastian sighed, sounding tired of this argument.

"Let's just sleep," Cole said. "Time goes faster that way."

The two boys settled down on the ground as they had on and off during their time there, Bastian lying close behind Cole, his body pressing against his back. With a little effort, the blond shifted one large wing to cover the both of them. He'd gotten better at moving them over the past day, and they'd proven useful for keeping the cold air out, but now the heat felt suffocating to Cole. He was getting very weak, and the wicked hunger that twisted inside him was becoming nearly impossible to ignore. As they lie in silence, all he could think of was the weight of Bastian's arm draped over him, the heat of his body against him, and the slight bulge he could feel where his ass pressed into the other boy's lap. He wanted to push back hard against him, wanted to grind into him until Bastian lost his sense of dignity and grabbed hold of his hips. He wanted him to push inside him right where they were. He wanted him so much that his mind became foggy. He shouldn't be lying with him.

"Has Marla ever talked to you about me?" Bastian's voice was only a whisper, but it still made Cole jump just a little after the long minutes of silence.

"No. She said she wanted all of us to get along, but she never talks about private things. Why?"

"The day I had Alistair break your door, she brought me to her office. She told me about you living underground when she found you."

A sick feeling of betrayal made Cole want to pull away from the other boy. He didn't like thinking about that time of his life. It made him remember the faceless strangers he would lure into corners of the subway system to feed from, and how desolate it had made him feel. A filthy sensation made the hair on his body stand up.

"Did she say anything else?"

Bastian paused.

"She said you were found on the same day that Venja found me." Bastian's arm seemed to tighten on him just a little. "She found me underground as well. In Paris. In the catacombs."

For a moment, Cole forgot about his hunger and his shame. His heart fluttered and beat in his throat. All he could do was lie still and listen to Bastian's voice against his ear.

"I don't remember getting there. I don't remember being a child. I just remember waking up underground. It was like a switch had been flipped on inside me. I hadn't been sleeping. I hadn't been injured or born. I just started to be. I know it's confusing, but I thought that you might understand."

A shiver ran from the heels of Cole's feet up to his scalp. He did understand. That was exactly how he'd felt. It was so hard to explain to Marla, or to Milo, that he hadn't "woken up." He had "begun to exist." But now Bastian was using those same words he'd tried to rely on to explain the sensation.

"I do," he said, his hand tightening on Bastian's forearm where the other boy held onto him. "I really do understand, because that's exactly how I had felt."

"Maybe that's why I've not been panicking. Being down here is nostalgic. It's comforting in a way. Especially with you here."

The tender feeling that Bastian stirred inside him peaked, and he found himself wanting to turn over, to hold him, to kiss him. But then he felt the quiver of hunger and told himself that it was only his greedy body talking.

"I think you hit your head in the fall," Cole said after a few seconds. "Even if what Marla said is true, we're nothing alike." The silence from the other boy made Cole think that he may have hurt his feelings. It was fine, though; he needed that distance between them now. He needed Bastian to be disgusted with him so he would resist if it came to the worst. "You're the last person I want to be trapped down here with." His chest ached and his limbs trembled as he tore himself out of the taller boy's arms.

His legs barely supported him as he stood, but their lights were off, so he knew Bastian wouldn't be able to see them shaking.

"I'm going to look around again. You stay here and sleep. I don't want to hear your voice for a while."

Cole's chest hurt, like a chasm darker than their prison had opened up under his ribcage. He stumbled, but pushed on, wanting to be as far away from the other boy as he could get. He needed space, and he needed to sever the little tendrils that were trying so desperately to bind his heart to Bastian's. When he reached the far side of the cavern, he saw a sliver in the stone he remembered squeezing through during his first search. With the bit of strength his limbs had left, he nestled himself into the rocky womb, folded his arms across his stomach, and closed his eyes. Maybe if he died in this stone sarcophagus, he would wake up in another underground tunnel somewhere else. Maybe he wouldn't though. That might be best for him. And for Bastian.

26

It had been hard to not follow Cole, but he'd ripped himself from his arms so quickly that Bastian hadn't known what to do. Maybe he shouldn't have told him about his conversation with Marla. He knew the topic of what Cole was and where he came from was sensitive for him, but he'd just wanted the other boy to feel like he wasn't alone. He'd wanted to connect with him somehow.

He rolled onto his stomach, his body feeling cold without the smaller boy in his arms.

He'd felt the strange connection to Cole from the very beginning, though he'd tried to use the boy's confusing aura as a wall to keep from admitting it. But for every second he spent with him, Bastian felt another tiny thread binding them together. He wondered if Cole felt them too, or if he was just being creepy. He pressed his face into his folded arms. He *felt* creepy. But sometimes he saw something in Cole's eyes that made him think that he might feel the same way, and he hoped that Milo had been wrong.

No. Milo is wrong. He has to be wrong. Cole is too gentle to not be capable of loving someone.

His face felt hot against his forearms and he cut his train of thought short. It was going in strange directions that he wasn't ready to explore yet. His memory of Berlin's disapproving face made it easier to cut short. He would give Cole the time alone he needed, then he would apologize for overstepping his boundaries.

When Bastian came around, his body ached from laying on the hard ground. His ribs felt bruised—sleeping face down on stone wasn't the best choice. His groan sounded loud in the silence of the cavern and as he moved to sit up he noticed that the ache in his wings was almost completely gone now. How long had he been sleeping? Opening his minicomputer he saw that it had been almost five hours. Regulating his sleep had become difficult in the pitch dark of the cave. That also meant that he was nearly four hours late checking in.

Turning his earpiece on, he opened the transmission.

"Sorry for the late check in."

"It's about time."

Great. Of course I get Milo.

"Yeah, sorry about that. I didn't mean to sleep so long." Bastian fumbled in the dark for his flash light.

"Is Cole still sleeping?" His voice softened just a little at the mention of his friend. "I'd like to talk to him if he's not."

The muscles around Bastian's stomach tensed as he was reminded of his last conversation with Cole. He still needed to apologize.

"Hold on, I'm getting my light now."

Once his fingers finally stumbled over the hard plastic of his flashlight, Bastian flipped it on and surveyed his immediate surroundings.

"I guess he's not sleeping. He went to explore a bit before I laid down. He must still be out." While he said it calmly, his heart had started to race. Would he still be gone after so much time? Was he that angry with him? Or had something happened?

"What do you mean he's 'out?' You guys are stuck in a cave together, where could he have gone? Why weren't you keeping an eye on him?"

"He's a big boy, Milo. He can take care of himself. Besides, there's nothing down here to get into trouble with. We've been over every inch of it." Bastian got up quickly, despite his own words.

"If you've been over every inch, why is he exploring?"

Bastian hated how sharp Milo was.

"He got mad at me, okay? He left to be alone for a while." He thought Milo might like that news.

"Then why hasn't he checked in?"

"I don't know, Milo. Okay? I just told you he wasn't with me. How could I know what he's doing if he left to be alone? Chill out. I'm looking for him now."

"I swear to God, Bastian, if you let anything bad happen to him while you're down there—"

"I've got it under control, Milo. I'll radio back once I've found him."

Bastian heard the other boy start shouting again, but turned off the radio before he could get his sentence out. The last thing he needed was Milo adding to the worry building inside him.

"Cole?" The name came bounding back to him, reverberating in the closed space, but there was no answer. He called for him again and again, and as he began running out of places to look, his heart started pounding. Where was there for him to go? He couldn't have gone in the lake, could he? Surely the sound of water would have woken Bastian up. "Cole! Answer me; this isn't funny!"

He was just about to turn back to their camp, where he fully intended to jump into the lake to look for him, when his light passed over a sliver of pale skin showing through a crack in the stone wall. The gravel at the foot of the wall shifted as he climbed the small slope to the fissure, and inside he found Cole, folded into himself, fast asleep.

"Christ." Bastian huffed a sigh of relief, then steadied himself as he reached through the opening to shake Cole's shoulder. "Hey. Come on, it's time to wake up." He didn't move, so he shook him harder. "Cole. Get up, Milo's worried about you."

Bastian's mouth went dry when the other boy remained unresponsive. Moving his hand from his shoulder to his cheek, Bastian tilted the other boy's face toward him. He looked asleep, and as he slid his fingers down his neck, dipping them under his jumpsuit collar he felt a heartbeat, but it was very weak and very slow.

"Shit."

Leaning into the opening in the stone wall, Bastian collected Cole's limp body. He stumbled as the gravel beneath his feet shifted, and he thought he may have injured Cole's leg as it was dragged through the narrow sliver in the rock. If he was hurt, he didn't show it. He didn't show anything. Sitting at the base of the gravel, he pulled Cole more properly over his lap so the other boy sat with the back of his neck in the crook of his elbow. Bastian patted his face gently, then more firmly when he didn't respond.

"God dammit!"

Standing with a little effort, Bastian hoisted Cole's chilled body into his arms and set a quick pace back toward their camp. It was hard to be sure what was wrong with him, but recalling the times Bastian munched on his own rations while Cole simply sat aside and watched, he could make a good guess. He wouldn't have gone on a mission without some of the medicine Milo made for him, though. Even if the two of them were fighting, Bastian was sure their resident genius would not let his friend go without anything.

Bastian laid the other boy onto the ground more gently than he probably needed to, then went for the bag he'd barely seen his companion touch. Shining the light into the opening he removed the left over first aid, the gauze and the extra bandages. He removed the spare canteen and the tiny tool set. Then, at the very bottom his fingers touched the smooth surface of glass. He would force the liquid down Cole's throat, the other boy would wake up, and they would never tell Milo about it. He lifted them out of the bag.

They were broken.

He set them aside and turned the pack inside out, looking for any secret pocket he may have missed. Nothing. Bastian threw the bag to the ground several feet away and rubbed his face with both hands. His fingers were shaking as he turned his radio back on.

"Milo, do you copy?"

"Where's Cole?"

Bastian wiped his mouth and chin, as though the words tasted bad. "I found him, but we have a problem."

"What happened? What'd you do to him?" His voice had grown high in his panic.

"I didn't do anything. I found him, though, unconscious. He's totally unresponsive. His heart is beating, but it's weak, and he's cold to the touch."

There was a pause on the other end of the radio—not what he'd expected. When Milo spoke again, his voice was shaking.

"Alright. Go into his bag. He should have two doses of medicine. Give him one. If he doesn't come around in a few minutes, give him the other."

It was Bastian's turn to be silent for a moment. His throat constricted around the words.

"They're broken, Milo. I found both of them in the bottom of his bag. They must have cracked during our fall."

More silence.

Bastian waited for the other boy to shout at him. To tell him to look again, maybe even to tell him that there really was a secret pocket he'd not known about. He looked at Cole's face. He looked peaceful, and Bastian wondered if this is what he'd wanted from the beginning. He wondered if he dreamed like that, or if he finally had some peace from the self-hatred he seemed to always be fighting. What he'd not expected was for Milo's voice to come back through the radio in one severe command.

"Feed him."

"What?"

"We don't have any other choice. We're still at least thirty hours out from you guys. He won't make it that long."

Bastian looked at Cole's face again. He really did seem peaceful.

"I don't think he would want me to do that."

"So you're going to let him die?"

"That's not... he's not even awake to give me any sort of consent!"

"He's *going* to say no, Bastian. He thinks he's tainted. That he'll destroy anyone who touches him." Milo paused and his voice was a little softer once he continued. "You and I both know that's not right. You *do* feel that way, don't you? You care about him?"

It was strange hearing Milo say that without sounding disgusted. But he was right.

"I do."

"Then you need to do this for him whether he wants you to or not. We don't have a choice."

Bastian covered his mouth again and took a deep breath through his nose. Milo was right. Cole would die if he didn't feed. He had to do this for him.

"What do I do?"

Milo cleared his throat, as though he were struggling to keep himself composed.

"You'll need to rouse him first. It'll be dangerous to start while he's unconscious." It sounded like he was speaking from experience. "What you need to do is start with self-stimulation. Then you'll need to use your fingers to deposit some of the Cowper's fluid into his mouth."

"What?" Bastian wasn't entirely sure what Milo meant, but his face grew hot nonetheless.

Milo huffed. "Pre-cum, Bastian. Put some pre-cum on your fingers and feed it to him!"

"Oh," was all Bastian said. He was no stranger to intimacy. He and Berlin had dabbled in just about everything there was to dabble in, but somehow hearing Milo tell him so bluntly that he had to jack off and rub his own fluids into Cole's mouth made him burn with embarrassment.

He stared at Cole's sleeping face. How was he supposed to get himself off while sitting over his unconscious friend? It felt wrong.

"Once he's awake, he may try to kiss you. You saw in the locker room how persuasive he can be. Don't do it. If he doses you, any intention you had of being gentle with him will be gone. And if you hurt him, I'll kill you."

"Right." Bastian was barely listening to Milo's threats as he pulled his torn jumpsuit off his shoulders.

The air was chilled, but his body was already running hot, though not the way it did when he was aroused. It was a more bashful kind of heat, and a guilty one. Lifting the other boy off the hard ground, he pulled him close. At the very least he wanted this to feel a little more affectionate. He already felt like he was taking advantage of him, he at least wanted Cole to look like he might be comfortable. Sitting back on his heels, Bastian cradled the other boy in one arm, his head resting on his bare shoulder and his body propped up by Bastian's thigh. He could feel Cole's breath puff across his collarbone and pressed his mouth into his black hair, wanting to apologize for what he was about to do.

Keeping his lips buried in the other boy's downy hair, his free hand pushed his jump suit down past his hips. A familiar shiver ran through his body as he wrapped his fingers around himself, but for a moment he wondered if his guilt would allow him to become aroused at all. Then he breathed Cole's scent in through his nose and he hardened instantly in his own hand. He was ashamed at how quickly he it happened, but all he did was breathe the other boy in again. As he felt the first tiny drop of moisture on his fingers, he tightened his grip, grunting faintly into Cole's hair to keep Milo from hearing him on the other end of the radio. With one firm, slow pull of his hand he milked a bead of pre-cum from himself.

Taking a breath to steady himself, he looked back to Cole's sleeping face, swallowed, and brought two wet fingers to his mouth. He thought he should be as clinical as he could manage, but as his fingertips touched lips that were so much softer than he'd expected he found himself brushing the shining liquid across his bottom lip.

Cole didn't move as Bastian traced the soft skin of his mouth with his sullied fingers, but as they pushed between them and touched the smooth muscle of his tongue Bastian saw his eyelids flutter. Like a child seeking nourishment, Cole's mouth opened, allowing Bastian's fingers to rub across the pad of his tongue, then his lips closed around the digits, gently sucking them. Bastian let out a breath of relief. No matter how questionable his actions might be, he was glad to see Cole doing more than imitate a corpse.

"Is he coming around?" Milo must have heard his sigh.

"Yeah, a bit." Without direction, Bastian pulled his fingers from the weak grip of Cole's mouth and brought his hand back to his forgotten arousal, milking a few more drops from himself before feeding them to the other boy again.

This time his mouth closed around him with more force, and one soft whimper escaped the black-haired boy's throat.

"Alright. If he's this bad, you should probably let him feed orally at first."

Milo's voice had been strained, like he hated saying those words, but Bastian still snapped into the radio when he heard him.

"What?"

"You know what I'm saying. Don't make me spell it out for you."

"I'm not sticking my dick in a sleeping person's mouth."

"Please, Bastian." Milo sounded like he was talking through his teeth. "You have no idea how much I hate this. But you need to shut up and do what I tell you."

Bastian swallowed and took a few deep breaths to prepare himself. As he looked back down at Cole's face he saw that his eyes had opened, heavy lidded and distant looking.

"Okay," he said as he shifted, lowering Cole's head down to rest on his thigh.

It was awkward, but as he brushed one hand through the smaller boy's hair he used the hand he'd pulled from Cole's mouth to guide the head of his dick to the lips that still shined with pre-cum. Cole didn't move at first, but as Bastian brushed the wet slit across the other boy's mouth, he stirred, and Bastian felt the hot tip of his tongue brush against him. Trying to keep himself still and composed, Bastian let out a slow breath, wondering if he should guide himself past the other boy's lips.

Then Cole's hand moved to grab a fistful of the jumpsuit that sat pooled at his waist. With only a small mewling as warning, Cole shifted, surging forward and pulling Bastian deep into his mouth. Bastian jerked and grunted as he felt the sensitive head of his prick brush the back of Cole's throat. A tremor shook his body, and he was just about to pull the other boy off when his radio crackled in his ear.

"Don't stop him. He can get intense when he feeds, but as long as it doesn't hurt, don't interrupt him."

Bastian brought a hand up to cover his own mouth, not wanting Milo to hear him moan into the radio. Berlin never liked giving head, but this was by no means Bastian's first time on the receiving end. Still, as Cole's hot mouth pulled up along his shaft, as his teeth raked across the sensitive skin, his whole body buzzed with desire. Did it have something to do with the toxins Milo had mentioned? If it did, Bastian couldn't be bothered right then to care.

Bastian knew this is what Cole did to sustain himself. He'd seen him doing this very thing to Alistair in the locker rooms. But it was still hard to wrap his brain around. He looked so innocent most of the time. His unblemished, pale skin looked so pure, so stainless, that seeing his reddened lips wrapped around circumference of his dick made his body shake with the effort of his restraint. He didn't need Cole to kiss him to shake his composure or his control. Just the black eyes that moved up to Bastian's face were enough to make his mind go blank. He moved his hand from his own mouth down to brush across Cole's cheek, then down to his chin where he cradled him as he thrust very lightly against the soft palate of the smaller boy's waiting mouth.

Cole moaned around him and Bastian had to fist the fabric of his jumpsuit to keep from ramming himself down the other boy's throat. He wouldn't do that though, not to Cole. Not to the boy who clung to his side while they played scary games, the boy who smiled so softly when Bastian touched his hair. He opened his mouth to say something to him, but before he even knew what he might say he remembered that Milo could hear everything and instead he brushed his thumb over one of Cole's supple cheeks, hoping that his feelings would get across.

Closing his eyes again, Cole met the soft thrusting that Bastian gave him and after a few moments he began whimpering around his flesh, his hands gripping Bastian's thighs, and the blond new that he was begging for him to hurry. Bastian didn't need any encouragement. His free hand moved to the ground behind him where he propped himself up, his head dropping back as the coil in his stomach snapped.

Bastian's body jerked as Cole's mouth continued to work around his suddenly sensitive member, seeming desperate to swallow every drop that had been shot against the back of his throat.

"Cole, wait. Wait, that's enough." Trying not to be too rough, Bastian eased the other boy off him, watching as his mouth worked around the taste residue he'd left. His small frame shivered and his eyes fluttered. "Cole? Can you hear me?"

The eyes that rose to meet Bastian's were different this time. They were darker than the shadows at the edge of the cavern, but they shone now, wet with tears. Then his chin shook as he sucked on his bottom lip, still tasting what he'd done.

"Oh god, shhh." Instantly, Bastian's arms gathered Cole up, lifting him onto his lap.

"No." Cole's voice was very weak, and the hands that tried to push him away had no strength in them.

"Crying is normal at this point." Milo's voice was so dead that

Bastian felt guilty for a second. In the heat of the moment he'd forgotten that the other boy could hear them. "Once you arouse him, though, he'll stop resisting. His instincts to feed will take over."

Bastian's chest hurt as he pulled Cole more tightly against his chest, the sound of the other boy's weak sobbing tearing him up. "Isn't this enough?" His own voice shook a little. "He's come around. Can't we just wait it out now?"

Milo was slow to respond, like he wanted nothing more than to say that it really was enough.

"If you stop here you'll have to do this again every five or six hours until we get to you. The medicine only lasts as long as it does because I've added a lot of other things to it. This isn't enough to sustain him."

Bastian grit his teeth and moved Cole's squirming body so he sat with his back to Bastian's chest. He wrapped his arms tight around the other boy, successfully pinning him so he couldn't wriggle away.

"Shhh." He shushed him over and over against the shell of his ear, rocking him just a little in an attempt to calm him. Eventually Cole seemed to give up his fight, though his body still jerked now and then with small, mewling sobs. "You're okay, I've got you." The words felt dirty in his own mouth. He was the reason Cole was upset, yet there he was, trying to comfort him. "I know you don't want this, Cole." He whispered in hopes that Milo wouldn't hear him. "But I can't just sit back and watch starve to death. You know, that, right?"

"I don't want you to." Cole's voice was so tiny that it made Bastian hurt. "Please, just let me go."

"Reasoning with him right now is useless." Milo's voice sounded harder now. "Just do it and get it over with."

Bastian pushed his eyes into the crook of Cole's neck, struggling with himself.

"Cole, I'm so sorry." He thought he felt the other boy shiver under the words he breathed against his neck, but then Cole jumped as Bastian's hand moved across his thigh, his fingers tracing the half hard bulge he felt under the thin fabric of his jump suit.

"No! Bastian, please don't do this." His words were so sincere, but his head dropped back against the blond's shoulder, his hips rising to meet his hand.

"Shhh. I swear I won't do anything to hurt you."

"That's not the point!" Cole sobbed again and Bastian's hand gripped his thigh, his mind and body torn in too many directions. "Please, don't do this to yourself. I'm disgusting. I don't want to make you do this."

"What?" Cole's words seemed to cut through the fog of guilt inside his head.

"Don't let him talk you out of this, Bastian." Milo's voice cut in, and Bastian almost ripped the radio out of his ear. "Do it now. Hold him down if you have to."

"Will you shut up a second?" Bastian snapped at Milo, then lifted Cole off his lap, rearranging him like he were a rag doll. Pulling one thin leg across his lap, Bastian maneuvered Cole so he sat facing him, one leg straddled on either side of his body. Cole resisted, but was still weak, so when Bastian's hand caught his chin he couldn't pull away. "Look at me, Cole."

The smaller boy stilled, only the tears that clung to his lashes dropping to his cheek.

"Why would you say that?"

"I have to fuck people to live." Cole's face crumpled under the weight of his tears. "How is that not disgusting? There were so many of them. And now I've poisoned Milo. I don't want that to happen to you, too."

"Hey." Bastian's hands moved to cradle Cole's cheeks, his thumbs brushing the tears from his face. "Don't ever say that about yourself. You've not done anything wrong. It doesn't matter how many people you had to feed from. And Milo helps you because he cares about you."

"I just don't want to be here." Cole's hands moved to hold onto Bastian's wrists where he was cradling his cheeks. "I just wanted to go to sleep. I didn't want to wake up. I didn't want you to wake me up."

It hurt even more as Bastian recognized the pure truth behind Cole's words. It hurt bad enough that he didn't know what to say, so he kissed his forehead, then his cheeks. He kissed his face over and over until his tears slowed down.

"I thought I told you not to kiss him."

Bastian ignored his earpiece. "You're the only one who wants that. Who would hang out with me when I can't sleep if you didn't wake up?" Bastian swallowed, embarrassed by how intimate his words felt. "I'd miss you. We'd all miss you. Well, except for Berlin."

Cole actually managed a tiny puff of tearful laughter.

"You're not doing anything wrong to me. I'm not under any sort of influence. I'm not poisoned. I just want to help you."

Even in darkness softened only by a discarded flashlight, Bastian could see the faint red in Cole's cheeks. His tears had stopped now, and his fingers fiddled nervously around Bastian's wrists. He could still hear Milo's warning in his ear, but he barely managed to fight his urge to kiss the other boy. Softly, he brushed his lips across the warmth of his cheek, then he kissed his jaw, then under his chin as Cole let his head tilt back. Bastian found his fingers shaking just a little as they moved to undo the collar of Cole's jump suit, kissing down his neck as he pulled the zipper past the small dimple of his belly button.

When he felt Cole shiver, Bastian's arm pulled him close, pressing his body more firmly into his own. He paused as he felt a hardness press into his stomach. Cole must have felt him still, because one of his hands moved to his own face, hiding his shamed expression as he tried to push himself away from the blond.

"I'm sorry, I'm just..." He moved to hide in the crook of his own elbow and Bastian couldn't wrap his brain around the endearment he felt toward the unexpected bashfulness Cole showed.

Gently, he moved Cole's arm away from his face. "It's okay. You're hungry, right? It's natural for you to feel that way." Watching the horned boy's face, he pressed his other hand between Cole's legs.

Narrow thighs trembled as Bastian outlined the other boy's shape through the fabric separating them. Cole's gasp was so soft, and Bastian couldn't stop himself from leaning forward to brush his tongue over the throat that Cole exposed to him.

"It's okay to be hungry, Cole," he said as his lips brushed down to the soft curve of his collarbone. "I'll give you anything you want."

Bastian found his own breath growing heavier as his hands moved to pull the opened jumpsuit over Cole's shoulders. He wished it was brighter so he could see just how pink the other boy's nipples were. Even in the poor light they looked like pale drops of peach in a sea of milky skin. His mouth sought them out immediately. Finally, Cole's hands moved to Bastian's hair, his fingers raking over his scalp. The soft hum of arousal made Bastian instantly hard.

"W-wait," Cole gasped. "You don't have to do that." He shook as Bastian's hand pressed more firmly between his legs, making the jumpsuit feel even more constricting.

Bastian was hardly listening, his mind enamored with the smooth hardness in his mouth, the gentle curve of Cole's back as his hand traced the boy's spine down until he was following the curve of his ass toward the heart of Cole's need. Even through the fabric of the jump suit, he could feel the warmth as his fingers dipped between the backs of his thighs, pressing into the soft flesh behind the mound that grew tighter and harder as he paid him more attention.

"Bastian." Cole had raised up on his knees so he could spread his legs a little wider. His hips twisted, trying to decide which direction he should be pushing. "Please, get this thing off me."

Pulling his mouth away, Bastian took a moment to admire the red, puffy nub he'd left, then looked up at Cole's face. "Can you stand?" he asked, and was unsurprised when Cole shook his head. "Alright, turn this way."

In silence marked only by the sound of their breathing, Bastian maneuvered the other boy so he sat across his lap. With one arm, Bastian supported him, with the other he pulled the jumpsuit down his body. Cole hissed just a little as he eased it over the erection that laid flat against his stomach once free. Even there, Cole was pale, the tip the same red as his swollen nipples, and suddenly, Bastian wanted to taste it—wanted to know if it tasted as good as the rest of his skin did.

Bastian watched Cole's face as his hand finally wrapped unhindered around the straining shaft of his dick. He wanted to watch the arousal take the other boy over, and as he felt the body in his lap bow into a soft arc he felt his own body tense. He wondered if it was just his own desires or if it was Cole's eerie powers of seduction that had his heart racing so fast. Either way he was completely taken by the way Cole's mouth opened around his gasp for breath.

"No." The dissent was weak, and the hand that tried to grip Bastian's wrist was soft. "Please, I don't want this. I need you to hurry."

Bastian had completely forgotten about the third party listening in on their intimate moment until he heard a crackling in his ear.

"If you're bothering with foreplay you're wasting your time."

Bastian ignored Milo, refusing to give up the sweet view of Cole's head thrown back, his hips rising to meet the hand Bastian had fisted around him. It wasn't a waste of time if it made him writhe like that. He bent forward to suck on the small swell of Cole's Adam's apple, the vibration of his voice tickling his lips as his fingers moved from the base of his shivering cock to the swell of his cheeks. Cole whimpered in a way that sounded so helpless, his legs spreading and shaking as they tried to find purchase on the ground. Bastian moved to look at his face again as his middle finger pushed between the supple curves of flesh to where his small ring of muscle was waiting for him.

"Don't ignore me, Bastian." Milo seemed intent on ruining the mood. "He gets nothing from foreplay. You're supposed to be feeding him. You two aren't making love. Don't get confused."

Bastian knew Milo was upset by the intimacy of what they were doing, but he couldn't imagine doing anything to Cole that could even walk the line of being rough. "That doesn't mean he can't enjoy himself," he said quietly into his radio.

Cole's whimpering stopped for a moment as Bastian pushed one finger inside him.

"He doesn't want to enjoy himself. He hates having to do this and you're only prolonging it, so stop playing around and get on with it."

Cole squeezed Bastian's fingers tight as he added a second one. He wanted to be sure that he wouldn't hurt the other boy, but Cole seemed to only grow more impatient and a moment later his hand moved to the hair at the back of Bastian's neck, tugging on him.

"Bastian, please hurry. I need you to fuck me." The words seemed so foreign on Cole's innocent lips, and for a second, Bastian thought he would have to kiss them off his mouth.

Instead, he heard himself growl softly as he moved the smaller boy so he was straddling his lap again. He shoved his jumpsuit down, freeing his own aching dick. Slender fingers brushed over the wet head of it immediately, and Bastian had to take a moment to catch his breath as Cole leaned in close to him, brushing his lips over his ear.

"Hurry, Bastian. I want it. I want this inside me."

He was begging so softly in his ear that Bastian wondered how anyone could resist him. He recognized the desperation, though. He was lost in his feeding, just as he'd seen him in the locker room. But he wouldn't let that cloud his judgment. He would be gentle with him, no matter how badly he wanted to shove him into the hard floor and fuck him raw. He would only offer him tenderness, suddenly feeling like Cole hadn't gotten enough of that in his life.

"Hold onto me." Bastian's voice was gruff from the effort of restraining himself as he guided Cole's thin arms around his neck before bring his hands down to lift the other boy up by his thighs.

The cascade of whispered begging continued as Bastian maneuvered him over his waiting shaft. They only stopped when Bastian felt the heat of Cole's opening pressing down around him. They both went quiet, both held their breath, as Bastian lowered him slowly, inch by inch onto him. When Cole sat flush against his lap, they both caught their breath. Bastian could feel the muscles inside him quivering and clenching around him, the heat making his head spin.

Bastian didn't realize his eyes were shut until he felt Cole's chilled hands on his cheeks. Looking up at the black-haired boy, he felt his heart stumble and felt a flipping in his stomach. His face was so close, his nose brushing his, his eyes glossy with arousal, and he thought he saw stars in the black void of his eyes. They looked infinite. They looked like the dark place Bastian had lived before he'd woken up in the caverns. For a second, he thought Cole was feeling something similar, then he bowed his head and brushed his lips so softly over Bastian's, and it was over for him.

He didn't even think to pull away, letting the overwhelming feeling of oneness consume him as his hands moved to Cole's hair, pulling his mouth more firmly against his. Cole's fingers moved down Bastian's cheeks, opening his mouth as he wound his arms around his neck.

Everything was a blur after that. Bastian thought he heard Milo shouting at him through his earpiece, but the only sound he could hear was his own heart beat and the sound of the breath they shared. Bastian's arms looped around Cole's narrow waist, holding him steady as he thrust up into his heat, and Cole gasped and mewled into

Bastian's mouth, neither of them giving up even a second of their kiss. Cole tasted like honey and moonlight. His mouth suckled at Bastian's tongue in a way that set fire to his whole body. Bastian thought that he could have reached his climax from just the sharp edge of teeth that raked cross his lower lip.

The cave filled with the sound of their breathing and their bodies straining against each other, and when Cole finally pulled his mouth away from his, he whispered, wet-lipped against the blond's mouth.

"Come inside me, Bastian."

It was over. Twining the fingers of one hand into Cole's hair, he squeezed him so tight against his body, holding him still as he pushed one last time into him. Light burst behind his eyelids, only aware of the way Cole's body shook in his arms, the soft cry that he seemed to wring from him. Before his body had stopped pulsing his essence inside the other boy, he was already showering the Cole's face with kisses. Dark, sated eyes met his, and then Bastian descended on his lips again. He kissed him softly, and Cole responded with such tender brushes of his lips.

Reverently, Bastian's hands moved to Cole's cheeks, brushing the tears from his flushed skin. He felt something looking into the depths of his eyes, but his body seemed unsure how to express whatever it was. As cold air passed between them, Bastian felt the quickly chilling proof of Cole's ecstasy on his chest and stomach. He was relieved that at the very least, he'd been able to give Cole pleasure. Milo was saying something in his ear, something about Cole sometimes crying after a feeding, that it shouldn't be something to alarm him, but Cole only gazed back at him with the same sort of wonder he thought he felt on his own face.

27

It was shady, but Cole could feel warmth in the air and could smell the sun on the grass around him. Everything smelled green.

"You glow in the sunlight." Bastian's voice sounded in his half-sleep, the deep tone soft and so tender that it drew Cole's eyes open.

Above him, Bastian's face seemed to shimmer like gold in the sunlight, one giant, pristine wing unfurled over their reclined bodies like a canopy, rays of light filtering through the broad feathers.

"How can you say that?" Cole heard his own voice, but couldn't recall choosing any words. "When you're so radiant?"

He was radiant. His eyes seemed deeper, bluer than the cloudless sky Cole could see beyond the white feathers that shielded them. It was the same Bastian that Cole had played games with, that he sat across from at breakfast. But this figure was different. His blond hair was long, cascading over one shoulder in a thick braid as wide as Cole's wrist. It fell over his collarbone and laid in a coil on Cole's chest as Bastian leaned over him on one elbow. Cole forgot how to breathe for a few seconds as lips moved to brush across his.

"You're perfect."

Cole woke up in his own bed. The lights were out and it was pitch black, even though his clock said it was still the afternoon.

That's right. I took a nap.

Two days had passed since he and Bastian had been dug out of that cavern, and Cole still couldn't look the other boy in the face. He avoided the dining room and slinked off in the middle of the night for his showers. The only time he saw Bastian was when they had mandatory training, and even that felt like too much. Just being in the same room made Cole's body burn all over.

He napped because he couldn't sleep at night, his head full of thoughts of Bastian's hands on him, of his heat inside him. Now, he shifted in his bed, his body prickling and alive in a way that he wasn't used to. The dream had felt so real, and he wished he'd not woken up at all.

He looked pretty good with long hair. Not sure where it came from, but I wouldn't mind if he grew it out.

Cole closed his eyes, and for a second he thought he could smell the sunlight from his dream, thought he could feel the warm brush of Bastian's hands on his cheeks. He took a breath to calm the fire that smoldered in his chest. Usually, Cole didn't masturbate—it did nothing to sate his hunger—but now as he shifted under the weight of his blankets, his hand couldn't keep from wandering as the thought of Bastian's body against his filled his mind again.

Cole pressed his face into his pillow as he worked his fist around the persistent erection that plagued him almost constantly when he thought of Bastian. As he tried desperately to purge the fire from his body, his other hand moved to squeeze one nipple between his fingers, remembering the hot pull of Bastian's mouth. He'd never touched himself there before, and even Milo had only ever given those small nubs a passing sort of attention. But, the way Bastian had so carefully teased him made it feel like he'd been worshiping the hard flesh he now rolled between his fingertips. He felt poisoned by the ecstasy Bastian had planted inside him.

With one long, muffled keen, Cole came into his own hand, providing his mind with a few promised hours of clarity. He sighed, turning onto his back. He would have to figure out what to do before long. He only had until the end of the week, then he would have to feed again. He couldn't rely on Milo any more, and the idea of asking Bastian was too embarrassing.

No. This isn't about embarrassment. If I go to him he'll just end up like Milo.

Bastian was spending most of his free time in the labs now that he had wings for Marla to play with. That would make it easier to avoid him as his next meal. He smiled a little as he recalled the expressions their teammates had worn when they'd been pulled out of the cavern. Berlin, in particular, had been awestruck by Bastian's wings, crossing himself and muttering "Heiligen Engel," as he approached him. Cole learned later that he'd called him an angel. He had scoffed at the idea then, but now, if he was asked what an angel might look like, he very well might describe Bastian.

Cole jumped in his bed as a loud knocking at his door broke his train of thought. Milo hadn't come to his room since they'd returned from Lechuguilla. He wondered what might be bringing him by now. He didn't answer, unsure if he was ready to talk to his friend.

"Cole, you've got three seconds before I let myself in. Get decent."

Marla.

Cole panicked, wiping his sullied hand on his bedsheets and getting his pajama pants re-situated. He'd just managed to cover the stain on his bed and get settled sitting on top of the comforter when he heard the key click in his door and Marla stepped in.

"Why is it always so dark in here?" She flipped on the light and Cole squinted at her. "This is enough of..." She waved her hand vaguely in his direction. "Whatever it is you're doing in here. I want you to come for dinner."

"I really don't want to."

She hummed as she rubbed her chin for show. "Don't care. You're coming. Get dressed. You have five minutes before I come back here and drag you to the table myself." She turned back to the door. "Hiding out in your room is just going to make whatever gaps you feel between yourself and the others bigger."

Cole threw himself back onto his bed as the door shut. Marla only ever wanted the best for him, but right that minute it felt like she was going out of her way to sabotage him.

Just as he'd expected, sitting at the dinner table was awkward. He intentionally placed himself between Sabin and Alistair, thinking it would be easier to not have to be so close to Bastian or Milo. What he'd not considered was the fact that now he had to sit facing both of them. He kept his eyes on his plate, or on Marla as she kept them up to date on the research being performed on the Hi'iska Daaparu and the scheduled fumigation of the cave system. He was mildly interested in the progress, so it was easy to focus on.

Bastian continued shifting at the table, though, threatening to draw Cole's attention. The few times he broke down and threw a glance his way, he noticed how uncomfortable he looked sitting at the table with the wings he was still getting used to. He wondered if they would ever disappear again, but he didn't have the courage to ask. Whenever he did fail and look over at Bastian, his eyes always darted immediately to Milo afterward, afraid that the other boy would be glaring at him. Cole wondered when he'd grown so used to the jealousy he saw bubbling behind his friend's glasses. But Milo never looked toward him. Not once during their dinner did Milo even glance in Cole's direction. It was selfish of him, he knew, since he was the one who had told Milo to stay away from him for a while, but it still hurt to not have that safe place to return to.

"Cole." Marla's voice brought him out of the selfish wallowing he'd let himself fall into. "Since you've been hiding out, it's your turn for kitchen duty."

With those words said, the others started getting up from the table, each of them ready to go back to whatever they'd been doing before Marla's "family dinner" had interrupted them.

"Okay," was all Cole said.

Marla wiped her mouth with her napkin then got up. "Bastian. You stay and help." Both boys whipped around to look at her, but she only smiled at them, winked, then walked out of the room with Venja.

For the first time in days, Milo finally looked at him, and Cole felt a pang of guilt. He waited for his friend to protest, but a moment later he followed Marla out of the room. Only Berlin hung back.

"I'm going to help also," he announced, stepping between them to begin collecting plates.

The only thing that could have been more awkward than being alone with Bastian, was being alone with Bastian and Berlin. Cole wasn't sure how to handle it

186

"You don't need to hang round." Bastian's voice on the other hand, was confident as he addressed the darker boy.

Berlin didn't stop collecting dishes, didn't even bother looking at Bastian. "Ich kann Sie nicht allein mit diesem Dämon verlassen. "

Bastian heaved a sigh and rubbed his eyes with his forefinger and thumb. It seemed like he'd dealt with this before.

"Er ist kein Dämon."

Cole never liked it when they held conversations in German. He always felt like they were talking about him. In most cases he figured it was paranoia, but this time he was pretty sure he wasn't imagining it. Berlin raised his voice, his hand sweeping in Cole's direction, though he never spared him a glance. In response, Bastian ran his hands through his hair like he wanted to pull it all out. He thought for a moment that the blond was trying to calm himself down, but then he shouted louder than Berlin.

Cole had learned a long time ago not to stand around where he was unwanted, so instead, he walked around them, grabbed a handful of plates, and left for the kitchen. He could still hear them shouting as he ran hot water in the sink, but at the very least he wouldn't have to watch them gestureing toward him like he wasn't there to hear. When he'd looked up the word Engel, he'd also seen what Dämon meant. He wasn't stupid. Berlin was calling him a demon.

The deep sink was full of hot water when the shouting finally died out. He didn't bother asking about it when Bastian brought the last of the dishes from the table in to him.

"Sorry about that," he said as he took a spot beside him.

"It's not any of my business." Cole could feel the pressure in his chest constrict around his lungs. When had it become so painful to be near Bastian? He used to seek the other boy out for the calm it kindled inside him, now it was torture just to stand beside him.

"Berlin seems to have it in his head that my wings make me an angel. He thinks I have higher standards I have to meet now." He said it like it was a joke.

"I guess that would explain his bad attitude." The words felt cold in Cole's mouth. "If he really believes that, it makes sense that he wouldn't want you hanging around with something as unclean as me."

Bastian braced his hands on the side of the sink, leaning into them like he needed to support himself. He seemed annoyed, but it was hard to tell if the feeling was aimed at him or just a residue of his argument with Berlin.

"Is that why you've been avoiding me? Do you feel unclean about what we did in the cave?"

"I don't really want to talk about that, Bastian." Heat rushed into Cole's body and all he could think of was the way Bastian's eyes had looked as they'd made love—like the sky in his dream, blue and infinite. The plate in his hand slipped and splashed water onto his shirt.

Made love? What the hell am I thinking?

Before the shock of his own thoughts had dissipated, Bastian handed him a small towel.

"Nothing has to change between us, Cole. I helped you because you're my friend. Just because we both enjoyed it doesn't mean what we did is wrong."

The gentle words were just like him. Cole had learned very quickly that his stern looking face hid a very generous and gentle personality. And yet, hearing him call what they did "a favor for a friend" still hurt. He didn't know why it hurt, but he was sure his chest was about to cave in on itself.

"I'm not upset about it." He wondered if Bastian could detect the lie in his voice. Then again, he wasn't really sure if he was lying or not. "I just…want to forget that it happened."

Bastian paused for a long time and for a second Cole hoped he would refuse. He imagined the Bastian from his dream with his long hair, looking at him with those adoring eyes. He thought that Bastian would grip his hands, maybe even kiss them, and say that he refused to forget something that meant so much to him.

"If that's what you want, then that's what we'll do." Bastian's voice was soft as he turned his attention back to the now cloudy water. He didn't say anything else about it and Cole was disappointed with himself. He thought that maybe he shouldn't have lied.

28

Cole had been lying. Bastian had been able to tell immediately, but he wasn't sure what the truth might actually be. It didn't seem like he was playing hard to get. You'd have to be blind to miss the turmoil Cole was struggling with, and it hurt to know that what they did in the cave had added to that pain.

When they were done putting the dishes away and straightening the kitchen, Cole had left immediately, presumably to go back to his room. Bastian wasn't tired, though. No, that wasn't quite right. He was exhausted, but he knew that he wouldn't be able to sleep. He'd not slept well since he and Cole had been rescued from that cavern. Marla had spoken with him and Cole separately and had told him that the experience could leave some latent issues in him, but he knew that wasn't it. When he tried to sleep, he wasn't bothered by thoughts of the darkness, or of being trapped. Instead, his mind was filled with thoughts of Cole. Thoughts of those narrow limbs wound around his neck, the soft bow of his back, the sound of his panting breath in the dark.

Bastian went to the TV room, planning to play games until he couldn't stand being awake any longer. But it was too quiet and the couch beside him felt too cold

Maybe I just can't get him out of my mind because it felt so good to

sleep with him.

It had been a while since he'd last been with Berlin. Maybe his body had just been too hungry. Maybe he needed to get someone else's body in his head to force Cole's out. His chest ached a little and he realized that he didn't *want* to forget Cole's body. He would sleep on it and decide in the morning. He'd been working to sever the physical ties he had with Berlin. It would only make things more complicated if he went back to him now.

The muscles in Bastian's back felt strong. He could feel the power in his shoulders extend far into the wings that he held open to protect Cole's incandescent skin from the harsh rays of the sun. He looked so delicate laying in the bed of grass. His hair pooled around his head like a dark halo, long and silky. Only his eyes could rival the depth of that darkness, two drops of liquid ebony, deeper than the waters that dot the caves beneath their feet.

Bastian could only distantly remember those lakes, or that cave. It seemed like a dream from another life.

"You're perfect." He heard his own voice, deep and reverent. He'd not meant to say those words, though he knew now that those are the words he'd wanted to say to Cole for weeks. He wanted to tell him that because he wanted him to believe it.

He'd expected the soft features of the other boy's face to darken with the self-hatred he always struggled with. Instead, he smiled, soft and spellbound. Bastian had never imagined he would see such a deep affection in the tiny star-fields of the other boy's eyes. He glowed.

Thin, pale fingers brushed across Bastian's face, his touch cool in the warmed air around them.

"I'll love you forever, Bastian. No matter what the laws say."

Bastian sat straight up in bed, the blankets flying off him in his panic. A dream.

Was it a dream?

Bastian could never describe the feeling he had when his body discerned truth and lies, but he felt it now, deep in his gut. He felt truth radiating from the memory of that dream. Did that mean he wanted it to be true? Did he want Cole to say those words to him?

It was the middle of the night, but Bastian got out of bed anyway. He wasn't sure why the idea of wanting Cole to love him startled him so much, but he needed to clear whatever was storming inside him away, and fast. As he slipped into the hallway he wondered if Milo hadn't been right. Had Cole poisoned him somehow when he had kissed him in the cave? He felt the other boy's presence growing stronger inside him and it scared him.

Berlin's room was unlocked, and sneaking inside gave Bastian a comforting sense of nostalgia. He didn't wait for Berlin to wake up or to invite him into his bed. Instead, Bastian pulled the blankets back and slid in beside him, immediately moving one leg over the other boy so he was straddling the narrow hips that accentuated the broad set of the rest of his body.

"Bastian?" The other boy's voice was low and scratchy from sleep. "What're you—"

Bastian didn't let him finish his sentence, closing his mouth over his friend's lips. Kissing Berlin was comfortable. He'd done it so many times in the past, but it didn't thrill him the way kissing Cole had. He didn't feel the fire that had burned inside him when he'd been with the black-haired boy in the cave. The body underneath him stiffened for a second, but then Berlin responded, kissing him back, his hands moving from his thighs up to his waist. The fuzzy arousal was starting to build up in Bastian's mind and he pressed harder into the kiss. He wanted to wipe his mind of everything, just for a few minutes if that's all he could get.

Then Berlin's hands slid into the mass of feathers that rested against Bastian's back and he pulled away.

"Wait, Bastian; I can't do this."

Berlin sat up, his hands softly pushing Bastian off of him as he did so.

"What do you mean, you can't do this?" His feelings weren't necessarily hurt, but he did want to shake the other boy. "You weren't complaining the last time you snuck into my room to have me suck your dick."

"Well yeah, but that was before."

"Before what?" Bastian didn't need to ask that question. He knew, but all he wanted was to drown himself in something filthy, and

Berlin's sudden piety was making it very difficult.

"Before I realized what you are! You can't seriously expect me to sully an *angel!* I'd end up in purgatory forever to work something like that off."

Bastian wanted to scream. He was so tired of hearing Berlin talk about him like he knew what was going on.

"I'm no different than I was when we went into that cave."

Berlin grabbed Bastian by the wings and pulled them so they unfurled just a little.

"I would call this a bit different."

Bastian pulled himself away and planted himself on the bed beside him.

"Besides," Berlin continued. "You were the one who suggested we stop fooling around."

"I know." He had said that. He really had no excuse, other than desperation.

"I'm still your friend, though." It was unusual for Berlin to sound gentle like that. "You've been acting weird since we dug you out of that cave."

"I know," he repeated.

Berlin huffed, then shifted in the bed, folding his legs beneath himself. Once he was situated he put one hand on each knee as though to prove that he was serious and offering his full attention.

"Okay. I'm listening. Tell me what's going on."

Bastian couldn't help but smile just a little. "It's hard to explain."

"That's fine. I'm Catholic. We're great at understanding stuff that makes no damn sense."

Bastian wished he'd gone to Berlin sooner. Even though he was being an ass about Cole, he was still his best friend. Fighting, for them, was part of the natural order. He shouldn't have let it get in the way of the good things.

"I can't stop thinking about Cole."

"What? You mean this isn't about..." He waved vaguely at the wings Bastian had learned to fold neatly against his back.

"Well, I mean, I think they're involved in this somehow. I told you it's complicated."

"Okay." It was obvious that he was trying to not go off on his 'Cole is a monster' tangent. "So how are they related?"

"I'm not really sure. A while back Marla told me that Cole and I were found in the exact same way, on the same day even. We were just on opposite sides of the planet. It just… seems strange. And now I can't get him out of my head. I think about him all the time and when we're in the same room I start sweating. My heart races. God, I even feel sick to my stomach sometimes and all I can think about it grabbing him and…" He shook his head

"Okay." Berlin seemed to be taking the news well, or at the very least he was faking it really well. "Let's not argue about whether Cole might be a demon or not right now, but we *do* know that he feeds off your danglies, okay?"

Bastian pinched the bridge of his nose. Leave it to Berlin to ruin the mood of any serious conversation.

"What? He does. And even Milo said that he can use toxins on people to get them hooked so he can ensure his next meal. I'm not saying you were wrong for feeding him in the cave, but maybe he dosed you while you were down there. I bet all this obsessive stuff is just a side effect of that."

It was definitely a possibility. Milo had warned him not to kiss Cole at all while he was feeding him, and once that gate had opened they had kissed until he thought he might pass out. Kissing Cole had almost been better than the actual sex. His mouth had been so warm, and the heat of it had filled something in his chest that he'd never felt with anyone else. Somehow, though, he knew it wasn't as simple as that.

"I've been having dreams about him." Bastian felt his face go hot as he said those words out loud for the first time.

"Since when?"

"Since we got back from Lechuguilla."

"It's probably part of all that poison bullshit."

"That's not it, though. These dreams aren't about having sex with him or anything. They're weird. I mean, we're us, but it's different. We look different. I *feel* different in those dreams. I feel like they're things that have happened, but that's obviously not the case. I mean I've not even known him that long."

"What sorts of dreams?"

Bastian shrugged. "I don't know. The one tonight was just us laying together in the grass. We were just..." *Why is it so embarrassing to say this?* "Kissing. He said he loved me. Said that he would no matter what the laws say. It didn't really make any sense."

Berlin was quiet for a while, and Bastian was relieved that he was at least taking the conversation seriously.

"So you're having dreams that feel a lot like memories. And you both suddenly woke up in random ass places on the same day in our world."

"Hold on a second. What do you mean by 'our world,' exactly?" He had a feeling he knew where Berlin was going with this, and he wasn't in the mood to hear about it.

"Look. *To me,* it sounds like you're dreaming about a past life. Well, maybe not in the way we normally think about it. But we can all tell that you two are nuts about each other, and frankly it pisses me off. I think you're dreaming about whatever was going on before you two woke up here. And with this talk about laws, and with the new developments here," he waved his hand at Bastian's wings again. "I think that you two were lovers. And honestly, it probably pissed God off. He probably booted you and sent you both to Earth as a punishment."

Bastian took a deep breath and massaged his eye sockets until they hurt. No matter how stupid Berlin sounded, he really was trying to help.

"What?"

"You pissed God off by getting freaky with a demon. Which proves that what I've been telling you from the beginning is right. Don't put your dick in evil, man. Bad things happen!"

"I'm leaving."

"I'm telling you. Even if it sounds crazy, I bet you money I'm right!"

Bastian didn't answer. Instead, he went back to his room, his sex drive totally shot now.

That is the most ridiculous thing I've heard from him yet.

And that was saying something after he'd been convinced that Alistair was possessed when they first met him. Apparently super human strength is a sign of possession in the Catholic Church.

Ridiculous.

He tried to imagine what a life with Cole might look like, and suddenly the green field from his dream came to mind. Maybe the soft heat he felt when he looked at Cole was the remnants of the love he'd felt in that dream. Maybe it was the remnants of a love from a life before the one they both knew.

He shook his head.

Berlin's superstitious thinking is getting to me...

It was an unbelievable but not unpleasant idea.

29

Several days passed, and the dreams about Bastian continued. Sometimes they would be lying together in that vast field of grass, other times they were embracing in the shadowed nooks and crannies of some massive palace. Sometimes they were wound together, straining against each other, tangled in blankets. No matter where they were, every time he woke up those dreams felt a little more real than they had the night before. And every time, he felt the pull that Bastian had on him grow stronger.

Milo rarely left the research facility located in the lower levels of Haven these days, and while Cole stood by his decision not to feed from him anymore, the loneliness was getting to him. He wondered if he was angry that he'd let Bastian feed him. He knew that Milo had suggested it, but it was impossible to keep his feelings of guilt from pecking at him.

No matter how he felt, though, his time was up. While he wasn't desperate yet, he was hungry, and he knew that he would have to feed before the end of the weekend.

The security inside Haven was strict. Even getting down to where Marla's office was could be a challenge sometimes. No one was allowed to come or go without permission and an escort. Yet, somehow, Alistair had managed to crack their system. Cole wondered if Marla and Venja had just given up and started letting him come and go on purpose. Maybe they thought he would be too big a handful if he got angry about it. After all, what would they be able to do against someone as strong as Alistair?

Cole had never been very interested in leaving Haven. His experiences outside the facility weren't exactly good, but he knew the sorts of places that Alistair usually snuck off to. And that was exactly why he needed the other boy's help.

The hall was quiet. Cole thought he could hear Milo's keyboard through the closed door, but he ignored it. Milo had made it very clear that he wasn't interested in seeing him one-on-one, and Cole wasn't about to go to him now. He knew that Milo would probably try to stop him if they spoke. Quietly, Cole approached Alistair's door. He heard some faint music coming from the other side, which meant, at least, that he'd not left yet. He knocked softly at first, then when he got no answer he knocked a little harder.

The door whipped open so fast that Cole jumped where he stood. Alistair seemed taller standing so close to him now, but he wasn't tall and broad like Bastian. He was narrow, delicate looking.

"Yes?"

"Hey…" Cole just remembered how bad he was at this. "I was, um, hoping I could talk to you?" Alistair didn't move. "In private?"

Pale green eyes narrowed just slightly at him, but then he stepped aside.

"Come on then."

Cole scurried into the dimly lit room. Candles burned in the corner and clothes lay about the bed and floor, some song with a heavy bass played quietly from small speakers hooked to his phone.

"What is it?"

His mouth was a little dry. Cole thought he probably should have sorted out what he was going to say before he came.

"Are you going out tonight?"

Alistair didn't seem surprised that he knew about it, which only supported Cole's suspicion that Marla had started consciously letting him get away with it. He was obviously dressed for a night out. He typically wore loose fitting house pants and large-necked sweaters.

But now he wore a tight fitting black tank top that made his red hair seem brighter and his pale, freckled skin seem lovelier. The black pants he wore weren't as tight as his top, but they hugged his hips and gathered at his calves, the pockets down the side and the combat boots he wore giving the whole thing a vaguely punk esthetic. The boots gaped unlaced and Cole got the impression they would stay that way—they matched the intentionally messy look of the outfit.

"Maybe." His answer was obviously a formality.

Cole looked up and down Alistair's body, then at the clothes strewn about the room like he was reminding Alistair that he wasn't stupid.

"Why do you ask?"

"Well," Cole said as he tried not to fiddle his fingers. "I was hoping I could go with you."

Now it was Alistair's turn to look Cole up and down. "Absolutely not."

"What? Why?"

"Do you even know the sorts of places I go to? You'd be eaten alive, or kicked out for your bad taste in fashion."

Cole had never given his clothes much thought, but he still felt insulted.

"I think I have a pretty good idea of where you go."

"So you know where I go but you still want to tag along? What? Are you looking for some action?"

Even though he knew exactly what he was trying to accomplish by sneaking out with Alistair, the words still made his face flash with heat. Before he could say anything, though, Alistair began laughing.

"You are, aren't you?"

Cole swallowed. "I'm going to have to feed soon, and I've decided that I can't rely on Milo any more. The side effects are getting to him. And I can't wait much longer either, or I might lash out like I did to you. So... yes. I want to go with you to find someone who I can feed from. Someone I won't end up hurting."

Alistair was still laughing quietly to himself, shaking his head and not paying much attention to Cole's very serious explanation. For a moment, Cole was sure he would turn him away, then the tall red-head pulled his hair up into a messy bun at the top of his head and smiled at him.

"Alright. I'll take you. But I'm going to dress you."

Being part of Haven, Cole had stood up to many intimidating forces in his time there, but he'd never been as nervous as he was facing Alistair and his vast wardrobe.

30

Talking with Berlin had been a bit of a relief for Bastian, even if he still didn't agree with his ridiculous ideas. It was nice, though, to have someone he could be completely transparent with. Over the handful of days that passed, he'd talked with the other boy a few more times, and the more Bastian told him, the more he started wondering just what his feelings for Cole might be. He cared about him, usually more than he cared for any of the others. He might have even dropped the big "L" word if he wasn't still living under the shadow of Cole's toxins. Could all of these things he was feeling really be caused by something like that?

Marla had let Cole skip the dinner table, something she let him get away with now and then. Berlin had hurried to eat so he could make it to the TV room in time—the football season was starting back home in Germany, and Berlin never missed a match unless they were on a mission. Sabin, as was usual, excused himself quickly as well, which left Bastian with Alistair and Milo.

Thinking so much about the toxins that people kept talking about, Bastian thought he should ask Milo about them more explicitly, but the other boy had been reclusive lately. Chances were he didn't want to talk to him.

"I'm going out tonight." Alistair said quietly as he got up from the table. "Tell Berlin to keep his mouth shut about it this time, would you?"

"He won't notice anything until the match is over."

Alistair only huffed a vaguely irritated laugh then left the room, leaving Bastian alone with Milo. The last time he'd been alone with Milo they'd gotten into a fist fight. Now was his chance to ask him about the toxins though. Yet, somehow, all he managed to do was quickly finish his meal. Asking Milo anything about Cole felt like a very serious breach of propriety.

He was just about to drop his plate in the kitchen and flee the room when Milo spoke up.

"Are you free right now?"

Bastian had to fight the urge to look around for anyone else those words might have been directed to, but he knew they were alone.

"Yeah, I guess."

"Good. Come to my room with me. I want to talk to you about something."

Milo didn't wait for him. He got up, leaving his empty plate where it was, and marched out of the dining room. For a minute, Bastian thought he should refuse. He wasn't exactly being inviting, and while he knew he could take Milo in a fight, he wasn't looking for another bloody nose. Nevertheless, he followed him.

Bastian had never been inside Milo's room, but it was about what he'd expected. A massive computer set up with multiple screens took up the majority of one side of the space, but the bed and dresser were no different than what Bastian had. His eyes lingered on the bed, though, and he wondered how many times Cole had been wrapped in those sheets.

"I've not slept with him since before our trip to Lechuguilla."

Bastian jumped at the sound of his voice and wondered if his face really gave him away that obviously.

"I still want to," he continued, "but the longer I stay away, the easier it gets."

"I'm sorry." Bastian wasn't sure what exactly he was apologizing for.

"It's not your fault." Milo leaned against his computer desk. "You didn't cause this problem. You just forced me to recognize it."

Bastian nodded, glad that Milo didn't seem angry with him. He sounded depressed, but not angry.

"And what problem are you talking about exactly?"

Milo's lips grew thin for a moment, then he changed the subject.

"You've been the talk of the town down in Research, you know. I'm sure you're at least a little aware of that after all the poking and prodding they did once we got you out of that cave. But I'm guessing they haven't given you any real details, have they?"

"Do the details include the results of my prostate exam?"

Milo didn't laugh. Instead, he collected some papers from the desk and passed them to Bastian. They all looked complicated and were covered in graphs and numbers. They made no sense him.

"They've been really interested in your DNA here lately. Wanted to figure out if you're some sort of hybrid, or if you have a gene mutations that caused the wing growth. Turns out you have quite the package."

"I didn't come here to flirt and talk about my package, Milo." Teasing him wasn't a great idea, but Bastian still didn't care much for the other boy.

"God, he deserves better than you." Bastian could barely hear him, but when Milo continued he spoke louder. "I meant your genetic package. When someone's DNA copies itself, there are usually tiny mistakes. It's normal. Everyone one gets those little mess ups. Your DNA has none of those mess ups."

"What can I say? I drank a lot of milk growing up."

"Will you take this seriously for two seconds? We've not talked about it because we've not known what it means, but Cole's DNA is the same way. Whatever you guys are, you're bred from the same stock."

The look on Bastian's face must have been horrified, because Milo sighed and rubbed his forehead.

"I mean you're likely the same *thing.* I don't mean you're related."

Bastian stared at the papers for a while, wishing they would somehow start making sense to him. They didn't, but then again he'd never been very interested in the sciences. At the very least he wished he understood what he meant by the "same thing." He didn't even know what he was, so knowing that Cole was the same made little sense. Then Berlin's ramblings came to mind. He knew what Berlin would say at a time like this; "Demons are just fallen angels." He had to laugh a little. It felt like a soap opera.

"Also, I noticed something interesting as well." Milo took the papers from him, shuffled through them, then presented him with one from the bottom of the stack. "The other researchers didn't have any interest in it, but I noticed. This includes a listing for your oxytocin levels."

"That's the hormone that makes you happy, right?" He at least knew that much. He remembered hearing that it was released when you exercised, had sex or fell in love.

"Yeah. It plays other roles as well, though. It helps with bonding after child birth and builds ties with family and lovers. But in unnatural doses it can cause possessiveness and obsession. I was interested in it because that's exactly how the toxin Cole produces work. It makes the oxytocin levels in his victims spike so they are compliant and so they want to keep coming back. It ensures a continued source of nourishment."

Bastian knew that Milo was talking about Cole in a strictly anatomical way, but it still made him bristle. He didn't like how accusatory it sounded. He could feel his heart rate pick up a little and he had to fight his urge to defend the other boy.

"I'd been ignoring the constant rise in my oxytocin levels. Probably because they were also blinding me. But yours were totally normal. Even though they were taken not long after you fed Cole. Maybe it's because your DNA is so pristine. Maybe it's because the two of you have some other connection. But your body seems unresponsive to his toxins."

"Unresponsive?"

"That's right. When he's desperate and turns to pheromonal persuasion you've not had any reaction, have you? In the locker room he tried it on you. I'm sure he gave you a nice dose when you were in the cave, but you remained completely lucid, right?"

"I don't think that's right. I mean, I've not been able to get him out of my head. You said this causes obsession and stuff, right? That's exactly what it feels like. In the locker room I could barely stop myself, and when I was feeding him I totally lost mind and..." He stopped when he saw the pained expression on Milo's face. "Sorry."

"It's fine. Like I said, it's getting easier as my body goes back to normal." He was quiet for a second. "But, have you ever thought of hurting him? Of locking him up? When you were feeding him did you think that you should just wrap your hands around his neck? Just squeeze until he disappeared so no one else could have him and you wouldn't have to feel so sick with your desire to own him?"

Bastian's face must have looked more horrified than he realized, because Milo didn't even wait for an answer. He let out the smallest puff of a laugh, a sound that felt far more miserable than anything Bastian would have expected.

"If you've not felt those things then the toxins didn't work on you. And that's exactly why I'm staying away from him. I wanted to do everything for him, but not because I love him. It was because I wanted to own him. I wanted him to only have me to rely on. I wanted to isolate him from everyone else because I thought he belonged to me. So I guess I owe you my gratitude. I still hate you right now, and I still want him back. But it's slowly going away. I'm hoping that at some point I can be close with him again. The way we were when we first met."

Bastian wasn't sure what to say. He couldn't imagine the anguish the other boy must be suffering if his obsession was even greater than what Bastian felt toward the black-haired boy. It was confusing, though, because in the end, he *did* still feel obsessed with Cole. Was he just affected more gently than Milo?

"God, you're so stupid." Milo snatched the papers from Bastian's hands before he even had the chance to be offended. "The sort of obsession *you're* feeling is because you're in love with him." He slapped the stack of papers onto his desk. "And honestly, he probably feels the same way about you."

A thousand different objections flew into Bastian's head, but only a strangled "What?" managed to escape him.

"And honestly, toxins or not, it pisses me off."

"Hey. What's so bad about me?"

"It doesn't matter. What does matter right now is that I know Cole and I know how he thinks. He won't come to me for another meal, and he won't go to you either because he likes you too much. That means he's going to find some way to feed from someone else."

Bastian didn't want that. The gentle smile he'd seen on Cole's face in his dreams, the soft voice he'd heard whispering such sweet words, came to his mind. He didn't want anyone else touching him.

"So if you actually care about him at all you need to go sort this out with him."

"Wait. Didn't you tell me he wasn't able to fall in love?"

"I just told you that I'd been intentionally cutting him off from forming bonds with other people. I was lying. I thought you were supposed to be able to tell that. I shouldn't have ever lied to Cole about that, but he believes it now. Which means you're going to have to convince him."

Bastian was surprised. He'd *not* been able to tell that Milo had been lying. Was he giving him a blessing of some sort? They were quiet for a second, then Milo moved back to sit down at his computer.

"You should go. Cole's pretty stupid too. I'm sure he's hatching some kind of stupid plan already. Go sort it out before I change my mind."

At any other time, Bastian would have told Milo to watch his attitude. He would have told him that he had no authority to give him or Cole permission to do anything. But he could see the pain the brunette was still working through, and honestly he felt bad for him. He hoped that he would eventually get over whatever effects Cole had on him. He thought that Milo might be a good guy once he was back to normal.

"Thank you."

Milo didn't answer him, not that Bastian expected him to, and after another moment, he left the room.

Bastian had gone back to his own room after that, heart hammering in his chest. Was Milo right? Was he really in love with Cole? He'd been so busy with Berlin's stupid theories about angels and demons that he'd not stopped and think about what his obsession with the other boy really meant. The dreams he had made him feel warm and giddy, but they were only a shadow of the feelings he'd had in that cave. The breathless wonder he'd felt when his body had connected to Cole's was something that still made him dizzy when he thought about it. He'd written it off as a side effect of Cole's powers, but now he wasn't so sure.

He wasn't sure if it was love, but he did know how delicate Cole's heart was, and he knew that he would do nothing but hurt himself in his attempt to protect everyone else.

It was late by the time Bastian had talked himself into confronting the other boy. The only problem was that Cole wasn't in his room. Bastian knocked for several minutes, then let himself in. It was empty. The TV room was empty. The kitchen, then gym, the shower room. Bastian was just beginning to panic when he bumped into Berlin who was coming back from one of the larger media rooms that Bastian hadn't thought to check.

"Hey! Was Cole watching the match with you?" He knew the question was stupid the second it left his lips and Berlin did nothing to hide his distaste.

"No. But I did see him run off with Alistair earlier."

"Run off? Where?"

"I dunno. Wherever it is Alistair goes to get lucky, I guess."

Bastian felt something shutter inside himself.

"It's still so unfair that they just gave up on keeping him here. Maybe I should sneak out some time. Just because—hey!"

Bastian shoved his way past his friend, not listening to him anymore. He knew that Cole would go so far as to starve himself to keep from feeding on people he cared about. But he wasn't seriously stupid enough to go pick up a stranger. Was he?

31

Cole had begun avoiding the streets of the city the moment Marla had picked him up. He didn't like being out, especially at night.

Alistair walked several yards ahead of him, as though he wanted to deny any association they had. His strides were long and confident, elegant in the way every other part of his body was. He looked stylish, like he knew what he wanted and like he would definitely get it. Cole, on the other hand, felt foolish dressed up. Alistair had done his best, but Cole still wondered if he wasn't playing some sort of joke on him. He'd put him in a black tank top and draped him in a dark top that refused to stay on his shoulders. That in and of itself was not bad, even comfortable, but the shorts that Alistair had insisted on were outrageous.

"You have good legs. You're short, but they're a great shape and supple. You should definitely show them off."

That's what Alistair had said when he was dressing him, but Cole had never worn such tiny shorts and the moment he'd tried to pull them down, Alistair had swatted his hand away.

"If you embarrass me by picking a wedgie or something in that club I'll leave you there, you got it?"

Cole had kept his hands at his sides after that. He felt like an idiot, and he was sure that anyone who glanced his way thought the same.

All he could do, though, was remind himself that he needed to do this. If he cared at all for Milo or Bastian, he had to suck it up and do the right thing.

The club that Alistair seemed to frequent wasn't far away, and they got there after about twenty minutes of walking. Even from outside, the four-story building thumped with music, lights flashed in the slivers that were left where windows had been covered from the inside. A line wrapped around the side of the building.

"Is there always a line like this when you come?"

"Ignore them." Alistair caught Cole's wrist and pulled him toward the front of the line.

Cole could hear people talking as they walked past, but Alistair never hesitated. He walked to the front of the line and past the large man by the door who Cole could only guess was a bouncer. Cole could tell the man was surprised—he watched his eyebrows shoot up his forehead—but he didn't say anything as Alistair dragged him through the dark glass doors. Inside, the space was dark and hazy, and instantly the music was so loud that Cole felt his whole body vibrating in time with the bass. At a small window, Alistair paid his entry fee, then after a huff of annoyance paid Cole's as well.

After they paid, Alistair pulled Cole into a small nook where a few plush chairs sat. He leaned close to shout in his ear. Even then Cole could barely hear him.

"You owe that entry money back. If you want drinks find someone to buy them for you."

Cole tried to tell him that he wasn't interested in drinking, but he was sure he'd not said it loud enough.

"Don't talk to me while we're in here. Walk home when you're done."

And then Alistair left, disappearing into another room where the lights and music seemed to be coming from. He fought the urge to pull on the tiny shorts he wore. Now that he was there he felt a little less foolish in them—lots of others were wearing outfits far more revealing than his—but they were still uncomfortable. Now he just had to figure out how to choose a partner, and then how to seduce him. He tried to remember how he'd done it in the past, but he'd always waited until he was desperate back then. And even now he only ever tried to seduce anyone when he was starving—when his mind was foggy. His body always took over. He knew, though, that a kiss would hook them. He just had to find someone who would kiss him, and then everything should fall into place.

When they'd left Haven, Alistair had told him not to worry about his horns, even though Cole had put up a fuss about going out in public with them. Now he understood why. The club they were in was draped in black and decorated with gothic arches, stained glass windows, bloody crucifixes and dark, haunting paintings. The guests seemed to be into the aesthetics as well, because most of them wore black clothes and heavy, dramatic eyeliner. As he entered the main room with its high cathedral ceiling and wide dance floor, Alistair's strawberry blond hair stuck out in the sea of black. Cole, however, fit right in.

Cole made several laps around the dance floor, not sure how to proceed. He could smell the arousal in the air, though, and he supposed that he wasn't the only one there to find a partner. Through the crowd he saw Alistair dancing with a tall, shirtless man. Alistair's thin hands were wound tight in dark hair, his body rolling against the other man who held him tight about the waist. Cole found himself fascinated by the way their bodies ground together, and he wondered how Alistair could look so thin and delicate while still knowing what the lithe body was capable of. Even though his hunger was under control, he still felt a stirring in his gut as he watched the way Alistair's body moved. He wondered how someone could ooze sexuality like that. He wondered if that was how people saw him when they were drugged.

"Makes you a little jealous, doesn't it?"

Cole jumped where he was standing as the warmth of someone's breath washed over his ear. A hand moved to the narrowest part of his waist and for a second he couldn't move.

"They look like they're enjoying themselves."

The man's voice was deep, and something about it reminded Cole of Bastian, how he'd imagined he might sound without his German accent. As he turned to look at the man who finally pulled back from his ear, Cole realized that wasn't the only thing about this other boy that reminded him of Bastian. His hair wasn't blond, but it was a light enough brown that Cole could stretch the comparison. He was similar in height and build too. It made Cole suddenly ache for Bastian. He wished it was his hand on his waist instead of this stranger's.

The brunette seemed to notice his staring and took it as a compliment, because he smiled. He leaned in close again, his lips brushing Cole's ear. "I'm Asher," he said as he brought a hand up to run his fingers down the curve of Cole's horn. "You're a pretty little thing, aren't you? What's your name?"

Cole wondered if "Asher" was this boy's real name or if it was some club name he used, but it didn't matter. Asher seemed interested, and the resemblance he had to Bastian made the choice easy for Cole.

"Cole."

"Very cute." Asher's hand moved to Cole's chin, his fingers brushing over the soft skin of his cheek. "Do you like to dance?"

"No." There was no reason to drag this out longer than was necessary.

"Interesting." Asher smiled. He was handsome, and he seemed gentle enough. "Do you want to come upstairs with me? It's quieter. We can talk."

This was exactly what Cole had come here for. And Asher had even made the whole situation easier for him because he'd kept Cole from having to approach anyone. Still, his stomach clenched, and he felt a small tremor starting in his hands. He didn't want to be there. He didn't want to go away with a stranger. He wanted to go back home and sit on the couch with Bastian and play games.

"Yeah." Cole hoped he didn't sound as sad as he felt.

Asher smiled, though, and took Cole's hand. If Cole looked sad, he didn't seem to care. He led him off the dance floor and up a set of stairs that were hidden in the back corner.

32

Sneaking out of Haven had been easier than Bastian had expected, and he thought he should tell Berlin about it when he got back. Doors were left unlocked, guards were distracted with books and phones. He wondered if it was always like this, or if they were just leaving the back door open for Alistair to come back. Either way, Bastian made it out onto the streets quickly. The door to Haven opened up onto a nondescript alley. He knew it was to keep anyone from getting suspicious, but it was still surprising to know that a single, rusted metal door led down into the labyrinth of halls and rooms that sat under his feet now.

It had been easy getting onto the streets, but now he was faced with a new problem. Even as late as it was, the sidewalks kept a steady stream of pedestrians. Certainly the roads weren't packed, but there were enough people out that Bastian was very aware of their curious glances. Of course, he *did* stick out. As he checked his phone for locations that might have drawn Alistair's attention, he realized he should have taken at least a few minutes to think about his appearance before he'd run off. As it was, he was wandering the streets of New York City barefoot, wearing a tank top, pajama pants, and a massive set of wings on his back. He did his best to ignore the stares, keeping his new appendages as still as he could. Maybe people would think they were just a costume prop and he was just that weird guy they saw talking to himself sometimes.

It was hard to guess which club Alistair might have gone to, but there was a place nearby with a cluster of clubs and bars, and with Cole tagging along, Alistair probably wouldn't have wanted to go by train anywhere. Bastian kept his pace to a casual, brisk walk for a long time, not wanting to bring any more attention to himself than he was already getting, but the more he thought of Cole alone in one of these clubs, the more antsy he got. Eventually, he gave up caring about the other pedestrians and broke into a run.

The map he'd looked at had shown the cluster of nightlife, but once he got there he felt a wave of panic wash over him. The streets were thick with people bar-hopping and socializing. Bars sat with their doors open and patrons spilled out of them onto the streets. How was he supposed to find Cole in this mess?

Ignoring the funny looks and curious shouts from the people he passed, Bastian began a quick once-over of the street, trying to think like Alistair—trying to figure out where he would go if he were looking for a good time. The clubs all had lines of people waiting to get inside, but at the end of the road he saw one massive building with a line wrapping around the side of the building and down the street. He knew Alistair's taste, and he knew that he would go for the most popular, most coveted spots. Starting at the end of the line, Bastian scanned the people waiting to get inside, hoping that he would catch his friends before they actually got in. It was a waste of time. He knew Alistair better than to think he would wait in a queue like a regular civilian.

When he got to the front of the line, the bouncer, who was letting maybe a quarter of the people waiting inside, stopped him.

"Hold it, Cupid," he said, putting one meaty hand on Bastian's shoulder. "We don't let cherubs into the club. Especially barefoot ones. Beat it."

Bastian had always been strong. Maybe not like Alistair, but even with the size difference he knew he could take this man in a fight. Confidence was not something new to him, but now there was a new feeling inside him. A surety he couldn't quite place. His hand moved to the bouncer's massive wrist. He squeezed, but not in an attempt to injure him. Instead, he looked the man in the eyes and the heat of righteous confidence rose up to his mouth where it released as a single command.

"Move."

As though cast under a spell, the man's face went slack. His hand released Bastian's shoulder, and he stepped out of the way. If he'd not been in such a hurry, Bastian might have wondered how he'd done it, but all that mattered now was getting inside and finding Cole. The man at the ticket booth who had seen his interaction with the bouncer didn't stop Bastian, and even the other patrons moved aside for him as he walked into the dark club.

Finding Cole would be hard. Everything was dark and hazy with smoke given off by some hidden fog machine. He couldn't even shout for him, the music too loud for him to even hope to be heard. There were a few nooks and crannies that he checked before moving into the main room. Immediately, he plunged into the mass of shifting bodies that rose and fell with the beat of the music. While people all around him had hair dyed black, rendering Cole's hair impossible to pick out of a crowd, Alistair's vibrant mane stood out. He looked shocked when Bastian ripped him away from the man he'd been dancing with.

"Where's Cole?" Bastian shouted as loud as he could to ensure that Alistair would hear him, but also because his anger and panic was bubbling to get out of him.

"I don't know. I saw him wandering off with someone."

"You weren't keeping an eye on him?"

"I'm not his babysitter. He's the one who asked to come here. I'm not going to stop him if he's looking to get laid." Bastian had to do everything he could to keep from hitting his friend, but in the end, if Cole asked to go, it wasn't Alistair's fault.

"Where did you see him going?"

"That way." He motioned toward the back of the club. "Probably upstairs."

Bastian didn't know what was upstairs, but it sounded far too intimate for his liking. He let go of the redhead and pushed his way toward the back corner. Upstairs he found a mezzanine that ran the circumference of the dance floor, railings and chairs giving people a place to look down on the action of the main floor. Against the exterior walls, however, were small sitting areas and dark coves where he saw couples sitting together or making out. This was definitely more intimate than he wanted. The music was a little quieter there, but still loud enough that his eyes were his best chance of finding Cole. As he worked his way around the area he interrupted several couples to ensure he wasn't missing the other boy anywhere. What if he was too late? What if they'd left the club to go somewhere more private?

Then, muffled under the base of the music, Bastian heard a familiar voice, a sound that both lifted his heart and dropped a stone into his gut. In the back corner he saw a couple pressed back into the shadow behind a pillar. Bare, milky legs flashed in the dark and Bastian heard Cole's frantic voice.

"Please! Stop it, I've changed my mind. I don't want to do this."

Bastian didn't run, not wanting to make the scene he was about to cause any worse than it was going to be, but he made a beeline for them. As he got closer he could hear the other man's voice, he could see his hand pressing against the tight fabric of Cole's shorts. He could see a hand that didn't belong shifting down into places that were far too intimate.

"Just relax, okay? I'm not gonna hurt you. You're gonna feel really good." The brunette's mouth moved down onto Cole's neck and Bastian thought he must have bitten him because Cole shrieked only to be muffled by a hand clamping down over his mouth. "You don't get to seduce me and then tell me I can't touch you." With a jerk that shook Cole's body, the other man broke the button on his shorts and pushed them down around his hips.

Refusing to let him get any further, Bastian ran the last few yards, and through a haze of red that seemed to fill up his line of sight, he yanked the other man away from Cole by a fistful of hair. "Get you fucking hands off him!"

Asher stumbled away from Cole as Bastian slung him back by his hair.

"What the fuck?" He stumbled and regained his footing. "What the hell are you supposed to be?" He looked over Bastian's shoulder at Cole. "Do you know this guy?"

Bastian could hear Cole panting behind him, could hear the tremor in his breath, and he shifted to block him from the other man's view.

"Yes. He knows me. Now leave before I beat the shit out of you."

Asher bristled all over and took a few steps back toward Bastian, reaching out to grab him. "Listen here, you ponce-ass piece of shit." He balled his fist, obviously ready to either threaten or fight Bastian.

Then the hot surety rose in Bastian's throat again, and in a voice that boomed in a way that couldn't be human, he stepped toward him, his wings pressing out to their full length, and shouted "Leave him!" The room shook even over the music, and everyone on the mezzanine stopped to look at them. Asher stilled instantly, his face pausing in a look somewhere between wonder and horror. Then he backed away, turned and walked back to the stairs. The others on the floor slowly got up and followed him. They didn't seem panicked, but obedient. Bastian wasn't sure what he'd done, but as he heard the soft gasp behind him, he realized he didn't care.

Turning around, he wondered if he was going to hug Cole or shout at him. But then he saw the other boy slumped against the wall, one hand holding his shorts up, the other covering his face, his chest jerking around his muffled sobs. His heart ached. It hurt to see Cole crying, but frustration and anger still simmered inside him.

"Why are you crying?" The questioned sounded harsher than he'd intended. "What he was doing, that's what you came here for, right?"

Cole shook his head.

"You're telling me you didn't come here for a meal?"

He only shook his head again, and Bastian knew what he was doing. He knew that if he answered out loud he would be unable to hide his lying from him.

"Say something!"

"I came here to get away from *you*!" Cole's voice cracked as he moved his hand away from his reddened face.

Bastian froze, something inside of him twisting under the pain of those words. They hurt because he knew immediately that Cole was telling the truth.

"Yes, I came here to feed, but I did it so it wouldn't be you."

"You hate the idea of me feeding you so much that you'd rather come here and pick up a stranger?"

"Yes!" Cole ran his hands through his hair, gripping his own horns like he wanted to pull them out of his skull. Tears continued to spill over his cheeks even as he shouted. "You're driving me crazy. You're the only thing I can think about. I dream about you. I jerk off to you! I can't get the feeling of you off of me and when I lose it again I know you're the one I'll go after! I don't want that. I don't want to hurt you like I did Milo..."

Bastian's anger fizzled.

So he's the same. We've infected each other.

"Cole." His voice was soft now as he took the other boy's thin wrists in his hands, easing them away from his horns. "I'm sorry I shouted." He watched Cole's dark eyes waver with uncertainty, but the smaller boy didn't fight him. "I'm not going to let you feed from a stranger. And I'm not going to let you starve yourself."

"No!" Cole's eyes filled with tears all over again. "You're not going to feed me. I won't allow it..." His voice faded as Bastian moved his hands to his cheeks.

"I'm so happy that you can't get me out of your head. Because I feel the same way." Bastian could feel him shiver ever so slightly under his touch. "I dream about you every night. I'm always thinking about how soft you are. " He dropped his forehead to Cole's. "How sweet you are."

"Stop." His voice was weak as he closed his eyes around the fat tears that still clung to his lashes.

"Cole, I think this is love."

The words seemed to strike Cole like razors because he tried to squirm away.

"No. You're confused. I do this to people. You shouldn't have kissed me. I should have fought you more."

Pressing a hand to the back of Cole's neck he drew him into a soft kiss, and despite his words, Cole only stiffened for a second before relinquishing himself.

Bastian wound an arm around Cole's narrow waist and pulled him in close to his body. He could feel the heat of him through the thin fabric of his tank top and could feel the muscles in Cole's back quiver under his fingers. He kissed him slowly, trying to express the gentleness of the feelings he had for him, the warmth and tenderness he felt when he was with him. As he pulled away Cole's eyes stayed closed and Bastian watched him suck his pinkened lips between his own teeth, as though he were savoring the taste Bastian had left there.

"Your toxins don't affect me, Cole." Obsidian eyes fluttered open to look at him. "Milo told me tonight before I came here. He's done my blood work. The feelings I have are for you, not your pheromones or your toxins."

Cole shook his head weakly and Bastian moved his hands back to his cheeks to still him.

"Just for a moment, forget about all of that and tell me how you feel about me."

"Bastian…you know it's impossible for me to fall—"

"No. Don't say that any more. I think you and I both know it's a lie. Forget it, and tell me how you feel." He pressed a hand flat against Cole's chest. "Here. It hurts, doesn't it? When you think about being separated from me." He dropped his forehead to Cole's again as his hand moved from his chest down to his stomach. "And here. When I'm close to you like this, it flutters, right? I can feel you shivering." He brushed his lips so lightly over Cole's as he spoke that neither of them could be sure if they'd actually touched. "Please, Cole. Tell me the truth."

As though he were confessing the greatest sin of his life, Cole's body shook with one hard sob, his hands clung to Bastian's shirt in a weak attempt to hold himself steady, and he finally admitted it.

"I love you, Bastian. I'm sorry, but I love you."

Bastian had never felt such immediate relief in his life, even as his heart ached under the sadness in Cole's voice. Wrapping his arms tight around the smaller boy, he drew him as close as he could before they might melt together.

"Don't ever apologize for this, Cole. Love should be so much happier."

Cole's arms wrapped around his neck and he held on tight, as though letting him go right then would shatter what they had just created. It felt right to finally have him in his arms and for a second he thought the black hair that tickled his noise smelled like the field from his dreams.

They stood like that for a long time, neither of them ready to let the other one go. Finally, Bastian pressed his lips to Cole's ear and whispered, "Come home with me."

Cole was silent for a long time and Bastian wondered if he was going to put up another fight. He'd not exactly been subtle with his meaning. But after a moment, Cole nodded against Bastian's neck. Reluctantly, they let each other go and the sudden bashfulness in Cole's eyes made Bastian's body hot all over. For a second he considered dragging the smaller boy into one of the dark recesses of the club and having his way with him there, but this was about more than sex. He needed to make love to Cole, not fuck him. Instead, he brought his hands down to the open button of Cole's shorts and refastened them.

"I'm going to have to disinfect everywhere that asshole touched you."

He could hear Cole catch his breath at those words and it only made his decision to take Cole home where he could love him properly harder. He took Cole's hand, squeezing it softly, as though that bit of pressure was his promise to him.

"Don't let go of me."

Silently, Bastian led Cole back downstairs, out of the club and back to their home.

218

33

Sneaking back into Haven was even easier than sneaking out, though Bastian was walking with such intense purpose that Cole thought they wouldn't question him even if they were caught. His hand was sweating where Bastian held onto him and he wanted to wipe it off, but was unable to pull away from him. He'd never intended to say those words to the blond boy, and now in the silence he wondered if he'd made a mistake. He wasn't sure if he believed Bastian's story about not being affected by his toxins, but even if it was true, he was sure that Bastian deserved someone so much better than him. He deserved someone who was unsullied.

His chest hurt, and as though Bastian could hear his thoughts, he squeezed his hand tighter.

Cole rarely went into other people's rooms. He didn't like how powerfully private places smelled like their owners, but now Bastian was leading him into his darkened bedroom. Part of him hoped Bastian would leave the lights turned off but he led him a few steps inside, then turned on a small lamp beside his bed. The light was dim, but did nothing to hide the embarrassment he could feel burning his face. He wondered what he was supposed to do, what Bastian *planned* to do. He'd never slept with anyone when he wasn't shaking and desperate for a meal. He tried to remember what he did when his mind became foggy and ravenous, hoping he could take some cue from that. He swallowed, vaguely recalling the taste of Bastian in his mouth.

"Sit with me." Bastian's command was so gentle that it felt like the humblest request.

Cole followed the blond to his bed and sat at the edge of the mattress. A moment later, though, Bastian tugged him gently by his hand until Cole was laying against him where he sat reclined against the headboard. He lay with his arms around Bastian's waist, his body resting between the taller boy's legs, his head resting on his chest. Bastian held him about his shoulders, one hand moving to his hair at the back of his neck, measuring the length with his fingertips.

They sat like that in silence for a long time, neither of them ready to separate, then Bastian's voice vibrated against Cole's ear.

"Tell me about your dreams."

Cole wanted to look at him, surprised by his sudden request, but he didn't.

"It's embarrassing."

Bastian chuckled, the sound rumbling in his chest. "Well then let me guess what your dreams are like." His pause to think felt fabricated. "We're lying in a field together." Bastian's arms suddenly tightened around Cole as he flipped him over so he lay on his back, the blond boy perching over him on one elbow. Slowly, Bastian extended his wing, covering both of them like a small feathered tent. "And I'm shading you like this. Telling you how much I love you."

Cole felt goosebumps break out across his body as déjà vu washed over him. For a second he forgot how to breathe. All he did was stare, the wonder he felt reflected back at him through Bastian's eyes, then the blond smiled, his face radiant even in the dim light of the lamp.

"It's a little overwhelming, isn't it? Being like this for real." He took Cole's hand and guided it to his chest where shivering fingers were met with the heavy beating of the other boy's heart. "It feels like it's going to beat right out of my chest."

"How do you know about this?" Cole found his fingers clinging to the fabric of Bastian's tank top.

Bastian let out a long breath, seeming relieved as he dropped his forehead to Cole's chest. "So you *have* been having the same dreams. I was afraid I would be wrong. I didn't believe it at first when Berlin suggested that we must have known each other before we woke up like we did. But I think he's right." He moved back up to look at him, his hand moving to Cole's cheek. "Cole, I think we've loved each other all along. We'd just forgotten."

Somehow, in the deepest part of Cole's body, he knew what Bastian was saying was true. And if it wasn't, he didn't care anymore. He loved him right then, and that's all that mattered.

Lifting his head, Cole placed a single, soft kiss on the other boy's lips.

"I love you. Whether that's true or not." He touched the tanned skin of Bastian's cheek with his fingertips. "Whether I should or not."

Bastian's response was a soft smile, a whispered "good," and a kiss far deeper than the one Cole had given him.

And then the nervousness and the sweet words were gone, and the only thing Cole could do was desperately hold onto Bastian as he pressed down on him, as his tongue brushed the roof of his mouth. Cole wasn't hungry, yet he suckled the other boy's tongue like it would provide him all the nourishment he would ever need. Just as Cole thought he would faint if Bastian stole any more of his breath, the blond's mouth released him, moving instead to his jawline, then his neck.

"That man left marks on you here."

A small pang of guilt turned Cole's stomach, but then Bastian's mouth closed over the small kiss marks Asher had left on him and he bit just hard enough to make him gasp.

"I can't believe you actually went out in these tiny shorts." A hand moved up Cole's leg, squeezing his thigh and running his fingertips under the snug fabric there. "Honestly, I'm amazed I got home before laying my hands on you."

Somehow those words felt like the most tantalizing of promises.

"Bastian...I've never done this when I'm not hungry. I don't know..."

"It's fine." He planted a kiss on Cole's mouth to quiet him, then pulled the loose fitting shirt off over his head. "Just do whatever makes you feel good."

He could feel himself blush, but he desired him enough that his words still slipped out. "I want to touch you." His hands tugged at Bastian's tank top, and with a smile, the larger boy conceded.

Moving to his knees, Bastian pulled his shirt over his head, the muscles in his stomach and chest tightening as his body stretched and twisted. Before he'd even thrown the shirt to the floor, Cole's hands moved to his sides, following the angular lines of his body up to his shoulders, then down over his chest and abs.

As though Bastian were mirroring his thoughts, the winged man bent over him, whispering reverently as he pushed Cole's under shirt up under his arms. "God, you're beautiful."

Compared to Bastian, Cole's body was pale and narrow. He knew he was strong, capable, but now beneath Bastian he felt fragile, like he may break into pieces any second. Bastian's hands felt big as they moved to Cole's waist and pushed up over his ribs until this thumbs each brushed a nipple. Had Cole felt that jolt when he'd touched him like that in the cave at Lechuguilla? He watched the other boy's lips fall on the hardened bud, kissing it, drawing it between his lips, moving to the other to do the same thing. Then teeth brushed his skin and bit down just hard enough to make Cole shudder.

"Bastian." He wanted to tell him to unzip his shorts for him. The sensation of his mouth had gone straight to his dick, and now he strained against the zipper of his pants. His words died in his throat, though, as Bastian's hands moved to knead the flesh of his thighs again, his mouth continuing its work.

Instinctively, Cole's legs eased apart, and he felt himself begin to shake as thumbs pressed into the hollows at the inside of his thighs. His hips shifted and rolled forward, making him gasp as he ground against the inside of his zipper. He wondered if sex was always this embarrassing, and he only felt his face heat up more when Bastian raised his head to chuckle at him.

"I'm sorry, Cole. Is it uncomfortable?" One hand moved from his thigh over the bulge in his shorts and Cole felt his body jerk as he gasped. "These tiny shorts are so cute on you, I didn't want to take them off. But they're tight now, aren't they? Do you want me to get rid of them?"

"Yes."

"Then what do you want me to do?" His hands moved to the

button and he pulled the zipper down so slowly that Cole thought he might cry.

"I don't know." He realized he had no idea what to do without his instincts and hunger guiding him. "I just want you."

As though the sincerity of his words had left the other boy's gentle teasing useless, Bastian descended on him, catching his mouth in another deep kiss as blind hands guided the last barrier between them off of Cole's body. Vaguely, he noticed Bastian toss the shorts over his shoulder, but he was immediately distracted as his lips left him, only to trail down his chest to his stomach. He caught his breath as hands pushed his hips into the mattress.

"What are you doing?"

"You did this for me in when we were in Lechuguilla. I want to do it for you now." As he finished his sentence, lips brushed across the soft head of his dick, and Cole had to hold onto the bedsheets to keep from rolling away in embarrassment.

"Has anyone done this for you before?"

Cole could only shake his head. Once someone was drugged by him, foreplay wasn't exactly on their minds. Milo had offered to do it in the past, but they'd decided against it because of the heavy dose of toxins he would probably get. Now, as Bastian's breath made his erection twitch against his stomach, he wondered if it was true that he was immune.

Then the heat of his lips closed around him, and he didn't have any room left in his head for thoughts of toxins. All he could think about was the soft pull of Bastian's mouth as the blond drew him deep into the back of his throat, his strong hands gripping Cole's hips as his body arched off the bed, searching for more of the heat that Bastian was giving him. His mind filled with static and his fingers pressed into blond curls, Bastian's name tumbling off his lips in shock. Was he supposed to feel this hot all over? Were his legs supposed to shiver like this? Is this how it felt when he was lost in his hunger? He didn't remember it ever feeling like this.

With one slow push, Bastian pressed Cole's thighs apart, and as he raked his teeth up his length he passed his thumb over his opening, the sensation straightening Cole's spine. Holding still became harder as Bastian's tongue swirled and wrapped around him, as his fingers squeezed and spread the soft cheeks of his ass, only so they could dip in and rub against the core of his desire. Finally, as the shaking moved to his chest and nervous tears stung his eyes, he managed a pathetic whimper.

"Bastian, wait."

Without hesitation, the blond let the head of Cole's dick slide from his mouth, watched it twitch against Cole's soft stomach as he licked the taste from his lips, then looked up at him.

"You okay?"

Embarrassment burned Cole's cheeks and he had to cover his face. "I'm sorry. I'm just so nervous. I can't stop shaking."

With a soft, sympathetic coo, Bastian moved back up Cole's smaller body. He propped himself on one shoulder so he was laying beside him, then pulled him into a firm embrace. Cole pressed his heated face into Bastian's collarbone, whispering a weak apology, only to have Bastian shush him.

"There's nothing to apologize for."

Cole let his body settle for a minute, listening to Bastian's steady breathing, feeling his erection pressing hard against him through the pants he still wore. He wanted to rip his pajamas off, but just the thought of that made his chest catch fire. There was something beautiful and infuriating in the knowledge that Bastian would never press him, that if he kept still, Bastian would probably let him sleep right there in his arms without a single word spoken about what he might want from him. What Cole wanted, though, was Bastian. Even if he shook himself apart, he needed to be with him.

Squeezing his hands between them, Cole brushed fingers down either side of Bastian's face, then kissed him, chastely at first. Then he opened his mouth to brush the tip of his tongue around the insides of Bastian's lips. He could taste himself there and it made him ache.

"Please don't stop. Just keep kissing me."

Bastian groaned as Cole felt him throb against beneath the cotton of his pants. He did exactly as he'd been asked, and he kissed Cole until the smaller boy thought he was going to faint. As Cole was finally let up for breath, Bastian's fingers traced his swollen lips, his mouth kissing a line to his ear where he whispered. "Open your mouth."

Cole's lips parted and Bastian's fingers pressed inside, rubbing against his tongue. The sound of the blond's breathing against his ear made Cole's skin crawl with desire, and he sucked at the digits he'd been presented as though they would feed him for the rest of his life.

"Just like that," Bastian whispered against his skin as he kissed his way down Cole's jawline, then back to his ear where he sucked at his earlobe, mimicking the pull of Cole's mouth as he gently thrust his fingers against the pad of his tongue. "I'm going to put these inside you. Make them ready for it. You're so perfect." Bastian sounded as entranced with him as Cole was with Bastian, and he continued showering his cheek and ear with kisses, moaning softly when Cole whimpered around his fingers.

As Bastian finally pulled his wet fingers from his mouth, Cole turned opened lips toward his lover's waiting mouth, suckling at the tongue presented to him in place of the digits that now moved down his side. With one tug on his hip, Bastian rolled Cole onto his side, pulling a leg over him so that he lay open, exposed to the lubricated hand that pressed against him. Cole's head rested on Bastian's bicep, and as he felt those warmed fingers press against him, he was held steady by the blond's arm wrapped around the back of his neck. He dug his fingers into Bastian's shoulders, tried to catch his breath through his nose, but could do little more than shiver as strong fingers moved inside his body.

When Bastian finally released him, Cole's head fell back, and he gasped for breath as the other boy began a slow, deep thrust with his fingers. It was hot and made his body thrum with the need to move, but Bastian's free arm wrapped around his waist and held him flush against his own hard body.

"Tell me if I hurt you." Bastian's voice was strained as he watched Cole's face, bending for only a second to rake teeth across his throat before moving his eyes back to his face, watching him as he eased a third finger inside him.

Cole felt the moaning that had been cascading from him seize for a second as his body was stretched and prepared. He could barely breathe as he waited for his body to relax. Was this how he felt when he was feeding? He was certain it had never felt this overwhelming.

Finally, as his lungs spasmed back to life, he gasped for breath, straining against Bastian's body where he was unrelentingly held. And as though that were his cue, Bastian went back to work, pressing deep inside him, brushing places that made his body jump as bolts of pleasure tried to tear him apart from the inside.

Bastian nipped at his ear again, his voice strained and rough as he whispered to him. "You're shaking all over. Are you gonna be able to handle me actually doing this?"

It was at that moment that Cole realized he would fall apart if he didn't have Bastian inside him right that minute. His hips pressed back hard against his fingers and he brought a hand up to grab a fistful of blond curls. His own voice sounded alien in his ears, raw, but so soft, lacking the hysteria he had in the throes of his hunger.

"I want you, Bastian," was all he managed before the blond pushed him into the mattress, his fingers withdrawing just long enough to shove his pajama bottoms down and free his already leaking cock.

Cole felt trapped in a way that thrilled him as Bastian laid his firm body over him, his hands drawing Cole's legs around his waist. And before Cole could get a single begging word out, he felt the other boy's heat press inside him, the way made easy and soft by the fingers that now held Cole by his hip.

A tremor ran up Bastian's back that Cole could feel where his own shaking hands were holding onto him, and they both held still as they caught their breath.

"Gott, Ich will dich so sehr..." His breath was hot in Cole's ear.

They stayed like that for a long time, and once Bastian had reined himself in, he moved up to his elbows to look into Cole's eyes. Cole felt a new wave of embarrassment when he saw the reverence in the blond's expression, but instead of the urge to hide, this time he kissed him, softly, chastely.

"I love you," he said again, and he wondered how he could have ever been uncertain about his feelings.

The wave crashed again, set loose by those words, and they grasped at each other, Bastian's hands moving to lift thin hips off the mattress as he rocked into him, driving Cole's breath from his body every time he pressed to the hilt. They couldn't stop now; their bodies drove them closer together, every muscle in Cole's body wrapping around him, trying to draw him closer to him, deeper inside him. Bastian met every pull and gave him everything he could—his body, his breath, his heart.

Those moments as they drove each other higher felt infinite and fleeting. They clung to every second, reveled in every thrust, every gasp, and when they finally hit the precipice, Cole tore his mouth from Bastian's. A single "no" passed his lips before his body arched, soft ribbons of his own come drawing lines on their stomachs. He didn't want it to be over, even as he spasmed and twisted his fingers in Bastian's hair. Over him, the blond jerked and pushed hard inside him. Bastian growled in his ear, cussing in German as Cole toppled him over the edge with him.

Cole was used to relief flooding his body at the moment of climax when he fed, but now he felt something much warmer than relief. Bastian rested his weight on top of him, neither of them worrying about the mess Cole had shot between them. Cole could feel Bastian's heat inside him, and he drew his legs around the other boy's hips, not ready to release him yet.

Bastian puffed a gentle laugh into the side of Cole's neck.

"Don't do that unless you're planning to go again."

The warmth inside Cole bubbled up inside him and came out as a soft laugh. He'd never felt this wash of joy after a physical encounter, and he knew that it must be the love he felt for the other boy growing and blooming inside him.

"That might not be so bad."

"Don't tempt me," Bastian said as he mouthed at Cole's neck, the feeling suddenly ticklish instead of tantalizing, and Cole squirmed and laughed beneath him. Propping himself up on his elbows to look down at Cole's face, Bastian smiled in a way that made his eyes shine like a sunlit ocean. "Stay here with me tonight."

Cole's heart fluttered and all he could say was "okay."

34

Waking up could be a struggle in the underground dorms where there was no light to signal morning, but now Bastian's body eased out of the bog of sleep. For a second, he wondered what had woken him up, then he felt Cole shift beside him and nestle deeper into his chest. A smile pulled at Bastian's mouth, and he was glad for the darkness—he liked that his foolish expression was hidden, even if there was no one else there.

It was too dark to see the boy who had suddenly become so dear to him snuggled up under his chin, but he bowed his head and rubbed his nose into the downy hair that tickled him. Berlin was crazy to think that Bastian was an angel; if there was such a thing, then surely this sweet-smelling, delicate boy was it, not Bastian. His arm tightened a little around Cole's narrow shoulders and the black-haired boy shifted and hummed, his voice hushed and sleepy.

"Bastian?"

"Shh. It's not morning just yet, Cole. Go back to sleep."

"Mmm," was all Cole managed before his weight settled back into the curve of Bastian's body.

Bastian didn't know anything about angels or demons. He didn't know whether the dreams he and Cole shared were true. But he did know that there was no one as precious to him as the pale boy that lay in his arms. He also knew that if Berlin was right—if he and Cole had been punished by God for merely loving each other—then he would never worship that god.

He would choose Cole over that god.

Every time.

MICHELLE KAY

MICHELLE KAY